THE NEW BREADMAKERS
The sequel to THE BREADMAKERS SAGA

Having survived everything that the Depression and the Second World War has thrown at them, the people of McNair's bakery are now facing an uncertain future. With the Coronation of 1953, a new age is beginning, and all is by no means well in the lives of the bread-makers. Catriona McNair's husband is making her life a misery; her friends Julie and Sammy have been involved in a search for a long-lost daughter; Alec Jackson, the happy-go-lucky reformed philanderer, finds himself caught up in one of Glasgow's worst tragedies; and the youngsters are challenging convention in the name of romance.

THE NEW BREADMAKERS
The sequel to THE BREADMAKERS SAGA

The New Breadmakers

The sequel to

The Breadmakers Saga

by

Margaret Thomson Davis

Magna Large Print Books
Long Preston, North Yorkshire,
BD23 4ND, England.

British Library Cataloguing in Publication Data.

Davis, Margaret Thomson
        The new breadmakers – the sequel to The Breadmakers Saga.

        A catalogue record of this book is
        available from the British Library

        ISBN   978-0-7505-3715-5

First published in Great Britain in 2004 by Black & White Publishing

Copyright © Margaret Thomson Davis 2004

Cover illustration © mirrorpix

The right of Margaret Thomson Davis to be identified as the author of
this work has been asserted by her in accordance with the Copyright,
Designs and Patents Act, 1988

Published in Large Print 2013 by arrangement with
Black & White Publishing

Magna Large Print is an imprint of Library Magna Books Ltd.

Printed and bound in Great Britain by
T.J. (International) Ltd., Cornwall, PL28 8RW

ACKNOWLEDGEMENTS

Many people were kind enough to help with my research. For instance, Eddie McGarrell MBE whose 50 years of experience working for the Red Cross at various events, including football matches, was of invaluable assistance.

I'm also grateful for other help with the football parts of the story given by Tommy Malcolm from the Football Museum, Mae and John Pitcairn, and Adrienne and Tom Whitehill.

Ex-policeman Norman Richardson also gave generous help and advice.

Bill Findlay shared his knowledge of local history.

Special mention must be made of Jeny Faulkner, Registering Officer of The Society of Friends (Quakers), who gave me details of a Quaker marriage.

Thanks also to Molly and Joe Fisher who helped me so entertainingly with their memories of the library service.

My thanks to all of the above and apologies to anyone I may have omitted to mention.

1

Catriona could hardly look at her husband Melvin's gaunt, moustachioed face without feeling hatred. Then she'd feel guilty. After all, he was quite a few years older than her and he'd had a bad time during the war. He'd been a prisoner for most of the time although, to hear him talk, it was the high point of his life. His time of glory. She'd lost count of the number of times he'd told her about his daring attempts to escape. His eyes glowed with a fierce intensity every time he recounted the well-worn stories of secret tunnel-digging, wire-cutting, forged papers and stolen German uniforms. Sometimes she wondered if any of it was true, if it was all just made up. After all, she could hardly imagine anyone less heroic or selfless than Melvin.

She'd long since detected in his manner an admiration for the Germans. She even believed that, if he'd been a German himself during the war, he would have been a member of the SS or the Gestapo. He was a bully and he admired bullies. He'd bullied her since they met when she was just sixteen. He'd bully anyone if he could get away with it. She'd once heard it said that some people have to stand beside a dwarf to feel big and if they can't find a dwarf, they'll make one. That's what he'd been trying to do to her for years – belittle her, humiliate her, make her feel small.

Well, not any more.

He'd treated her like a slave, nearly killed her. He'd been the death of his first wife, Betty, and had nearly managed it with Catriona too. Fool that she was, she had kept trying to please him and be as perfect as he kept making out Betty to have been. At the beginning, he'd insisted on keeping pictures of her on the mantelpiece. He'd made Catriona read the poor woman's love letters. Every week, without fail, he'd taken her to pay homage at Betty's grave.

After the war, when they'd moved to the West End, at least all that had stopped. He was now too intent on making an impression on the present. While he'd been away at the war, they had been bombed out of their tenement building, losing not only their home but also the family bakehouse that had been their livelihood. She had been forced to move, with their son Andrew and Catriona's eight-year-old step-son Fergus, to her mother's. Her mother hated Melvin and had done everything she could to stop Catriona marrying him. After the wedding, she had never stopped trying to persuade her to leave him. Now she concentrated on making Catriona feel guilty about baby Robert's death in the air raids.

'Long ago, I warned you that God would punish you by taking away someone you loved. I told you you should have the children stay at my place. I warned you. I told you that building in Dessie Street was far too close to the shipyards.'

Melvin must have been devastated when he'd received the letter in the camp telling him the awful news about losing his home and business, and the even worse news of Robert's death. She'd put off writing that letter as long as she could. Eventually she dared not put it off any longer. It would have been even more of a shock to him if he had turned up and been faced with the pile of rubble that had once been the home he'd been so proud of. It had only been one of the flats in the tenement building owned by his father, the master baker (all his father's employees and their families lived above the bakery), but no one had been as ridiculously house-proud as Melvin. 'This house is like a palace,' he often said.

The boastful words and the arrogant manner in which they were delivered echoed in her mind now and with this bitter memory came the equally hateful vision of the flat in Dessie Street. She had suffered, as Betty had suffered. No doubt before Betty had become ill and helpless Melvin had forced her to make a god of his stupid little house, just as he had forced Catriona to. Not a thing had ever been allowed to change. It had remained exactly as it was when his first wife had died there. Catriona could still smell the pungent odour of wax polish that always hung in the air. She'd had to polish everything. The doors, like the dark-brown linoleum, gleamed and shone, daring anyone to deface them. Like stepping stones, rugs were dotted here and there in the lobby, the living room, the kitchen and the bedroom. Everything in every room had been sparkling and immaculate. Oh, how she wished now that she'd allowed the children more freedom to play and run about, and mess the place up. But she had been too much like a child

11

herself. Dominated by her mother, at sixteen she had thought she'd escaped into marriage and a home of her own, only to discover that the pattern was repeated, as she was dominated by her husband as well. To make things worse, her mother and Melvin had continuously fought over her like two mad dogs with a bone. Melvin's main weapon was the threat to throw her out on the street. 'You came to me without even a change of knickers to your name and that's how you'll leave if you're not careful.'

She knew he'd take the children away from her, that's what terrified her. On one desperate occasion, she'd left him and gone back to her mother's house in Farmbank with the children, but it was even worse than living with Melvin. Her mother had taken over the children completely. In despair, she'd eventually gone back to the jungle of grey tenements and Dessie Street.

Her mother never let her forget that, as a result, she had caused the death of her dearly loved youngest baby, Robert. Robert would have been a schoolboy now with his cap and blazer and his schoolbag on his back, like Andrew. All she had left of Robert was the agonising memory of his round, baby eyes gazing up at her with adoration and trust.

'God will punish you,' her mother used to threaten. And, oh, He had.

She hated Melvin for insisting, eight years after they married and not long after his return from the war, on buying the big terraced house in Botanic Crescent, where they now lived. Admittedly, it was a nice, quiet crescent, looking out onto a bank of greenery and, beyond it, to the trees of the Botanic Gardens. But the place was enormous. It was too much for her. Even when his father had been alive and staying with them, it had been far too big and impossible for her to look after, especially in the way Melvin expected her to. She had just about killed herself in the attempt. She'd been worn down trying to nurse Melvin's elderly father, as well as everything else. He wasn't so bad during the day but he'd get up in the night, only to cause havoc doing frightening things like nearly setting the house on fire or wandering out of the house in the dark wearing only his pyjamas.

She hardly slept a wink for worrying about him getting up and setting the place on fire or going out and falling and injuring himself. Melvin was always in the bakehouse, of course, and never had to deal with his father's distressing symptoms, refusing to face the fact that the old man was ill.

'He just takes a wee dram too many at times, that's all.'

He'd brush aside her desperate pleas to have his father put under professional care, such as in a nursing home.

'You're not going to put my father out on the street, so just shut up. You're getting a right nag.'

That last dreadful night, she'd found the old man dead and had rushed out to the bakehouse to tell Melvin. The next thing she remembered, she had woken up in hospital. She'd suffered heavy bleeding for a long time. Now she was given a hysterectomy. Even her ovaries and appendix had been taken away.

'You were in a right mess,' the surgeon had told her.

For a long time after that, she was so weak that even Melvin realised she couldn't cope on her own with such a huge house, along with all the work she had done for the business by doing the books and helping out in the shop from time to time. Anyway, whether he understood it or not, she simply refused to be his stupid slave any more.

'I'll have to get some domestic help,' she told him. The best he could come up with was a woman for two mornings a week. It was better than nothing but still not enough. the house was on three storeys, with ten high-ceilinged rooms, counting the attics, plus cellars that she no longer ventured into. Nor did buxom Bella, the cleaning woman.

'Ye're rattlin' aroon' in the place like peas in a drum,' Bella said. 'Ye could have half-a-dozen families livin' here. Did ye never think o' takin' in any lodgers?'

Catriona laughed derisively. 'That's all I need, a crowd of lodgers to look after.'

'Naw, naw. I mean tae dae for themsels. This kitchen's aboot as big as Hampden Park. There's plenty room for them aw tae see tae themsels. An' it would bring in a bob or two.'

Catriona was glad Melvin hadn't been there at the time. The temptation to make more money might have overcome him.

'It's a thought,' she said. A nightmare thought. Crowded chaos in the kitchen. It was more than enough to try to keep the place clean and tidy in between Bella's visits. There were all the meals to see to as well. Melvin demanded to be fed at all sorts of odd times, and Fergus was often out very late at the dancing or some music club or other. He'd sleep late next morning as a result and then eat at different times from everyone else. But since he'd got the place at Aberdeen College of Music and Drama they only saw him for the occasional weekend.

She was thankful to at least be rid of the back-breaking routine of the old washboard, which had been replaced with one of the new twin-tub washing machines. For that she'd had to put up with, and was still putting up with, Melvin boasting about his generosity. She even had an electric iron instead of the old flat iron that had to be heated on the fire. And thank God for the Hoover! At one time, she'd had to take the rugs out, put them over the clothes line and beat them.

'Think yourself lucky,' was one of Melvin's favourite phrases. 'Not many women are as lucky as you.'

What a laugh! Sometimes he'd make a completely trivial remark and she'd snap back with some bitter sarcastic retort out of all proportion to his original comment. Her outburst would be the accumulation of days, weeks or months of silently simmering resentment about other more serious things he'd said or done. But Andrew and Fergus could not know this. She had always struggled to give them a peaceful, loving, secure home life – something that she'd never had herself. And, not knowing how she struggled to protect them from the truth about her marriage,

15

fourteen-year-old Andrew would turn towards her after one of these outbursts and say, 'Mum!' in shocked reproof. He got on well with his dad and after school, at weekends and during the summer holidays, he often helped out in the bakehouse or the shop. She fought to control her bitterness and to keep quiet.

Her main aim these past few years had been survival. It still was. She had come close to death and, ever since, her priority had been to protect herself. For the sake of Andrew, if nothing else. He was only a schoolboy and, in her opinion, not yet able to fend for himself. Admittedly, he'd always been sensible, even courageous. Fergus used to torment Andrew when he was younger. Andrew had been such a lovable little boy, with his chubby features, big round eyes and curly hair. She well remembered one occasion when she'd heard talking and had looked out of the sitting room to see the five-year-old Andrew stamping towards the bathroom repeating determinedly to himself, 'I am *not* afraid of ghosts. I am *not* afraid of ghosts.' Instead of coming to her for help and telling her that he was frightened to go to the bathroom because Fergus had told him there were ghosts in the cupboard ready to jump out on him, he'd struggled to cope with it himself. She'd found this out from her friend Madge's children.

Andrew had always been like that. He'd never been a worry like Fergus. He was a good boy to her and to Melvin. It saddened her to think that he might be getting the wrong impression about her relationship with Melvin and thinking that

16

she was the villain of the piece. She had to admit his dad was all right with him. As good a father as any, she supposed, although there had been a time when he had not been anything like the perfect father he now tried to make out he was. Andrew had been too young then to be able to remember it. She remembered, though.

'Fat little bastard,' Melvin had sneered. 'I don't suppose he's even mine.'

That had been after Melvin came home from the war, terribly affected by it. If he'd sometimes acted like a madman before the war, he certainly became much worse during and after it. All right, he must have suffered a lot. She tried to remember that and to feel some compassion for him. Before the war, he'd had the physique of a gorilla and had always been proud of it – he never tired of boasting about his muscular body. He exercised regularly, never missed his 'physical jerks' as he called them. But he came back a mere shadow of his former self, physically at least, hollow-eyed and balding, with sallow skin hanging loosely on an emaciated body. She could not help feeling some pity and compassion. She'd kept quiet and gone along as best she could with all his crazy plans of becoming wealthy and successful in business and his home being the envy of everybody in Glasgow.

Big ideas. Showing off. That had always been him. Now he'd purchased a television set with which to show off to as many of his customers as could be crowded into the house. When they went out, he was too mean to buy even a cup of tea if they were in town and she said she was exhausted.

'Do you think I'm made of money?' he'd say. 'There's plenty tea you can have at home.' Now this magic box was to display the Queen's Coronation, transmitted in black and white from London, for everyone to marvel at. No one else they knew was the proud possessor of a television. Tea and sandwiches were going to be provided and passed around – by her, of course – and never mind the expense. Not to mention all the work – the preparation beforehand for such a horde, the washing up afterwards and no doubt cleaning up of a sea of bread and biscuit crumbs from the carpet. It could sink forever under spilled tea and crumbs, for all she cared, but he'd go berserk about his precious carpet if it was left uncared for. He was still as house-proud as ever.

She longed to leave him. But where could she go? Not to her mother. That would be like going from the proverbial frying pan into the fire. How could she keep herself? She had to be independent some day, but how? Melvin had been telling her for so long that she was helpless and useless and would never be able to survive without him that she was afraid it might be true. Deep down, she believed him.

'You've lucky you've got me,' he kept telling her.

She began to look for secret areas of her life in which she could find some happiness. She clung to her friends. But they thought she was lucky as well.

2

Most of the customers that Melvin had invited to come and view the Coronation were from Partick. McNairn's new bakery was down nearer the Partick end of Byres Road. It had more working-class character than the other end, where Great Western Road was filled with large villas and equally roomy terraced houses, all of splendid architectural quality. Further along towards the centre of the city, the tenement blocks, mostly above shops, were commodious and very respectable. It always had been like that around there.

Partick, on the other hand, had a chequered history. At first it had been a village, then, with the deepening of the river, the rise of shipbuilding and the massive influx of workers that followed, the place had simply grown and grown. Eventually there had been a unanimous decision to make the area into a burgh so that something could be done about the unhygienic conditions that were causing so many deaths. Smallpox, tuberculosis, scarlet fever, diphtheria, measles, whooping cough, typhoid and cholera were constant threats. A major source of much of the infection was the milk supply and, once the area became a burgh in 1852, sanitary inspectors kept an eagle eye on the many dairies, cow keepers and byres. A register was kept of ice-cream shops and a whole host of other premises, including grocers, fish restaurants, newsagents and bakeries.

Partick had fought long and hard to remain a separate burgh. Nevertheless, at midnight on 4 November 1912, it ceased to exist and was included within the boundaries of Glasgow.

Catriona had seen the Provost of Partick's gold chains and official badges of office in the Kelvingrove Art Gallery and Museum, one of the few places she occasionally managed to escape to. If Melvin was on night shift in the bakery, it was difficult. He only slept for a few hours during the day and was liable to come padding barefooted and hollow-cheeked out of the bedroom looking for her and wanting a cup of tea because he couldn't sleep and his mouth was 'like a sewer'.

More and more, he was becoming like his father, who eventually worked days instead of nights. Melvin had made Baldy Fowler the head baker or manager on the night shift because Baldy 'knew his stuff'. He had been one of the few survivors when Dessie Street had been bombed. Not that Baldy had ever shown any gratitude for the fact.

'Isn't it just like the bloody thing,' he'd complained at the time. 'Life's not worth living for me. I don't care if I snuff it. But I'm the one who survives.'

He still hadn't forgotten his wife Sarah and the terrible day she had been hanged for the murder of his mother, even though it had happened many years ago and he was now courting a woman from Springburn.

Catriona remembered that terrible day as well. Poor Sarah had been nagged beyond endurance by 'Lender Lil', Baldy's ghastly money-lending mother. She could well understand how Sarah felt. Often in the past, she had felt like stabbing her own mother to death. More recently, she'd felt like murdering Melvin. She had come to genuinely believe that anyone was capable of murder. At least her mother's aggressive nagging and threatening of God's punishments weren't so constant now. She still reminded Catriona what God thought of her but now it was with a regretful sigh. As Grand Matron of the Band of Jesus, she appeared to have a direct line to God and inside knowledge of His every wish and plan. Catriona used to believe this, but not any more. Oh, there were still deep-rooted fears that, no matter how much she mentally pooh-poohed them, refused to be completely banished. But now, she fought against them as best and as often as she could. She knew that her mother used God to get her own way.

Catriona had come to the conclusion that He couldn't be much of a God if He allowed Himself to be so often manipulated by Hannah Munro. He had never listened to the pleas and prayers of Catriona McNair. No help, no mercy and certainly no love had ever been doled out to her. She didn't believe in a God like that. Practically every time she saw Sammy Hunter, she argued with him about her beliefs or rather lack of them. Sammy had been a conscientious objector and suffered much at the hands of the military in Maryhill Barracks where he'd been imprisoned for a time. His wife Ruth had been killed in the war. After her death, the Society of Friends, or

Quakers, had helped to get him out of prison. The Quakers were pacifists and held mock tribunals to help COs and prepare them for the ordeal they would face and all the questions that would be flung at them, when they were called to face the real tribunal. Sammy was just one of many they helped in this way.

After his imprisonment in the Barracks, Sammy had served in the Friends' Ambulance Unit for the rest of the war. After it ended, he'd kept in touch with the Society of Friends. Sammy had fiery red hair and a broken nose, and he looked like a prize fighter. He certainly could be argumentative and he held strong views, but he never brought up the subject of God or religion. It was her that could never resist taking every opportunity she could to vent her bitterness and argue about religion with him. If Melvin was there, he'd say things like, 'Will you shut up about bloody religion? It's bad enough when your mother goes on about it.'

Sammy was the only one she could talk to. He argued with her, but he never made any attempt to convert her. She was curious to know why. Wasn't that what religious people, especially members of religious sects, were supposed to do? Sammy said it wasn't. Love is the meaning of life and the light of God is in everyone, he believed.

Catriona found this very hard to swallow, especially when she thought of Melvin. It intrigued her that a man like Sammy could go along with it, although she could remember one incident about which he'd shown amazing tolerance and understanding.

His wife Ruth had been killed in a cinema when it received a direct hit and Alec Jackson, Madge's husband, had been with her. It was while Sammy had been in Maryhill Barracks and Ruth had been fed up and lonely. They'd barely got seated, apparently, when the bomb fell. To Alec's credit (and there never had been much to Alec's credit), he had given his name and Ruth's to the air-raid warden when asked, then had gone down on his knees and dug with his bare hands to try to find Ruth and get her out. He could have walked away without saying or doing anything. That way Madge and Sammy would never have known.

Ruth had been a very beautiful girl, sexy too. Catriona could well believe that her every move could be sexually provocative, especially to a man like Alec, with her hips swaying as she walked, her full, pouting lips and black, suggestive eyes. As far as she knew, though, Ruth and Sammy had been ideally happy together and they had been so proud of their little room-and-kitchen flat. Sammy had obviously adored Ruth. Her death had devastated him. His emotions kept coming to boiling point about the way she'd died. It added fuel to his hatred of war.

Immediately afterwards, everyone, even Madge, thought it best not to add to poor Sammy's grief by telling him that Ruth had been with Alec. It was not until years later that Alec had confessed to Sammy. Alec had been a terrible womaniser. Even Catriona, who had been quite naive in her youth, had realised it eventually. Madge had given Alec absolute hell, not only because of Ruth, but because he'd seduced Catriona in the early years of her marriage, during the time her mother had taken the children from her 'for their own safety'. Catriona had allowed him to persuade her to have sex with him. She'd believed it to be an expression of love at the time. He had been so gentle after all the brutal and completely insensitive sex she'd suffered from Melvin. At the time she had felt more vulnerable than usual and in need of some sort of comfort, but afterwards she'd suffered agonies of guilt, even though it had only happened on one occasion. All her previous so-called sins shrank to nothing compared with the sin of adultery.

Much to Alec's horror, she'd confessed to Madge, who immediately felled Alec with a blow to his handsome face. Madge was a big, strong girl.

'You rotten big midden. She's only a wee lassie,' she bawled at her husband, 'and she's worried about her weans.'

That one act of unfaithfulness had resulted in a pregnancy about which she'd had to deceive Melvin, to convince him that baby Robert, like Andrew and Fergus, was truly his.

Not that she had ever regretted having Robert. She had loved him dearly and always would. He had been such a good wee boy. She remembered saying to Sandy, the van man, when they were all sheltering in the bakehouse lobby just before the bomb was dropped, 'Look at that wee pet. Wide awake and not a whimper.' She had been sitting on the floor at the side of Robert's pram with her knees hugged up under her chin. Leaning her head to one side, she had begun to sing to the

24

baby. She could still see him staring up at her, wide-eyed with delight.

Wee Willie Winkie
Runs through the town,
Upstairs and downstairs
In his nightgown.
Tirling at the windows,
Crying at the locks –
Are all the weans in their beds,
For it's now ten o'clock.

What kind of God was it who could allow such a lovely and loving wee baby to be crushed to death, even as a punishment for her? Her mind shrank away from the memory and the torment, and drifted on to Sammy again.

He had certainly shown great tolerance towards Alec. He'd always had a horror, he said, of Ruth dying frightened and alone. She had always liked Alec and Sammy was glad that he had been with her. He'd even helped Alec, by then unemployed, down-and-out and very miserable, to find a job and regain some of his self-respect. They were now good friends and Alec obviously thought the world of Sammy.

Fine, fine. But that was just Sammy. Not God. Not bloody God, who had allowed her baby to die a horrible death.

She fought to gather her strength so that she could survive for Andrew and Fergus's sakes. And go on surviving. God or no God, by hardening herself and fuelling her hatred of Melvin, she would find the strength.

3

Catriona lost count of the number of people who were crowded into the sitting room. Children and some of the younger adults sat on the floor nearest to the television. Then there were rows of chairs. Crammed in behind the chairs, people stood pressed against the walls at the back. Catriona gave up trying to pass round tea and sandwiches and she too squeezed in behind the chairs.

Wide-eyed with admiration, everyone agreed that it was a magic box indeed. Here they were in a room in Glasgow and actually able to see what was going on in London – *as it happened*. This fact took a lot of believing and was really much more amazing and impressive than the Coronation itself. Glaswegians had never been greatly impressed with the Royal Family. For one thing, they were English. For another, they had more money than was good for them. As her mother often said, 'It's an ill-divided world.'

For once, Catriona tended to think the same way as her mother. Her mother always said, when referring to the soon-to-be-crowned Queen, 'If she came to my door tomorrow, I'd invite her in and make her welcome the same as I'd do with any decent woman. But I'd never bend the knee to her.'

The bishops bent both knees. There they were

at the Queen's feet in their magnificent robes. All around her were equally sumptuously attired peers in velvet and ermine cloaks and coronets. The Abbey too looked magnificent and Catriona couldn't help wondering what it, like the expensive robes, had to do with the life and teaching of Jesus Christ, the lowly carpenter, the young man who'd upturned the money changers' stalls and chased them out of the temple. All the wealthy, and by the looks of them snobby, characters who filled the Abbey probably thought they were miles better than anyone in this room. They were certainly of a different world, a world of privilege that Catriona could hardly imagine.

Afterwards, everybody said what a miracle it was, meaning the television and its ability to bring pictures live into the room. The only remark that Catriona heard made about the Coronation itself was, 'That crown must have cost a bob or two!'

Everybody told Melvin how grateful they were to him for allowing them into his house to see his magic box. They thanked her for the tea and sandwiches. Then they went happily back to their 'single ends' and room and kitchens in the tenement jungle of Partick. It was a far cry from the pomp and circumstance and show of wealth that they had just witnessed, but it didn't seem to bother them. They had enjoyed a good time and had been just as interested in seeing the inside of Melvin's big house as they'd been in seeing the inside of Westminster Abbey.

When they were gone, Catriona got out the Hoover and started attacking the carpet. Melvin hovered at her back, hands jingling coins in his pocket, determined to make himself heard, while she was equally determined not to listen.

'They won't forget today in a hurry – visiting a house like this. This will give them something to talk about for years. There isn't another television set for miles, you know.'

Catriona knew only too well that there must be plenty of other televisions – many no doubt bigger and better than Melvin's pride and joy – in the large villas along Great Western Road. But she had no wish to get into an argument with him just now.

'Did you see their faces?' Melvin enthused as he swaggered around. 'See how impressed they were? And not just by my television set. Their eyes were taking in everything from the moment you opened that front door. That hall out there is bigger than most of their whole houses. You could easily fit a single end or even a room and kitchen into that hall.'

Madge would have stayed behind to help wash up the cups or Hoover the carpet but, when she offered, Melvin had said, 'Away you go back to your own place. You and your mob'll cause more mess than you'll clean up. We'll manage.'

'*We*,' he'd said. That was a laugh. Madge laughed but not for the same reason. Big, blowsy Madge liked straight talking. She was a straight talker herself, and she was always ready to enjoy a good laugh.

'You're an awful man, Melvin McNair,' she said as she rounded up her crowd of children, all still at school but relishing the day off for the Coronation. They'd got a mug with the Queen's picture on it. All the children in every school had been presented with a memento of the Coronation. Some had a tin of toffees with the Queen's picture on the lid.

Until they were flung out on the street, Madge and her brood had squatted along with other families in one of the big villas on Great Western Road. That was after they'd got into arrears with their rent in their original house in Cowlairs Pend. After they'd been forced out of the squat, they'd gone to one of the Nissen huts in the Hughenden playing fields off Great Western Road. The playing fields belonged to Hillhead High School, but they'd been requisitioned by the Royal Air Force Balloon Squadron in 1939.

After the war, the Nissen huts had sheltered a band of squatters, travelling people – displaced humanity. They were the flotsam washed up by war, regarded as dirtying the skirts of respectable West End society. Many were ex-servicemen and their families who had lost their homes in the bombing and, after demob, had been unable to find alternative accommodation. Others, like Alec, Madge's husband, had been unable to get work, couldn't pay the rent and had been forced to quit.

Now, at last, they were settled in a nice council house in Balornock, up the hill from Springburn. Madge was as happy as a lark, especially with the fact that for the first time in her life, she had the luxury of hot and cold running water, a bath-room and a kitchenette with a wash boiler. No more taking turns in a zinc bath in front of the kitchen fire. No more trekking with a pramful of washing to the 'steamie'. The house was still full to overflowing with her seven children. It had two bedrooms, a front room and a living room. Alec and Madge slept on a bed settee in the front room. The bedrooms, one for the boys and one for the girls, both had bunk beds.

Catriona noticed that the small house wasn't any warmer than her mausoleum of a place in Botanic Crescent. Just like in Botanic Crescent, everyone in the Broomknowes Road flat crowded round the coal fire in the living room, roasted at the front and frozen at the back. Winter or summer, to go into the bathroom in either house was like walking into a freezer. It was a torment to bare one's skin, even to sit on the toilet.

Alec had a regular job now, thanks to Quaker Sammy, and was almost back to his former confident, cocky self, although Madge had him on a short lead and kept a vigilant eye out for any signs of his old philandering ways.

Catriona switched off the Hoover when she reached the bay window and gazed out at Botanic Crescent. She could see Madge's tall figure striding along towards Queen Margaret Drive surrounded by her family, intent on catching the next tram car to Springburn. From there they'd walk up the hill to Balornock and their flat in Broomknowes Road.

Their mutual friend, Julie, lived in the Gorbals, but she had been working all day in Copeland & Lye's department store, so she hadn't been able to join the television viewing. Julie was slim and smart, and could sound and act very 'posh'. As she herself said, she had to keep up with the wealthy customers in Copeland & Lye's and also, of course, with her mother-in-law. It was a strange set-up with Julie and Mrs Muriel Vincent, Catriona thought. Julie's husband had been an RAF pilot, but he had been shot down during the war. Mrs Vincent and Julie had never had anything in common. Now the only thing they shared was a terrible grief. Mrs Vincent was the only child of Catriona and Melvin's elderly next-door neighbours, the Reverend Reid and his wife. Always immaculately dressed, Mrs Vincent was a politely spoken, middle-class snob, who regarded the Gorbals as hell. She tried everything to prevent Julie's marriage to her son, Reggie. But after Reggie's death and for years now, she had clung to Julie as if Julie was her own flesh and blood. She even wanted Julie to come and live with her in her roomy flat in Botanic Crescent but Julie had always refused.

'She suffocates me, that woman,' Julie complained. But in her own abrupt, proud way, she still managed to be kind to the older woman. She even called her 'Mum' or 'Mother'.

'Och well,' she explained to Catriona, 'it keeps her happy.'

As far as Catriona knew, Julie had been brought up by her father. She'd once asked what had happened to her mother but Julie had just shrugged and dismissed the query with an abrupt, 'Haven't a clue!'

It was nearly ten years since Reggie had been killed, but Julie had never married again. She'd had an illegitimate baby, the result of drowning her grief in drink on the wild night of the victory

31

celebrations, VE night, as it was called. She had given the baby – a little girl – up for adoption and had confided in Catriona. Catriona had tried to persuade her against it at the time.

'You'll always regret it,' she'd warned. But Julie insisted she had to think of the child's future, not her own, and the baby would have a better life with a secure and loving family. Although she remained her usual perky self and put on a brave face, Catriona saw the suffering in Julie's eyes the day she had come out of the hospital without the baby.

Mrs Vincent had found out but had been intensely supportive. Catriona guessed Mrs Vincent felt that Julie was the last link with her son. And Reggie had told his mother how much he loved Julie and asked her to look after his young wife while he was away during the war.

Mrs Vincent had certainly done that ever since. Or as much as the fiercely independent Julie would allow her to. Julie was coming later in the evening to see the television.

At one time at the beginning of their marriage, when they lived in Dessie Street, Melvin had not allowed Catriona to have any friends. He'd been the same with his first wife. 'But oh,' Catriona kept assuring herself, 'I'm made of stronger, more stubborn stuff!'

4

The Stoddarts lived up the same close in Broom-knowes Road as Madge and Alec. It was over a year ago that they had all been to visit Melvin, watch the Coronation and admire his television set. The Stoddarts had even sat next to the Catholic O'Donnels without a complaint. They also lived up the same close and couldn't always be avoided. Like all the others in the street, the close had a shabby-looking entrance decorated with the cheapest, reddish-brown paint the Corporation could find. The brown colour went halfway up each wall and was topped by flaking whitewash. The tenants did their best to keep the place looking decent. They took turns washing the close, the landings and the stairs, and conscientiously decorated each side with squiggles of white pipe clay. Chrissie Stoddart had told Madge that these squiggles kept witches at bay. Or so the folk long ago believed.

At seventeen, Chrissie was the oldest daughter and she read a lot. Her mother was always complaining about that. 'She's like a walkin' encyclopedia, that one. All her spare time's spent down in Springburn Library.'

Both Jimmy Stoddart and his wife Aggie were fervent members of the local Orange Lodge. Madge and Alec and their brood were friendly enough to the family, as they were to all their neighbours, but they didn't go along with the Stoddarts' extreme anti-Catholic views.

After all, as Alec said, 'The O'Donnels are regular chapel goers and they're as good neighbours as the Stoddarts – better even. Anyway, everybody's entitled to their own thing.'

'Except you,' Madge said. 'We all know what your thing is.'

Alec rolled his eyes heavenwards. 'I'm talking about religion and religious bigotry, Madge.'

'Aye, well. Just you watch it.'

He'd enjoyed chatting up and flirting with his women clients when he'd been an insurance man. He'd loved the work. He had been his own boss, out and about, on the move all the time, swaggering through the Glasgow streets, always ready with a cheery word or a wink that set women of all ages giggling.

After the war, like thousands of other ex-servicemen, he couldn't get any job at all and, as a result, soon got into arrears with his rent and was kicked out. It was then that he and his family had been hounded from pillar to post, sometimes having to walk the streets with nowhere to go. It had been terrible for them all but particularly humiliating and degrading for him. For one thing, he'd always been a natty dresser, but he'd become shabbier and shabbier, dirty too, because in some of the places where they'd been forced to live, there had been no hot water or any kind of decent sanitary conditions.

To make things worse, Madge had never stopped nagging at him since she'd found out about his bit of nonsense with Catriona McNair, not to mention Ruth Hunter. And he'd never touched Ruth. OK, he would have, if he'd got the chance, but he didn't. He'd had the occasional bit of fun with a couple of others over the years, but all that had meant nothing. He'd always stuck by Madge and the weans, despite Madge's constant nagging. Sometimes, she went too far and he'd burst out with, 'You'll be blaming me for the bloody war next, Madge.'

He used to be so miserable, he was tempted to leave the lot of them. He could have hitch-hiked down to England and tried for a job there. He'd have managed fine on his own. Somehow, he could never do it, though. He knew Madge loved him despite the nasty way she sometimes carried on. Now she was going through 'the change', which didn't help.

'At least you'll no' be able to lumber me wi' any more weans,' she'd say, as if she wished he hadn't 'lumbered' her with any in the first place. Nothing was further from the truth, of course.

She had loved him and he had loved her, and they had loved all their cheeky wee sods of weans. He supposed he still loved Madge, although she had long since changed from the easygoing, happy-go-lucky girl she'd once been. Freckle-faced, big-hipped, melon-breasted Madge with her long, sturdy legs, toothy grin and candid stare had gone. At least now she was clean and passably decent in her dress – unlike when they used to wander out from the unsanitary camp of Nissen huts where they'd been existing and Madge would admire the posh villas along Great Western Road. These occasions were purgatory for him.

Madge would keep crying out to the children, 'Oh, Sadie, look at this one, hen. Look at its lovely big windows. How many rooms do you think this one'll have, eh?' Or, 'Agnes, would you just look at that. Oh, isn't that just lovely, hen?'

In the silent gardens and streets where no children played, Madge's voice, booming out with such excruciating loudness, made him cringe, even now, remembering. Not that they had needed Madge's voice to draw attention to themselves. Nine of them crowding along the pavement was more than enough. He remembered being acutely conscious of his own seedy appearance and of Madge's down-at-heel shoes and dirty ankles, and the children's motley mixture of ill-fitting clothes, the girls' skimpy coats, with dingy dresses drooping underneath, and the boys' knobbly wrists protruding from their jackets. Worst of all, he remembered Charlie, his mouth plugged with a dummy teat, his nose running and his dirty nappy dropping down at his ankles. He was especially fond of Charlie. During the war, the other children had grown away from him and resented him as a symbol of authority.

Madge kept shouting at them, 'I'll tell Daddy on you, ye rotten wee midden!' Or 'Daddy'll throttle you, I'm warning you.'

The older children became sulky and resentful. But the youngest, Charlie, just used to put out his arms to him. He was eight now and still a loving and lovable wee chap.

Each time they returned to the camp after one of these walks, he felt especially diminished. The grand houses all around emphasised the fact that he was no use as a provider. All he could manage for his family was a dark, corrugated-iron cave.

He'd thanked God, and Sammy Hunter, many times over the years for getting him out of there. Once he'd got a job, it became easier to get a house. One way and another, he'd eventually managed to get the Corporation flat which, in comparison with the iron Nissen hut, was sheer heaven. Oh, the bliss of a bath and clean clothes! Some of his self-confidence had returned and with it, his bonhomie and even a hint of his old jaunty walk.

He could easily have graduated from the store-room to the office by now. He'd been offered a move upstairs more than once over the years he'd worked for McHendry's. He was eager to jump at the chance, but Madge would have none of it. In the storeroom, he would only work with two other storemen. In the office there were girls.

'No way are you going back to being the smart Alec you were before, and fuckin' every girl you work with.'

It never failed to shock him when Madge resorted to using the 'f' word. It never seemed so bad when men used it, although it wasn't a swear word he was in the habit of using himself. But it didn't seem right coming from a woman's mouth, especially his wife and the mother of his children. He'd once said that to Madge and she'd retaliated with 'You know what you are – a fuckin' mealy-mouthed hypocrite!'

Whatever else he was, he was not that. All right, he was no angel, but he'd done his best for Madge and the weans. Madge could have got a lot worse than him. He knew men who regularly battered their wives. What about guys who regularly stole, burgled or mugged folk to get cash? Others drank and gambled their wages away. He only took the odd pint of beer with his mates and went with them to watch football matches. Madge would have stopped him going to the football if she could have managed it. Once, she'd even threatened to go with him. That was just laughable. A woman at a football match?

'Don't be ridiculous, hen,' he'd told her. Eventually she'd compromised by demanding that he took Hector or Willie along with him.

'It's not really a place for weans either, Madge.'

He had seen some family men at Partick Thistle matches with their sons, but even that kind of dad would surely have agreed that Rangers and Celtic games were far too dangerous for a twelve-year-old and an eleven-year-old. At Ibrox Park, a vast sea of men in coats, mufflers, bunnets and soft hats were packed in like sardines. If someone passed out in the crush, a white hanky was waved until the Red Cross men pushed through to rescue him. Vicious fights could, quite literally, turn the place into a bloody battlefield.

But even at a big event like an 'Old Firm' game, as the Rangers and Celtic matches were called, Madge insisted that either Hector or Willie, or both, accompanied Alec. It was to keep an eye on him, of course – not to see if he was going into a pub, only to see if he'd hooked on to another woman. Madge didn't care about anything except that.

He'd got used to Catriona now. After all, she

38

had suffered and was still suffering as much from Melvin as he did from Madge. But not for the same reason. Only Madge and, perhaps, Julie knew about the mistake he and Catriona had made donkey's years ago. Melvin had never found out. What Alec could never understand was why Madge had taken Catriona's side and ever since had been like a big sister to her. OK, Catriona had been like a stupid wee wean at the time and, OK, maybe he had taken advantage of that, but all the same...

Madge could be stupid and almost as naive as Catriona at times – she even thought Melvin was marvellous. Oh yes, Catriona's husband had suffered during the war but not her own. According to Madge, Alec had enjoyed the war – a girl in every port and all that. That was one thing that made him feel really bitter. Madge hadn't a clue what he'd gone through during the war. By God, he had suffered. No way would he ever join up again.

It was one of the things he had in common with Sammy. Sometimes they'd talk about the war over a pint in the Boundary Bar. He hated it as much as Sammy now although maybe without quite so much fire. It was a kind of resentful bitterness with him, while Sammy burned with fury. It took a few pints more, and a change of subject (usually to football), to calm Sammy down and get him in a good humour again. Then, as often as not, Sammy would come home with him to Balornock for his tea. Sammy was one friend that Madge approved of and he was always made welcome. He supposed it was his

39

Quaker credentials.

At times, he'd even been tempted (and what a laugh that would cause Madge) to go along with Sammy to one of his Quaker meetings. He never could – secretly he believed that he wasn't good enough. Sammy was a great guy, a tough guy, but there was a basic goodness about him that Alec knew he could never match. He'd met some of Sammy's Quaker friends and felt the same about them. A bit eccentric, some of them. They didn't seem to care about material things all that much. He'd certainly never spotted any fashion models among them. He didn't feel clever enough either. Quite a few of them were academics – although Sammy wasn't, right enough. Some of the things he heard about them really amused him. Like the woman in Bearsden (Bearsden of all places!) who helped to rehabilitate ex-cons. One of the things she did was to wash their clothes. He had to laugh. He could just imagine what that woman's posh church-going Bearsden neighbours thought of her and said about her. He bet none of it was complimentary or Christian.

Sammy often went to matches with Alec although, as a companion in that situation, Sammy could be embarrassing or even downright dangerous. Not at the local Partick Thistle matches – they got on fine there. But Ibrox or Hampden or Celtic Park was a different story. If it was an Old Firm game, there would be chanting and insults bawled at the Celtic players, or Celtic fans, from the Rangers side. If the perpetrator happened to be standing near Sammy, Sammy would accuse him of being a mindless bigot and say that he

40

ought to be ashamed of himself and no wonder there were wars in the world. Or he'd come out with something even worse. Alec had to desperately nudge Sammy and tell him to shut up or he was liable to start a war right there and then.

The folk doing the bigoted bawling had so far always been gobsmacked into silence at Sammy's nerve, but then, obviously deciding he must be a nutcase, they'd soon abruptly restart their bawling and chanting.

Much as he admired Sammy for his nerve and for everything else, and much as he treasured him as his best friend, Alec would rather go with Hector or Willie to an Ibrox match. He never liked saying so to Sammy, of course, and, as often as not, they did go together. Afterwards, he had to make sure they didn't end up either in a Rangers pub or a Celtic one. The Loudon in Duke Street was a Rangers pub and there was always the danger, if he and Sammy went there, that someone would start chanting or shouting obscenities about Celtic or Catholics. Sammy would, at the very least, tell them to shut up. This was the same as asking to be kicked in the head. If Sammy opened his big mouth and told someone what he thought of them in the Crown bar in Duke Street, which was a bar always packed with Celtic supporters, and especially if he didn't bother to hide the fact that he was a Rangers supporter, extreme violence – even murder – would be a distinct possibility.

Sammy scared the shit out of Alec at times. Admittedly, not everyone was a bigot. In somewhere like The Titwood, it would be safe enough.

41

There were just photos of the Queen's Park team there. But Alec was developing muscles he never knew he had from continually dragging Sammy away from potentially dangerous situations.

Madge always said, 'At least you'll never get into any trouble if Sammy's with you.'

He had to laugh!

5

Maybe it was Madge's twins' birthday party and Madge ordering such a fancy cake that had reminded her. There was hardly enough room for all the icing on the top, never mind the candles. She'd even asked for the year – 1957 – in pink icing, as well as both the twins' names and ages, and fancy scrolls all round. Julie, no doubt, would never need any reminder.

'What age would she be now?' Madge asked Julie.

Catriona hastily intervened. 'Maybe Julie would rather not talk about it, Madge.'

Madge shrugged. 'It was her that started it. She said it would be her wean's birthday today.'

'It's OK,' Julie said. 'She'd be twelve.'

Madge took a big slurp of tea and a bite of her biscuit. 'Ever wonder where she is or how she's getting on, hen?'

'Every day. Every single day.'

'Och, you regret it. I thought you would, hen. I go on something awful about my weans. I mean, they drive me nearly demented at times, but I wouldn't be without them. I could never have given one of my weans away.'

'Madge!' Catriona hissed. 'For pity's sake!'

Julie lit a cigarette. 'You were in a different situation to me, Madge. I'd just lost my man. I was devastated and I got stupid drunk on VE night.'

'But you said...'

'I know what I said at the time.' She gave a sarcastic laugh. 'A married man who adored me, but he couldn't leave his wife. Or was it that I couldn't split up his marriage? Something like that. I was just saving face, Madge. The truth is I just got bloody drunk. I've no idea who the father is, never did know.'

'I wish,' Catriona said gently, 'you'd have tried to manage. We'd have helped you, Julie. I told you at the time that you'd always regret giving up your wee girl.'

'Oh yes,' Julie said bitterly. 'Go on, enjoy the "I told you so's".'

'I'm not enjoying any such thing. I'm sorry I said that. It was thoughtless of me. I just wish things could have been different for you, that's all.'

'Aye, OK.' Julie sucked at her Woodbine, then blew a quick puff of smoke towards the ceiling.

Madge said, 'Have you thought about trying to find her?'

'Oh, I've thought about it. But how would I work that miracle? Do you think anyone's likely to tell me where she is? No chance, pal.'

Catriona nibbled worriedly at her lip. 'There'd be no harm in trying, I suppose.'

Julie took a deep breath. 'I said it at the time and I'll say it again: it's the child I've got to think about. It's what's best for her that mattered to me then, and I feel the same now. I'm a single working woman living in a wee room and kitchen in the Gorbals. What kind of life could I give a twelve-year-old girl? I bet she's living the life of Riley just now with some posh couple in a big villa in Bearsden. Or maybe even up north someplace and going to a posh private school. Good luck to her, wherever she is.'

'Nobody could give her a mother's love like you,' Catriona said.

'Oh, aye, in between working all day to make enough money to pay the rent and feed us, you mean?'

We would help, wouldn't we, Madge?'

'Sure we would, hen. Nae bother.'

'No bother!' Julie laughed again. 'That's all you need with your seven kids, and Catriona with her big house and two boys and her helping out in her man's business as well. Oh, aye, no bother at all!'

'She's OK.' Madge jerked a head in Catriona's direction. 'Talk about living the life of Riley? She's got a man that dotes on her and gives her everything she wants and more. What about that television set? She had that long before anybody else, and it was bought for cash as well. We had to get ours on tick. She's even got a bloody washing machine – and a telephone. A telephone!'

A hint of bitterness crept into Catriona's voice then. 'You've always thought I was lucky, haven't you, Madge?'

'You're damn right I have, hen. If you'd had the life I've had to suffer, especially with that big, two-timing midden I'm married to, you'd know exactly why I think you're damned lucky.'

'For God's sake!' Julie stubbed out her cigarette. 'Don't let's start a fight. We're supposed to be best pals, remember?'

Madge's big frame suddenly shook and bounced with laughter. 'Here, the pair of you would know all about it if I started a fight. I'd flatten you both before you could say Jack Robinson.'

'Or Alec Jackson?' Julie grinned.

'Watch it, you!' Madge warned, but still with bouncing good humour. 'You're a cheeky wee sod, so you are!'

They surfed away on the swell of Madge's laughter to speak about other things. How great it was that sweetie rationing had stopped, for instance. They kidded Madge on about how she used to pinch some of Alec and the children's sweetie coupons.

'Och, I'm a right rotten pig, so I am.' Madge took them seriously. 'Me and my bloody sweet tooth!'

They all agreed what bliss it was that sugar and eggs were now derationed. They all loved too the new dish that had been created for Queen Elizabeth's Coronation. It was called Coronation Chicken and was absolutely delicious. Their mouths watered at the thought.

'I'll be getting like the size of a double-decker bus before long,' Madge laughed. 'God, I enjoy my food, so I do.'

They had been having a lunch of tea, sandwiches and biscuits in the restaurant in Copeland & Lye's, where Julie was one of the sales ladies in the underwear department. 'It's time I went back to work,' Julie said. 'I'm not a lady of leisure like you two.'

'Now, that is a laugh!' Catriona said, without sounding amused in the slightest.

Julie took out her powder compact and studied her pert features and sad eyes and the tendrils of glossy hair curling from under her hat. Before rubbing her powder puff over her nose, she said, 'I thought I saw a grey hair yesterday.'

'You're needing glasses, hen. If you'd as many grey hairs as me, you'd have something to worry about.'

Catriona assured her, 'You're a good-looking girl, Julie. I can't understand why you haven't married again.'

'Girl? I hate to disillusion you, pal, but the three of us have long since passed the stage of being girls.'

'Don't be daft. You can't even be in your thirties yet.'

'There'll always be a bit of wean in wee blondie.' Madge jerked her head towards Catriona. 'Talk about luck.'

'Oh yes, my life of Riley again! My big house and my television set and my washing machine and my telephone, not to mention my saintly husband.'

'I was thinking about the way you've never been lumbered by a mob of weans. See them weans of mine? I could murder them at times, so I could.'

She shoved her red beret further back on her head. 'See all my grey hairs? That's worrying about them weans, so it is.'

Julie tucked her powder compact back into her handbag and took a last sip of tea. 'I'd better go. See you.'

'Not if I see you first, hen,' Madge laughed.

'Aye, right.'

She waved them goodbye and clipped away on her black, high-heeled court shoes. She knew she looked smarter than her two friends, in her black tailored costume and pristine white blouse. The knowledge gave her spirits a triumphant lift. She believed in keeping up appearances and had always succeeded in putting on a brave front. But her triumph was short-lived and her bravery superficial. Alone in bed at night, she often suffered tornadoes of grief and regret. She wept. Sometimes she'd give up trying to sleep and get up, make herself a cup of tea and sit nursing it on the fender stool close to the dying embers of the fire.

Her hole-in-the-wall bed in the kitchen was cosier than the one in the front room. The front room was always cold as the North Pole. Sometimes she didn't bother lighting the gas mantle in the kitchen. She just crouched underneath it, watching the feeble light from the black iron grate flicker around the cramped room. It picked out the ghostly form of the scrubbed table, the wooden chairs, the high shelf on which sat her best china and two china dogs, or 'wally dugs', as they were known to most Glaswegians.

The light made grey shadows of the sink and

the swan-necked tap under the window and, when she filled the kettle, she could gaze out on to the back court with its overflowing midden and the occasional darting of rats. It was the front room that had the view of the street below. The street was always full of interesting, lively bustle during the day and, on long summer evenings, she liked to sit there watching Glasgow life go by. At weekends, she sometimes went out to visit friends or with one or two of the girls at work to the cinema. It depended if there was a good picture on, or if the other girls weren't going out with boyfriends. A date with a man always took precedence. She'd once gone to the dancing in the Barrowlands Ballroom with Flora. Flora had been stood up by a bloke and, at the last minute, had persuaded Julie to go to the Barrowlands as a kind of 'I don't care' gesture of defiance.

Flora had insisted she preferred a girlfriend's company any day. She was lying, of course, and the disaster of an evening hadn't been helped by the manager ordering them off the floor for dancing together.

The older women who got married always left work to concentrate on the care of home, husband and eventually children. As a result, Julie either had to go out with younger women or fall back on her real friends, Madge and Catriona. They had stood by her through thick and thin for years and she was grateful to them, although pride had always prevented her from showing her feelings.

It had been true what she'd said to them about

48

her wee girl. She just wanted the best for her – always had done. Yet, at the same time, she longed to find her, to see her. She told herself it was just to make sure she was all right. But, oh, in her heart, she knew it was more than that. She felt again the agonising wrench when the nurse came and took the baby away. She suffered the acute pain as if it had happened only yesterday.

And she wanted her back.

6

'What's my bloody school got to do with it?' Dermot O'Donnel jerked out his cleft chin.

'Don't you dare swear at me, you ignorant, impertinent lout,' Melvin said. 'I have no intention of giving the likes of you a job in here.'

'The likes of me being a Catholic, you mean, and having proved it by going to St Joseph's school?'

'It's nothing to do with your religion.'

'Think I sailed up the Clyde in a banana boat?' Dermot sneered. 'If I'd said Bearsden Academy or even the worst Protestant school in Glasgow, you would have taken me.'

'No. I would not. Now, I'm busy and I've other men to see, so away you go and stop wasting my time.'

Dermot, who had hoped against the odds to join McNair's as a trainee baker, strode out of McNair's office at the back and pushed his way roughly through the crowd of customers in the front shop. His cap was jerked down, his mouth was a tight twist and his fists were clenched. He was furious. He burst into the Balornock flat, that was home to his mother, father, younger brother and two sisters, and crashed down into a chair.

Sean said, 'You didn't get it, then?'

'Bloody Orange bigot! Just because I went to St Joseph's.'

'He'd know you kicked with your left foot without needing to know what school you went to,' Sean grinned. 'Dermot O'Donnel isn't usually a Protestant name.'

'I bet he's a regular at the local Orange Lodge. Up at the front of every Orange Walk, with his bloody bowler hat crammed on his fat head.'

Sean fell silent and serious, remembering. It was at times like these that his brother Dermot could absolutely terrify him. Dermot seemed to thrive on trouble and, if there was no fighting going on, he made it happen by his suicidal (as it seemed to Sean) provocation. At every Orange Walk, one of the most fiercely kept rules was that no one was allowed to break the flow of marchers by crossing a road that they were marching along. He had been out with Dermot once and had stopped at the pavement's edge to wait until a Walk passed before crossing the road. To his horror, Dermot began pushing his way through one of the flute bands to cross to the other side. He was lucky not to have been torn to shreds. The nearest sashed, bowler-hatted men hadn't seemed to notice. Maybe they were too full of themselves, strutting along, puffed up with pride.

Or maybe it was because most of those nearest to the flute band were middle-aged or elderly and Dermot looked like an aggressive young bull, that most of them ignored him. Anyway, miraculously, no fight had resulted from that incident.

There had been plenty of other occasions when Dermot had got his way and there had been a barney. At only twenty, his reputation as a fighter was so well known that guys sometimes even came to the door actually wanting a fight, in order to prove themselves or enhance their reputations as hard men. Of course, they never managed to win. Dermot was one of Glasgow's top hard men and head of the Balornock Boys, a local gang who occasionally had vicious street fights with the Springburn Savages. He'd once taken on three of them at once. They'd come 'to teach Dermot a lesson'. Dermot had felled each one of them in a matter of seconds.

'Bloody cheek, coming up here,' he'd said afterwards, smacking his fists together and hitching up his shoulders. He'd obviously enjoyed himself. Sean couldn't understand it. Give him a good book any time.

Even at school in Balornock, Dermot, with his cropped bullet head, thick neck and wide-legged stance, had invited trouble – although, before long, nobody in the school would risk taking him on. Sean had been grateful that it had saved him from being bullied. As the brother of Dermot O'Donnel, nobody dared touch him.

But, since leaving school, he just wished Dermot would calm down, maybe meet some nice girl and get married. Personally, he'd wanted to go on to university, but his parents dismissed the idea and told him to stop being such a useless dreamer, get off his backside, get a job and start making some money. Well, he'd got a job in McHendry's office, thanks to Alec Jackson and Alec's pal, Sammy Hunter, who both put a good word in for him. The rest of his family weren't so extreme as Dermot and didn't mind him being helped by two Protestants and working for a Protestant company. Especially his sister, Ailish. She shared Sean's interest in books and they often had long talks about different stories they'd read. Although she just read novels, he had become more adventurous and had tackled a few biographies of famous men and even a couple of books on psychology. He knew about Freud and Jung and he was interested in what made people tick. But he still couldn't understand why Dermot was the way he was.

Well, maybe that wasn't quite true. Michael, his father, was heavily built and could get quite aggressive at times. Dermot had probably taken after him. Michael certainly had some strong views about religion and he often argued with 'Proddies' as he called them. Never with Alec Jackson or Sammy Hunter, though. Alec was too easy-going and Sammy was a Quaker so nobody knew what to make of him. The McKechnies were Jehovah's Witnesses and wouldn't listen to anybody about anything.

Why, Sean kept wondering, didn't he and at least one of his sisters – coming from the same parents and having had the same upbringing – not turn out like Dermot? To be fair though, behind all the terrible aggression and hatred of Proddies, especially Rangers supporters, Dermot was a generous guy. If he was your friend (or your brother), he would do anything for you, give you his last halfpenny. If only, Sean kept thinking to himself, praying to himself, if only Dermot would stop being so desperate for confrontation. To go anywhere with him was like teetering on the edge of a dangerous precipice. He'd had a few girlfriends who had no doubt been attracted by his rock-like features and hard, muscular body, but soon enough they all got fed up when they found that half the time they didn't get the peace to enjoy a night at the dancing or the cinema with him. Too often, there was some violent and un-welcome distraction in which Dermot was the centre of attention.

Now, of course, he was unemployed and couldn't afford to take a girl anywhere.

'I could speak to Sammy Hunter and maybe he would put a good word in for you. Or better still, Alec Jackson. There might not be any vacancies just now, but if they know your name…'

They knew his name all right. Who didn't? That was the trouble.

'You might be quite happy to work for a Proddy firm, Sean, but not me. I've had enough of them.'

'What do you mean, you've had enough of them? You haven't worked for any of them.'

'If Melvin McNair is anything to go by…'

'He isn't.'

'He's a right shit.'

'The boss of McHendry's isn't like that. I know, I work there, remember.'

53

'Aye, just as a favour to Sammy Hunter because he's in with the bricks. What do you bet they ask any other guy who applies for a job what school he went to? They all do.'

'You'll never get another job if you take that attitude.'

'It's the bosses have the attitude. Proddy bastards!'

'Och, for goodness' sake!' Sean gave up. Dermot was hopeless. There was no budging him.

Ailish had been sitting nearby reading a book and she shook her head in sympathy with Sean.

'What's up with you?' she asked Dermot. 'Why can't you just relax?'

'Oh, aye, you're all right,' Dermot said, his aggression fizzling out. He was more of a soft touch with his sisters. 'You in your posh Copeland & Lye's.'

'Yes, and I haven't a clue what their religion is and I don't care.'

After a moment's pause, Dermot said, 'Will they be needing any storemen there, I wonder? Or van drivers?'

In his last job at the garage, he'd learned to drive. He'd been getting on fine and was a good worker. But then he'd got into a fight with a customer and, as a result, he'd been fired.

Ailish looked worried. 'I don't know. But I'll keep my ear to the ground and try and find out.'

'Thanks, hen.'

Sean knew what Ailish was feeling. She wanted to help Dermot the same as he did, but she was worried about the consequences. Dermot was a magnet for trouble, even without the Balornock

54

Boys. He wasn't the type to fit into Copeland & Lye's in any capacity. Dermot would look more at home in one of Glasgow's toughest bars than in one of the city's most genteel and upper-class shops.

Now there was a thought. 'Here, how about being a barman, Dermot? I bet any bar would jump at the chance of having you there to keep order in the place. Well, maybe not *any* bar,' he corrected himself, then laughed. 'Forget the Rangers bars, but how about a good Celtic one?'

Dermot's craggy face immediately lit up with hope.

'What a bloody good idea! I'll give that a try. You're the one with the brains, right enough, Sean. No doubt about it.'

'Aye, sure.' Sean laughed along with his brother, feeling really pleased that he'd been able to help him.

Ailish said, after Dermot had gone whistling cheerily out of the room, 'That really was a brilliant idea, Sean. I'm sure he'll get taken on. Then, once he's earning again and in a steady job, he'll stop getting mixed up in these horrible gang wars, meet some nice girl and get married and settle down and have a family. Then he'll be fine.'

'Hang on! You and your imagination. You should be writing stories.'

'But it could happen, and it's what Dermot needs. If he had a home of his own...'

'I know. I know. But let's just keep our fingers crossed and hope for the best at the moment.'

'And pray.' Ailish was one of the least bigoted members of the family and the most sincerely religious. She had a picture of the Holy Mother above her bed and often she could be seen fingering her rosary beads and muttering her prayers. She tried to perform her devotions in private but it was a bit difficult when she had to share a small bedroom with her much bigger, much noisier sister Jessie.

Like Dermot, Jessie took after their father. At eighteen, she was hefty like Michael and Dermot, but neither father's nor daughter's flesh was as hard and muscular as Dermot's. Jessie was just fat. Their mother had a painfully thin body, thin grey hair and a jaundiced complexion. She suffered from asthma and was constantly struggling for breath.

Sean thanked God neither he, with his black hair, nor fair-haired Ailish had inherited either of their parents' hatred of Protestants. Especially living up the same close as Protestant families like the Jacksons and the Stoddarts, not to mention the Paters and the McKechnies. The latter two families thankfully kept themselves to themselves. The Jacksons were OK, but he could see big trouble erupting one of these days with the Stoddarts. For this reason, he dreaded occasions like the Orange Walk and Old Firm matches.

There was an Orange Walk every year on the anniversary of the Battle of the Boyne. Sean's heart weighed him down at the thought. All it would take on one of these occasions was the sight of Jimmy Stoddart swaggering out of the close wearing his bowler hat and orange sash to set Dermot off. All it would take to start the Battle of Glasgow was for Jimmy Stoddart to sing

'The Sash'. One of these days, Sean felt certain, all this senseless bigotry was going to end in tragedy.

7

Before 1958 was out, Sammy decided to join the Red Cross and work for them in his spare time. *Good*

'Are you a masochist or something?' Alec asked him.

'Och, I'm used to it.'

'How do you mean? You work at a desk in an office.' *Quakers*

'I served in the Friends' Ambulance Unit for a while.'

'Even so. They saw to the injured on the front line during the war, didn't they? That's a lot different from looking after the injured at Glasgow events like football matches.' He hesitated with mock thoughtfulness. 'Although ... I don't know.'

Sammy laughed. 'The Red Cross believes in looking after folk in need or in pain. It doesn't matter who they are or what side they're on. That applies all over the world. Even in Glasgow.' *True*

Alec couldn't imagine Sammy in a uniform of any kind. One of the guys who'd been at Maryhill Barracks at the same time as Sammy had told of how Sammy refused to put on the khaki. How he'd survived the punishments meted out to him for that and everything else, Alec couldn't imagine. He remembered only too well how Sammy had looked at Ruth's funeral. That's when the Quakers had got him out. What a mess his face had been in, and no doubt his body had been covered with injuries as well. 'After what happened in the past, I was surprised at you agreeing to put on any kind of uniform.'

'It's not the uniform that's the problem. It's what it stands for.'

Alec grinned. 'I was always a wow with the girls in the old bell-bottoms.'

'I bet!'

For a second, Alec felt terrible in case his thoughtless remark would make Sammy remember him and Ruth. But Sammy's response had sounded perfectly good humoured, with no hint of bitterness.

'Well, anyway, I don't envy you having to patch up all the injured at matches. You'll never have time to see the game.'

Sammy shrugged. 'I'll not be the only Red Cross man in attendance and the St John Ambulance'll be there as well.'

'Aye, and there'll be supporters of both sides having to be patched up. Just try and make sure, when it's an Old Firm match, that you don't cart any Rangers and Celtic fans off to the hospital in the same ambulance. You'll be more like a referee then than anything else.'

'Stop worrying, Alec. You're getting as bad as my mother.'

'God forbid!' Hastily he backtracked. 'I don't mean anything against your mother. You know what I mean.'

'Yes, I know what you mean.'

It seemed to be Alec's day for putting his foot in it. Sammy's mother was a poor soul, bullied by his father, terrified of him as well no doubt. Alec didn't blame her. No wonder she was always so anxious about her favourite son. If she lost Sammy, it would finish her. All her other sons had gone either to England or abroad – to escape from old Hodge Hunter, no doubt. He'd have emigrated to the North Pole if it had been him. What an old horror! The exact opposite of his pacifist son, Hodge had been a military man all his life.

Alec remembered well, and now with shame, how he and other boys would jeer and laugh at the Hunter family as Hodge put young Sammy and his brothers through the military-style drills in Springburn Park. Poor sods. As if they weren't having a bad enough time with their horror of a father, without the likes of him and his pals tormenting them.

'Fancy coming up to Balornock for a bite to eat?' Alec asked. They had been enjoying a pint in the Boundary Bar in Springbum after work.

'Madge'll be getting fed up with me turning up for my tea so often.'

'Nonsense. She thinks the world of you. It's the only time she gives me any peace. She thinks I can't get up to any mischief when I'm with you. With women, she means. To her, you're my bloody guardian angel.'

He'd done it again.

Sammy groaned and shook his head, making Alec quickly add, 'You know what she's like.'

'Yeah, yeah.'

'Are you coming then?'

'Well, if you're sure...'

'Definitely. I'm depending on you mentioning the walk.'

'The Quaker walk?'

'Well, this year's Orange Walk's past. Thank goodness we were on holiday. Doon the watter. All crushed together in a wee room and kitchen. Mad, isn't it?'

'It's a hill walk. Are you fit for it?'

'Bloody cheek!' Alec stuck out his chest and threw back his shoulders. 'I'm as fit as you, mate. I wasn't in the navy for nothing.'

'Yes, I know. It was to get away from Madge.'

Alec grinned. 'You're right there.'

'Do you think she'll believe you?'

'Well, it's true, isn't it? I am going.'

'You'd better. You're not on if you're hoping to use me as a cover for anything else.'

'Don't worry, Sammy.'

'You did that once before, remember?'

'OK. OK. But this time it's either a hill climb or an afternoon with the Stoddarts down the stair. It's Big Aggie's birthday. They've probably invited half the Orange Lodge as well. Have you seen inside their place?'

Sammy shook his head.

'It's like a shrine to Rangers. Jimmy's got pictures of players lining every wall in his front room and a big picture of Ibrox Park hanging over the mantelpiece. I support Rangers myself, as you know, but he's a bloody fanatic.'

'Oh, I don't know. I've got pictures of Partick Thistle all over my house.'

60

Alec laughed. 'Aye, that'll be right. Anyway, no way am I going to be stuck for hours with Jimmy and his cronies talking about football. He can make the most torrid matches sound a bore. I've said I promised ages ago to go to this Quaker thing, booked in and all that. Swore on the Bible that I'd be there.'

'Alec!'

'I won't be at the thing beforehand, though. I'll meet you outside. It just isn't me.'

'Why not?'

'Och, come on, Sammy. You know me.'

'OK, OK, I'll meet you outside.'

They were passing the Wellfield Cinema and beginning the walk up the steep incline of Wellfield Street. Alec jerked his head in the direction of the 'Wellie', as it was often called, especially by the local children. 'I used to get in there for the price of a few jam jars. Did you?'

'No. After school and at weekends, we had to do various army drills and manoeuvres.' Sammy's mouth tightened. 'Or I'd be on some sort of punishment. Standing outside the mortuary for hours in the dark was a favourite one. Not with me, needless to say.'

'My God, Sammy, every time I think of your father, I don't know how you put up with him. Even to this day.'

'What choice did I have? Especially as a child.'

Now there was his mother, Alec thought.

As if reading his mind, Sammy said, 'I've asked my mother to leave him and come and stay with me, but I think she's been frightened of him for too long. At first, she made the excuse that he

61

was an old man and she hadn't the heart to leave him now. But eventually she admitted that she was afraid he'd come after her when I was out at work, and she's probably right. It sounds ridiculous in a way, but I gave her a puppy and that seems to have comforted and helped her. She loves that dog, and it loves her.'

'Och, well, you've done your best, Sammy.'

At the top of the Wellfield hill, they turned left, crossed over to the Co-op, then went round the corner to the right and along past the line of shops to Broomknowes Road. They crossed the road again at the grassy patch called the triangle and went up Alec's close. The Jacksons lived one up, so both men clattered up the stone stairs past the Stoddarts' and the McKechnies' doors. John and Vera McKechnie had a son and daughter and all were devout members of the Jehovah's Witnesses. They would take a dim view of the Stoddarts' birthday celebrations. They seemed to take a dim view of everything everybody did.

'Hello, Sammy.' Madge greeted him with one of her toothy grins. 'The kettle's on.'

'I feel guilty eating here so often, Madge. I was just saying to Alec...'

'Och, be quiet. You know fine you're always welcome. Sit down.' She suddenly let out one of her enormous roars. 'Sadie, Agnes. Where are you, you lazy middens? I told you an hour ago to set this table.'

Huffy voices issued from one of the two bedrooms. 'How's it always us that's to do everything?'

'I'll "how's it always us" when I get my hands

on you,' Madge bawled as she made for the lobby in big muscular strides.

Alec shook his head in exasperation. 'She's got a voice like a ship's foghorn. I don't know where she gets the energy. It tires me out just listening to her.'

Willie, who had been doing a jigsaw puzzle on the floor, looked up with a cheeky, mischievous grin. 'I'll tell her what you said.'

'Who's her?'

'Mammy.'

'Well, show a bit of respect. Say "Mammy", not "her".' Alec turned to Sammy. 'See kids nowadays? A right cheeky lot. They're all the same.'

'I'm not cheeky, am I, Daddy?' Charlie sidled up to Alec and leaned against him.

'No, you're a good wee lad, son.'

A loud groan came from Willie. 'Wee sooky, Daddy's pet. Sook, sook...'

Sammy cut in. 'How about some pocket money? I've got some for each of you.'

A cheer immediately erupted and Alec had to fight to be heard. 'You don't need to do this, Sammy. You spoil them.'

'Och, what's the harm? Give me enough space to get into my pocket, folks.' All seven children had appeared as if by magic and were crowding excitedly around Sammy.

'Say thanks, or I'll murder the lot of you,' Madge bawled from the scullery.

Alec suddenly longed for a bit of peace and quiet. Sammy's mother must be mad to turn down the offer of a bed at Sammy's wee house in Springburn Road. Although it was in the busy centre of Springburn, Sammy's house was an oasis of calm and peace inside. Ironically, it was too silent and still for Sammy.

'If he made me the offer,' Alec thought, 'I'd jump at the chance.'

8

The trees in the Botanic Gardens were laced with snow. It was like a fairyland, brilliant white and sparkling. Catriona liked to stand at one of the windows and gaze across at it. That was when she had a minute to spare, which was not often.

Usually, when she had to go down to Byres Road, either for shopping or if there was some emergency in the bakery and she had to help out, she cut through the park. She did that today, her boots crunching into the snow and leaving a trail of footprints behind her. It was strangely quiet. Snow muffled every sound, even those of the trams and buses in Great Western Road and Byres Road leading off it. She passed the Kibble Palace, one of the largest glasshouses in Britain, named after John Kibble, its original owner. At one time, the huge, iron-framed conservatory had been the venue for many city meetings and functions. Concerts were held in it and Disraeli and Gladstone had made their inaugural speeches there when they were installed as Lord Rectors of Glasgow University. Eventually, to prevent further damage to the plants by so many visitors, a heating system had been installed and it was returned to its original function as greenhouse. There were many other hothouses in the park, containing an impressive selection of shrubs, trees and plants from all over the world. Catriona took delight in wandering around, admiring the wonderful collection of exotic orchids. Apparently, the Gardens also supplied much material for the use of the Department of Botany in Glasgow University.

Melvin, as usual, had left earlier to open up the shop. The bakers in the premises at the back would have been busy all night and would be ready to knock off when Melvin arrived. There were four bakers, including Baldy Fowler. Baldy now rented a room and kitchen across the road from the shop. Every time Catriona reached the main gate of the park and crossed Great Western Road into Byres Road, she couldn't help looking wistfully at the wee room and kitchen she'd once lived in there. Melvin had been away at the war and, after the Dessie Street shop and houses had been bombed, that's where she eventually ended up.

It was overcrowded, with Melvin's old father and Fergus having to share one room, and her and Andrew sharing a bed in the other, yet she had felt – for the first time in her life – free, independent, with such a peaceful sense of belonging. She had found the place herself, paid for it herself, and made her own decisions. She had friends to visit when she wanted and went out when and where she wanted. Not that she went out very often, not in the evening at least. But, during the day, when the children were at school, she could always snatch a few minutes' walk in her lunch hour, even just around the shops. She had enjoyed her job, working alongside Julie in Copeland & Lye's. In the evenings, she'd either take the boys out to the park (so handy being just across Great Western Road) or occasionally to the Lyceum Cinema, which was off Byres Road, just a couple of minutes round the corner in Vinicombe Street.

On Saturday afternoons, the boys often went to the matinee there. Everything was so handy. On other evenings, especially after the boys went to bed, she'd sit at the front-room window, her chin cupped in her hands, watching all the people strolling along talking and laughing together.

Everything changed when Melvin came home. He had to be the big man again and have a bakery and a house to show off. That was the reason he'd bought the ridiculously big house they were in now. She didn't work full time in the bakery. Even Melvin, crazy though he was, saw that it was impossible for her to do that and run the house in the way he wanted and also have his meals cooked and served up exactly as he liked them. But she helped out occasionally – by checking the books or serving at the counter if Sandra McKechnie was off sick. The poor girl obviously had trouble with her periods. She was an awful sickly colour at times. Catriona guessed she hadn't much of a life. Not that Sandra had complained or anything, but she always looked so miserable and neglected, with her pale face, lank hair and steel-rimmed glasses. Nowadays, her father was an elder or had some such important post in the Jehovah's Witnesses and he was very strict with the family. Apparently, singing, dancing and enjoying yourself in any way whatsoever was a sin. Sex before marriage was particularly heinous and the perpetrators were definitely destined for hell.

Catriona didn't think illicit sex was such a good idea herself, but she wouldn't have branded anyone as a dreadful sinner and bound for hell because of it. (Probably because she'd had a brief indulgence in it herself.) She believed sex education was important and worried about Fergus and Andrew, although Andrew was only fifteen. Nevertheless, she felt Melvin should have spoken to them about the facts of life and how to prevent unwanted pregnancies and other problems, and told him so. When Melvin couldn't (or didn't want to) cope with what she was talking about, he'd dismiss her with 'Aw, shut up!' or 'Don't be ridiculous.' This time, it was 'You're mad. Fergus is twenty-three years of age. He'll know more about all that than you do.'

That was probably true. But one thing was certain – he hadn't learned anything from Melvin. Years ago, she'd asked Melvin to speak to Fergus but at that time she'd just got 'Aw, shut up!'

She would have tried to talk to the boys herself, but she really didn't know much about the practicalities from a male point of view. Anyway, it was so embarrassing. She wished there were books on the subject. The only ones she'd ever heard of were by a Dr Marie Stopes – *Married Love* was one. She couldn't remember what the other was called, but neither seemed to fit the problem of educating two boys about sex.

67

Slowly, as if reluctant to leave it behind, she walked away from the building in which she'd once enjoyed her brief spell of contentment. Not long after she'd passed what had once been 'her close', she felt one of her tension headaches developing. It was then she suddenly thought to herself, 'I can't go on like this for the rest of my days. I've got to get away and live my own life.'

But how? Where could she live? How could she afford to pay a rent and keep herself and Andrew, who wanted to start his physiotherapy training soon? Fergus was due to leave Aberdeen College of Music and Drama and would also need money to survive. A sudden thought made her feel faint with apprehension. What if, by some miracle, she had enough money and they didn't understand, didn't want to stick with her? Andrew got on with his dad better than most people. And she wasn't Fergus's real mother, only his stepmother. She got on a lot better with him now than she used to when he was a child. He had been a terrible torment one way and another both to Andrew and to her. She had tried her best to be patient and understanding towards him, but he had been so very difficult to cope with that sometimes she'd lost her temper with him. Now he was older and, as far as she could see, had got over most of his personality problems, he seemed a much happier and better-balanced person altogether.

Fergus had been through such a terrible time before she'd come on the scene. Catriona would never forget Melvin telling her how Fergus's mother, Betty, had died of TB. She had lain on the settee in the living room, in the flat in Dessie

Street. Betty had been alone all day with only baby Fergus beside her. When Melvin finished his shift in the bakehouse, he'd come upstairs to the flat and start cleaning it and polishing the floor. Betty, he said, always felt guilty and would try to get up and do it herself, but he always assured her that he would manage. She wasn't to worry.

Why was he worrying about the bloody floor? Why hadn't he employed a housekeeper or a nurse or anybody while Betty was still alive and needed help? Why didn't he put Fergus into a nursery?

After Betty had died and a few years before Catriona and Melvin married, he had given Fergus to Lizzie, the horrible, neurotic next-door neighbour, to look after. By the time Catriona married Melvin, Fergus was five and already his character had been formed (ruined, in her opinion) by Melvin and Lizzie. He was a sly, devious torment of a boy. First of all he tormented her, then Andrew after he was born. She knew it wasn't the child's fault. She never gave up trying to undo the harm that Melvin and Lizzie had done. Eventually, she believed, it had paid off. He had still been a bit of a worry after he had started school – there had been complaints about him tormenting other pupils. However, when he reached his teens he became interested and then completely absorbed in music. It certainly kept him out of trouble, although Melvin had expected Fergus to follow him into the bakery business and eventually inherit and carry on 'the good name of McNair's'. To see Fergus, long-haired and dreamy-eyed, strumming at a guitar, made Melvin furious. 'It's all your fault,' he accused Catriona. 'You encourage him.'

That was true in a way. Fergus had been in seventh heaven (not that he was a person who normally showed his emotions) when he had been offered a place in Aberdeen College of Music and Drama, and she had encouraged him to accept it despite Melvin's opposition. Indeed, she had done everything she could to help him get there and it had meant fighting Melvin every inch of the way.

Fergus had grown into a tall, skinny lad of nineteen with a pale, lean face and dark, shadowed eyes. He and Andrew seemed to rub along quite well now. They never quarrelled and, in fact, Fergus seemed quite fond of Andrew and was even teaching him how to play the guitar. The lessons usually ended with them both becoming helpless with laughter. Andrew had no musical talent whatsoever and accepted the fact with his usual good humour. Andrew did have a talent for drawing, though, and had sketched a very good likeness of Fergus and presented him with it. Fergus looked really pleased and proud and had carefully rolled it up and packed it away in his rucksack to show off to his friends in Aberdeen.

It did her heart good to see the boys together on those weekends and she was genuinely sorry every time Fergus went away. He always kissed her goodbye and said, 'Look after yourself, Mum.' She smelled the mixture of tobacco and sour sweat from him but controlled the urge to tell him that he should wash more often. She didn't want to spoil the loving moment. Then Andrew would go back to school, and she felt alone, with little else but the hated treadmill of housework to fill her days.

She hurried down Byres Road, not taking time to look at any of the shop windows and only taking a quick glance along Vinicombe Street to see what was on in the Lyceum. Not that she managed to go very often. In fact, she'd only been once to the cinema since Melvin had bought the television. Melvin said that it was a waste of money going to a cinema when there was plenty of entertainment in his own house. It was always *his* house, *his* television, *his* shop, *his* everything.

Her headache tightened like a band of iron around her skull. She resolved to make herself a cup of valerian or lemon balm tea as soon as she reached the shop. She always kept a stock of these herbs both in the shop and in Botanic Crescent. Herbs had been one of the things she'd become interested in in her desperate attempt to find something that would help her get off the drugs that the doctor had given her. Antidepressants and tranquillisers could be addictive, she'd been told. Not by the doctor but by a customer in the shop who'd seen her swallowing some. She believed it and was trying her best to cut down with a view to stopping altogether.

The shop was busy when she arrived and redolent with the smell of new-baked bread and spicy buns. It was the smell that attracted so many customers.

Catriona made her herb tea in the back shop

71

All DRUGS are addictive

and took it through to the front to sip at it in between serving. Sandra McKechnie was off again. One of the customers, a Mrs Mulvaney, said, 'What's that you're drinking, hen? It looks a funny colour.'

'Herbal tea.'

'Herbal tea?' The echo sounded incredulous. 'What's wrong wi' a good cup of Co-op tea?'

'Nothing. It's just this is what helps me relax when I feel worried or have a tension headache.'

'Huh!' Melvin snorted. 'Would you listen to her? What's she ever had to worry her?'

Often Catriona remembered with infinite pity and understanding how poor Sarah Fowler murdered her mother-in-law. Many's the time, and this was one of them, when she could have committed murder herself.

'Here,' Mrs Mulvaney laughed, 'it's time you sold some of that in yer shop, hen. There's plenty folk around here that's got worried and sore heads. Ye'd make a fortune.'

Melvin glared at the woman. 'Aye, well, it's just as well it's not *her* shop. Selling dried grass could soon pull the plug on any business and it's just the sort of stupid thing she'd do.'

He didn't seem to know the meaning of the word loyalty and had never had any compunction about making a fool of her in front of people. He was the stupid one. He had no idea how much he kept tempting her, forcing her down the path of murder. He'd enjoy a right good laugh if she told him. He never gave her – or anyone else for that matter – any credit for anything. He was always the clever one. Well, maybe he wasn't all that clever.

The thought of Mrs Mulvaney and what she'd said about herbs stuck in her mind. She gave Mrs Mulvaney credit for what might be quite a good idea. There might well be a market for herbs and herbal remedies. Perhaps not to sell in a baker's shop but, if not in McNair's bakery – where? She didn't know the answer to that but the idea gradually formed into a dream. She began reading more and more, not only about herbs and herbal treatments, but about other alternative therapies too. It was a fascinating subject. There was such a wide variety of therapies, including aromatherapy, acupuncture and homeopathy.

'Your nose is never out of a book these days,' Melvin complained. 'I've spent a fortune buying a television for you to watch and you sit there with your nose in a book.' He snatched the book from her, looked at it and jeered, 'You're getting a right hypochondriac, reading all this weird stuff. It's a shrink you need to see. You're going off your nut.'

She dreamed about getting premises of her own one day and perhaps renting out consulting rooms to various therapists at the back and selling herbs and pills and potions in a shop at the front.

Oh, what a wonderful dream it was. But she could never make it a reality unless she had capital. She needed money. The only way she could think of was if Melvin died and she inherited the house and the bakery. She'd immediately sell the house. That would give her enough capital and also enough to buy a cosy wee place like the one she'd had before. She could become successful in her own right, she felt sure. In her dreams, she saw herself getting the capital and becoming successful. In reality, she knew that Melvin would insult her even from the grave. Years ago, he'd told her that he meant to leave everything to Fergus. And he would.

But there was bound to be some way. And if there was a way, she'd find it.

9

'Get that bloody animal out of here while there's food on the table,' Hodge Hunter's coarse voice sawed through the shadowy room. 'Do ye want to poison us all with the filthy beast?'

'Now, now,' his wife said, half laughing but in obvious distress, 'wee Patch is just as clean as you or me.' But she lifted the dog into her arms and hurried with it out of the room.

Sammy kept his head down and made a pretence of enjoying his food.

'You're a great cook, Mother,' he told her when she returned. 'Every Sunday you surpass yourself. I don't know how you manage it. This is absolutely delicious.'

The old woman's face lit up with pleasure and gratitude.

'Oh, I'm so glad you're enjoying it, son.'

'He'd say that even if it tasted like shit.'

'You know I mean it, Mother. I always look forward to your cooking.'

He wanted to say a lot more but his mother

always pleaded with him beforehand to try his best to keep quiet and not anger his father.

'It only makes him worse, son. He just takes it out on me after you've gone.'

For her sake, he did his best to keep quiet. He sometimes remarked to Catriona that his father and Melvin were a right pair. Melvin was one of the few people he'd ever seen his father get on with. They sometimes met at the ex-servicemen's club in town and reminisced about the war and their time in the forces. His father was also a Mason and always on his best behaviour at his Masonic meetings. There he was on good terms with one of the local ministers, a local doctor, a councillor and a lawyer. His father took great pride in being well thought of and respected by those he regarded as the local 'big-wigs'. He judged Melvin, as a successful businessman, to be in this category, even though Melvin was not a Mason. Ordinary working men, his father despised. Unless they had been in the forces or had 'fought for their country', as he liked to put it.

The weekly Sunday visit was a terrible strain on Sammy. It upset him deeply to see how his father treated his mother, but there was nothing he could do about it. His mother refused to allow him to do anything about it. The only compensation was the stolen time his mother spent with him during the week when she was out for her shopping. Instead of going to the Co-op in Balornock, which was nearer, she'd hurry down to Springburn, do her shopping and then come to his house. He'd cook her lunch and they'd talk. Sometimes he even managed to make her laugh.

She always brought the dog with her now and she would proudly show Sammy the tricks she'd taught it to perform.

As he watched her lavish love on the little terrier, he blessed the day he had given it to her. She spoke to it as if it was a true friend and it obviously gave her comfort as well as company. He had never seen her so happy, so content.

On his Sunday visits, he put up with his father's boasts about his important Masonic friends with as much patience and good grace as he could. This was somewhat easier to do as he didn't have such a critical opinion of the Masons as he had of the Orange Order. At least, as far as he could make out, the Masons weren't religious bigots. There were Catholics, Protestants and even, so he'd been told, Jewish Masons. True

However, the mere fact that his father went on and on so much about the Masons made Sammy vow never to have anything to do with them. The mere fact that his father was one of them soured his view. There must be something wrong with them if they accepted his father.

He escaped from the house and strode thankfully and speedily away, nearly forgetting to turn round and wave to his mother. Usually the sight of her thin, bent figure and pale, sad face at the window haunted him for the rest of the day, but now, clutching Patch in her arms, she waved back at him quite cheerily.

'That dog,' he thought to himself, 'is causing a transformation in her. I wouldn't be surprised if she begins to find enough strength to stick up for herself and tell the old man where to get off.'

He chuckled to himself. The way things were going, it seemed a real possibility. That made him happy. He began to whistle to himself as he strode along.

In Broomknowes Road, he bumped into Julie Vincent. She had been visiting Madge and was now on her way to see her mother-in-law. As they walked along together, Julie said, 'I enjoy having lunch with Madge and her crowd. It's a terrible contrast at my mother-in-law's. It's noisy and a bit chaotic at Madge's but...'

'A bit?' Sammy laughed.

'Well, OK, but my mother-in-law's place is like the grave in comparison. It always depresses me. And she still goes on and on about Reggie. Never mentions her late husband. It's always Reggie. It's not that I want to forget Reggie, or ever will forget him, but it's awful the way she lives in the past so much. You'd think her father and mother would tell her to snap out of it. Well, not snap out of it, not using those words exactly, but you know what I mean. Her father's a minister. He lives next door to Catriona.'

'Yes, I know.'

'At least I managed to get out of lunch there today and settle for an afternoon visit. You must feel the same about Ruth. You loved her, but you don't still go on and on about her, do you? What good does it do?'

'No good at all. We've just to get on with our lives the best we can. They wouldn't want us to be stuck in the past and made to feel miserable.'

'No, that's exactly what I feel, Sammy. I've tried to tell Mum that, but she just doesn't listen.'

'You've been good to Mrs Vincent, Julie. I don't know how you survive these Sunday visits. The minister and his wife are usually there as well, Madge tells me.'

'Yes. Talk about depressing? He says a long gloomy prayer when I arrive and then another one before he and his wife go away. I can't stand Holy Willies. Oh, I'm sorry, Sammy. I forgot. You're religious, aren't you?'

'Not a Holy Willie, I hope,' Sammy laughed. 'And I know what you mean about gloomy Sunday lunches. I've just come from one. My father is a regular church-goer and before every Sunday lunch, he murders Robert Burns's "Selkirk Grace".' Sammy mimicked his father's loud, coarse voice:

'Some hae meat an' cannae eat,
An' some nae meat that want it.
But we hae meat,
An' we can eat,
So let the Lord be thankit.'

Julie laughed. 'If you don't mind me saying so, he sounds pretty awful.'

'I don't mind you saying so because it's the truth. He's monstrously awful.'

'I suppose you put up with your Sundays for the sake of your mother.'

'Exactly. I'd never go near that place if it wasn't for my mother.'

'You've brothers, haven't you?'

'Yes, but they got as far away as possible as quick as they could and I don't blame them.'

78

'Sometimes I'm tempted. To get away from Glasgow, I mean. But, apart from Mrs Vincent, I like living where I am. She tried to persuade me to move in with her. Can you imagine it? Me buried in that atmosphere all the time. I'd go stark raving bonkers. She still tries, you know.'

'Oh, don't, Julie. Enjoy life. Make the most of it.'

After a minute, Julie said, 'You're a strange man, Sammy. A real puzzle. I've never known what to make of you.'

'How do you mean?'

'Well, you belong to some religious sect like the McKechnies who live upstairs from Madge. But you don't seem like them.'

'I should hope not! I don't belong to any religious sect.'

'What is it you belong to then? Madge has told me but I've forgotten.'

'The Society of Friends. Quakers.'

'Isn't it religious, then?'

He shrugged. 'Not in the way you imagine.' He thought, as he often did, of the nearest thing to dogma the Society of Friends had. It was a list of what was called 'Queries and Advices'. One came to him now: 'Let your life speak.' It was the one he found most difficult.

He and Julie had to separate abruptly because Julie saw a tram car coming. 'I'll have to go. Nice talking to you, Sammy.'

'And you,' Sammy called after her. He stood for a minute watching the stylish figure in the calf-length tapered coat and flat, wide-brimmed hat race along to the tram stop, catch the pole and swing on to the tram like a seventeen-year-old girl.

79

Yet she must be in her thirties or near enough. Unexpectedly, Sammy experienced a surge of loneliness. He was tempted to turn back and seek the noisy companionship of Alec's place. With some difficulty, he controlled the urge. There surely must be a limit to Alec and Madge's hospitality – for him anyway. He took advantage of their kindness far too often.

Reaching Springburn Road and his close, he took the stairs two at a time, plunged his key into the lock, then was suddenly weighed down by the silence inside the house. He could have wept. He longed for his wife. He remembered with startling vividness her loving caress. It was as if it was only a few minutes ago they'd been entwined in each other's arms before being wrenched apart. He felt the physical pain of it. Then the anger. Anger at the bomb that had killed her. Anger at the stupidity and the cruel waste of war. Rage at his father for epitomizing all that he hated about the military. It was men like him who refused to think, who only obeyed orders, who believed in force as the only method of solving any problem.

'A good soldier isn't paid to think,' he used to bawl at Sammy and his brothers. 'A good soldier obeys orders.'

'I know what I'd do with all your bloody Quakers,' he was in the habit of sneering now. 'Put them up against a wall and shoot the lot of them, as we did in the First World War. Bloody cowards!' ALL WAR IS MADNESS

He knew nothing about Society of Friends, of course. Very few people did. That was the worst of not going around publicising oneself or trying to

80

convert anyone. The fact was, right back from the time of Elizabeth Fry, members of the Society of Friends had been working on all sorts of reforms behind the scenes. Elizabeth Fry, for instance, was determined to do something to improve the lot of women prisoners in the hell-holes of jails at the time. With great courage she went in among the prisoners and worked with determination and patience to help them in every practical way she could. Eventually, she succeeded in setting in motion the reform of the whole prison system. Quakers had never lacked courage. In the past, they had been persecuted, imprisoned, tortured and killed. The authorities had forbidden them to hold their meetings, but they went on meeting together and, when all the adults had been flung into jail, the children continued, even the youngest going along. But nothing stopped them. When they were banned from universities, the legal and other professions, they went into business, becoming renowned for setting a fair price and sticking to it. People were surprised and suspicious at first but then began to trust them. Their businesses grew as a result. Firms like Cadbury's, Fry's, Clark's Shoes, Horniman's Tea, Huntly & Palmer's biscuits, to name but a few, were all started and made a success by Quakers. Most of the Quaker firms put their profits to good use, often building whole villages of decent, attractive houses for their employees – in stark contrast to the abysmal slums of the time.

Sammy blessed the day he had found the Society of Friends. It was the only place he felt he belonged. Not that he felt good enough, or courageous enough for that matter, to join. He had been what was called an 'attender' for years and, as far as the members were concerned, it seemed he could go on being an attender for the rest of his days. Nobody put any pressure on anyone to join. He wanted to become a full member and maybe one day he would. Meantime he was just grateful to be able to sit in the quiet meetings every Sunday morning. There he gained the strength to enable him to face his father across the lunch table, in the gloomy house on the rough track that led to Auchinairn. He tried to bring the peace of the meeting to his aid now in the empty silence of his house. But, in a meeting, any silence was meaningful and comforting because of the people there. And because of Christ's words, 'When two or more of you are gathered together in my name, I will be in your midst', he could believe that Christ was with him and the others in Meetings. But no one was with him here. Nothing helped here, in the home he and Ruth had shared and had been so proud of.

He sank down on to a chair and angrily cradled his head in his hands.

10

Sandra McKechnie dreaded being off work. She even felt apprehensive about going home afterwards. Sleeping all night in the bakery would have been far, far better. She had come to dread every hour in the gloomy flat in Broomknowes Road, where she felt unbearably oppressed by the crush of huge Victorian furniture, a legacy from her father's family, who had once lived in a large villa in Pollokshields. She felt overwhelmed by the dark-brown moquette settee and armchairs that sucked her into their cushioned depths. The brown chenille tablecover, with its heavy fringe and tassels, and matching curtains, that cut out the light, depressed her.

Everything was too big, too dark and too heavy – including her father. She was afraid of him but recently she had plucked up the courage to talk to her mother about what had been going on. At first her mother had been horrified and hadn't believed her.

'Your father's a Jehovah's witness and an elder in Kingdom Hall. How can you say such terrible things about him, Sandra? Your own father, who has done so much good work for Jehovah?'

That was what made it so confusing. They had all tried so conscientiously to do God's work and to spread the Good News. Sandra's brother, Peter, had been very clever at school and had been told by his teachers and the headmaster that he should go on to university. Peter had refused, replying that for the work he was going to do for Jehovah, he didn't need to go to university.

He had been courting a girl called Rose Evans for a time, but he had given her up when he'd fallen in love with Jessie Connors, who was not a Jehovah's Witness. Rose had reported him to the elders and poor Peter had been partly ex-communicated. He had been forced to give up

83

Jessie and was not allowed to speak in Kingdom Hall for more than a year. He was broken-hearted during that time, Sandra thought, not because of losing Jessie but because he was unable to put up his hand and answer the questions from the *Watchtower* study paragraphs during the services as usual. He was always first at every service to answer with an accurate quotation from the Bible. She always enjoyed the study part of the service and was intensely proud of Peter. He was so clever that she was convinced he knew the whole Bible off by heart.

Her mother said, 'Don't you ever repeat to Peter what you've just said to me. He'd be so shocked and horrified at you that he'd never get over it. Fancy you saying such things about your good Christian father,' she kept repeating in disbelief, 'who's always been so conscientious in your teaching!'

Yes, he had been conscientious in that, Sandra had to admit. Even during the usual training, from the ages of five to seven, she had not been as quick and as clever as Peter. Sometimes, she had not even been a very willing pupil. She had always been shy and anxious, shrinking away from having to accompany her father around all the doors in Balornock and Springburn and everywhere else in Glasgow, it seemed, to spread the Good News and sell the *Watchtower* magazine. It wouldn't have been so bad if he had always stood beside her at each door for support and protection. Once she'd reached the age of eight or nine, however, he would give her the magazines and tell her what to say. Then he'd knock at the door and quickly disappear out of sight, leaving her standing in acute embarrassment and fear to face whoever opened the door. She feared saying the wrong thing and letting her father and Jehovah down more than any physical danger that might befall her. She knew that they were God's chosen people. They accepted every word in the Bible and, not only that, they lived it too. Because Jesus had said, 'I am no part in the world, so you follow me', they made themselves separate from everyone else. They were witnesses to the word of Jehovah, and that was why they went round knocking at every door – they were witnessing. Sandra had never been very good at it. She was too nervous and shy. These were terrible faults – she ought to have courage in spreading the Good News of the Kingdom.

Her father, like Peter, was a wonderful witness. He knew his Bible and was totally committed in spreading the word. He was also dedicated in teaching her everything she needed to know, even about the structure of the organisation. They were part of a congregation of Christians who all believed exactly the same thing, all over the earth, completely uniform in everything except language.

Would they be able to help her? she wondered. Even the thought paralysed her. There were elders, like her father, but their duty was to serve the brothers and help them with spiritual difficulties and questions. Her problem was not a spiritual one. Her mind dodged fearfully, shamefully about, trying to avoid thinking about it. She would never know how, in the end, she had managed to blurt out the words to her mother.

'Daddy has started touching me – down there.' The mention of genitals or anything to do with sex was strictly taboo. 'And the last time, he actually ... went all the way.' Ugh Ugh Ugh

Her mother had been so shocked she had collapsed down on to a chair. She hadn't been able to utter a sound for a long minute. Then she'd gasped out, 'You wicked, wicked girl!'

After that, she had avoided Sandra whenever possible, even refusing to look at her. It was terrible. Sandra began to wonder if she had imagined what had happened to her or even if, despite her instincts to the contrary, it was all right. But it was not all right. Her father came to her room at night and penetrated her again and it was painful and shameful and made her feel sick. Then she began to physically be sick, vomiting every morning. She would just manage to get to work and the privacy of the shop lavatory before the other assistants arrived. There she retched miserably until she was drained and exhausted.

It was obvious, even to her, that she was pregnant – to her own father. It was too terrible. It was the wicked result of the sin of incest. Only one course of action seemed possible. She had to get rid of it on her own. There was no use speaking to her mother again. She wondered how she could do it, how she could cleanse herself of the wickedness. She searched her memory for anything she might have read in books or magazines belonging to girls at school. The girls had even picked out bits from the Bible to whisper and giggle about. She remembered something that

86

had been said about drinking gin and swallowing laxative tablets and having boiling hot baths. She decided to try all three and bought a half-bottle of gin and some laxatives. The gin had to be bought from another district, in case she was seen going into a local licensed grocer's.

It worked the miracle she needed. She thought she was going to die from the pain but death held far fewer fears than going on living the life she was now condemned to. She crouched on the shop toilet, groaning in agony as blood gushed from her. She began to feel faint. Then she heard voices in the front shop. One of them sounded like Catriona McNair. In a desperate panic, she managed to stagger up so that she could pull the plug and get rid of the clots of blood filling the lavatory pan. No one must know that it was anything more than her usual troublesome periods. Gratefully she saw the clots flush away and only a pale froth of pink remain. She struggled to clean herself and flush away the paper but, despite her struggles, she felt herself sink to her knees. The lavatory pan and the cramped, windowless confines of the lavatory shimmered before her eyes, then faded away.

When she awoke she was on a stretcher in an ambulance and Catriona McNair was sitting beside her. Sandra could see her lips moving, but her words sounded faint and far away. 'Sandra, you know you don't have to come into work when it's your time of the month. Even Melvin understands and doesn't mind. You shouldn't have struggled out.'

'What's happening?' Sandra tried to sit up.

'No, no, just you lie still and relax. You'll be all right. I panicked when I found you and phoned for an ambulance. One of the customers kindly offered to go and tell your mother. She'll take a taxi to the hospital and see you there.'

'I'm all right now. I don't need to go to the hospital.'

'Well, it won't do any harm to have a check-over. It's surely not right that you've to suffer like this every month. Maybe the hospital doctor will find some way to help you.'

Sandra's heart was beating fast and she was praying that the doctors would not be able to find out the truth of what had happened. It occurred to her then, for the first time, that what she had done might even have been illegal. She could hardly breath for the thumping of her heart.

They carried her into the hospital. Doctors examined her and before she could grasp what was happening, she was in an operating theatre and being anaesthetised. When she regained consciousness she was in bed in a ward and her mother was sitting, white-faced and wide-eyed, beside her.

They gazed at each other in silence until her mother blurted out in a tragic voice, 'They said you'd had a miscarriage.'

Tears blurred Sandra's vision and all she could say was, 'I'm sorry, Mummy.'

'It's not... No, it can't be. Have you had a boyfriend we didn't know about? Is that it?' A pleading note crept into her voice. 'That's it, isn't it? Tell me, Sandra. I won't be angry with you, I promise. Just tell me who it is.'

Sandra could think of no one, even to lie about. She didn't know any boys. Never had done.

'Sandra,' her mother repeated. 'Please.'

Sandra just gazed helplessly back at her.

'Oh, dear God,' her mother said at last. 'What'll we do?'

'It's all right now. The doctors have cleaned it all away.'

'Oh, dear God.'

'Please forgive me ... I didn't know what else to do.'

Her mother took her hand and held it tightly. 'Don't worry, Sandra. It wasn't your fault. I should have listened to you. But it was so hard for me. I mean, how could he?'

'It's all right now, Mummy.'

'No, it's not all right. This can't be allowed to go on. You need help – we need help. This isn't only a sin, it's a crime. As soon as you're able, we'll go to the brothers. We'll report him to Kingdom Hall and ask for their help and support.'

'Oh, Mummy.' Sandra was saddened beyond measure at the hard and bitter expression on her mother's normally gentle, pious face. It was all her doing. Guilt heaped upon guilt, shame upon shame. How could she face not only her father but all the brothers in the Kingdom Hall?

With all her heart, she wished she had died on the operating table.

'You what?' big Aggie Stoddart gasped. 'Left your good job in the Co-op?'

'That's what I said.'

'Don't you be cheeky to me, madam.'

89

'You asked me.'

'Are you mad or what?'

'What's wrong with being a librarian?'

'Fancy flinging up a good job in the Co-op!'

'I never wanted to go into the Co-op in the first place.'

'I always knew hanging about that Springburn library so much wouldn't do you any good.'

'Being a librarian is a good job.'

'Fancy flinging up a good job in the Co-op!'

Chrissie cast her eyes heavenwards, at the same time giving a sigh of hopelessness. There was never any use trying to explain anything to her mother.

'Wait till your daddy hears about this, my lady!'

In response to her mother's warning, Chrissie nearly said, 'What can he do about it?' But she stopped herself just in time. Her mother could be violent and many a blow across the head had been delivered in the past. Even now that she was seventeen, there was still the danger that she could be the recipient of her mother's fist.

'It's a good job, Mammy,' she repeated. 'Honestly. And it's not just a job, it's a career. I'm so lucky to get a start in Springburn. One day I might even make it to the Mitchell. That's my ambition.'

The Mitchell Library in North Street, off Charing Cross, had come into being originally on a different site, by the good offices and money donated by a tobacco manufacturer called Stephen Mitchell. It had to move several times as its numbers of books rapidly increased, until now its stock exceeded one million items and it was claimed to be the largest public reference library in Europe.

'You could have had a good career in the Co-op.'

'Mammy, I'm telling you, I'll have a good career in the library service.'

'It'll no' pay you any dividend. It's the Co-op divvie that's kept clothes on your back and shoes on your feet all these years.'

'I never said anything against the Co-op.'

'Well, then…'

'I just didn't want to work there all my life.'

'You're a lassie. You won't need to work at any job all your life. You'll get married.'

Chrissie wanted to say that she didn't want that option either. At least, not if she had to conform to the generally accepted idea that once a woman got married, she had to give up everything to concentrate on being a housewife and mother. Monday the washday, Tuesday the ironing. Each day had a specific job, every week the same, ad nauseam. Although things were beginning to change a little. At least for folk who could afford the new luxury inventions like washing machines and refrigerators and Hoovers. Her mother still took her rugs out to the back green, hung them over the clothes rope and beat the hell out of them. There was a wash boiler in the scullery of this house though and washing didn't need to be carted down to a wash house in the back green. It had been like Shangri-La coming to this Corporation house. For the first time, they had a bathroom – they were actually able to have a proper bath! They had to endure sub-zero temperatures in the narrow strip of a room but it was still the height of luxury and much appreciated.

Wee Jimmy Stoddart arrived home from work then. It wasn't that he was small. Everybody knew him as that only because he was a good head shorter than Big Aggie. He did shifts on the buses.

'Jimmy, you'll never guess what this silly ass has done.'

'Who?'

'Chrissie, of course. Who else?' So far, Maimie, the younger Stoddart girl, had never caused them any worry or trouble.

Jimmy stripped off his uniform jacket and loosened his tie. 'What's she done now?'

'Just given up her good job in the Co-op.'

'Have you gone mad or something?' He addressed his daughter. 'You've given up your good job in the Co-op?'

'Oh, for pity's sake!' Chrissie almost laughed. What a pantomime! 'I've got a better job, Daddy, and one that I'm really excited about. You know how I've always loved books.'

'You haven't gone and got a job in that Springburn library!'

'What's wrong with the Springburn library?'

'If it had been the Mitchell...' Jimmy thought for a moment. 'The Mitchell's a grand big place.'

'Jimmy!' Aggie protested.

'It used to belong to a tobacco lord. That's his big statue high up in front. They don't build places like that nowadays.'

'Maybe I'll get to the Mitchell eventually...' Chrissie began.

She was interrupted by her mother. 'Be quiet,

you. What's a building got to do with anything? She had a good job in the Co-op. See in that big Springburn Co-op, she could have worked her way up from the grocery to the millinery if she'd have put her mind to it.'

Big deal, Chrissie thought, sarcastically, but wisely kept the thought to herself. It wasn't that she had anything against the Co-op. She just wanted to work among books.

'I'm going out,' she announced.

'Where are you off to now?' Her mother eyed her with suspicion.

'For goodness' sake, Mammy. I'm just going down to the Wellfield.'

'With a boy?'

'No, a girlfriend.'

'What girlfriend?'

'Just a girl from work. You don't know her.'

In actual fact, she was meeting Ailish O'Donnel from upstairs. Her mother would not have approved of that. Her mother was worse than her father about Catholics. She passed the time of day pleasantly enough with Mrs O'Donnel or old Mrs Gogarty if she met them on the stairs or in the Co-op but she always said in private, 'No good comes of socialising with Fenians.'

As a result, the O'Donnels or the Gogartys were never invited to any of the Stoddarts' parties. Even at Hogmanay, the Stoddarts never first-footed the O'Donnels or the Gogartys, and vice versa. Although, if any of the Stoddarts happened to see any of the Catholic families after Hogmanay, they'd call out, 'Happy New Year!' They even shook hands.

They were always friendly and civil, in fact. They had to be, all living up the same close. It was only on special occasions like football matches or Orange Walks that hatreds erupted and spilled over. The day after the Walk, Jimmy and Aggie would be all shamefaced and apologetic for their 'Fuck the Pope' shouts and other abuse.

'Och, it wisnae me talkin', hen,' Aggie would say to Teresa O'Donnel or old Kate Gogarty. 'It was the whisky.'

Chrissie and Ailish were the same age and shared a love of books. Ailish worked in Copeland & Lye's, a job she enjoyed. It was a lovely shop with a balcony tearoom, where an orchestra gently tinkled while you sipped your tea and ate dainty wee sandwiches and cakes and scones from a three-tiered silver cake-stand. Nevertheless, Ailish was excited about Chrissie landing a job in the library.

'Gosh, what a bit of luck!'

'Yes,' Chrissie nodded. 'As Mark Twain said – "the harder I work, the luckier I get".'

Ailish giggled. 'Right enough.'

They met round the corner at the Balornock Co-op before linking arms and making their way down the Wellfield hill. They weren't going to 'the Wellie', as Chrissie's mother thought, but to the much classier Princes Cinema in Gourlay Street, off Springburn Road. Chrissie remembered one time, when she was still at school, she had secretly met Sean O'Donnel and they'd gone to the Princes. It was her first date with a boy and, although he was two years older than her, she suspected it was his first date too. He had bought a bar of Fry's Chocolate Cream and carefully halved it between them in the pictures. They had sat in rigid silence all through the film, both shy and nervous and not knowing what to say or do. She remembered their mutual relief when they parted. Her mother had found out afterwards and boxed her ears for stooping so low as to go out with a 'Pape'.

She could imagine poor Sean getting much the same treatment. Nowadays she sometimes asked Ailish, 'How's Sean getting on?'

'Fine. He's still working in McHendry's. He's in the office and doing really well. I wish I could say the same about Dermot.'

'What makes Dermot so aggressive, do you think? He always seems to be in fights. But maybe they're not his fault,' she added, without much conviction.

'Haven't a clue,' Ailish said. 'Sean and I are always trying to talk some sense into him but it's no use. Blokes sometimes even come to the door asking for a fight with him!'

'For goodness' sake!'

By the time they reached the cinema they were discussing in detail the new book of 1958 fashion that had been added to the Springburn library shelves. There were pointed-toed shoes, pillbox hats and suits with short, boxy jackets, three-quarter sleeves and wide, boat-shaped necklines.

They were still chatting after they were seated in the cinema and the film had started. People all around noisily hushed them and someone gave Chrissie a painful prod in the back.

She and Ailish liked to talk. They particularly enjoyed discussing novels they'd read. They were steadily working their way through the classics and had just finished Jane Austen. Ailish preferred the Brontes. They had argued about Austen and the Brontës quite a lot. Although outwardly Ailish appeared a quiet, sober-natured girl, Chrissie had come to the conclusion that her friend had hidden depths. Chrissie wouldn't be a bit surprised if Ailish had just as passionate a nature as her Brontë heroines.

'Anybody you fancy?' she had asked Ailish recently – meaning boys.

'Not really. I'd prefer a man, not a boy.'

'Ooh! You've better be careful and not get yourself into trouble.'

'I should be so lucky,' Ailish laughed. 'There's been one or two at work but they weren't interested in me.'

'I can't believe that. Especially with your lovely blonde hair.'

'Hardly blonde, Chrissie. Mousy more like.'

'Never! Honey-coloured maybe. And so curly.'

'I hate my hair being curly. I can't even have a pony tail. Your hair's lovely and straight and glossy and you've a lovely pony tail.'

'Sometimes I think of dyeing my hair blonde, but my mother would have a fit.'

'Once you went blonde, there's nothing your mother could do about it. But you're fine as a brunette.'

'You don't know my mother! Nobody'll ever fancy me like this.'

'Don't be daft! And we'll both meet somebody

eventually. But I'm in no hurry. Are you?'

'No, I want to enjoy my job and my independence. I wouldn't mind so much if it was OK to work after you were married. But no man would want that. They have to be your boss and get all your attention.'

'I know. And if you don't get married, you are branded a "spinster".'

'Makes me mad.'

'Me too.'

They linked arms to return back up past the red sandstone tenements on the Wellfield hill, both pretending they were ignoring the local talent.

11

Of course he blamed her. Years had passed since Melvin had been able to make love to her. He had become impotent. She remembered the last time he'd tried.

'I've gone right off you,' he'd said, before turning away from her. She had believed him at first. She had been conditioned for years, long before she'd met him, to believe that she was at fault, wicked, a target for God's wrath. A target not only on the day of judgement but here on earth. Retribution and punishment would be her lot. Her mother had promised all this. Her mother had always been God's right-hand man – or, rather, woman.

97

For some time afterwards, he'd tried to make her do revolting things for him to watch. At least she'd had enough courage to refuse to have anything to do with this perversion. Then he kept telling her filthy jokes that degraded women. She'd eventually managed to stop him doing that as well, mostly by just getting up and walking away. She knew it was all because of his own sexual inadequacy.

Melvin was impotent. As often as not, she felt sorry for him but she hadn't the nerve to suggest he seek help from a doctor. She knew him only too well. For a man to see a doctor about anything at all was 'soft' and 'unmanly'. He would have gone berserk if she had made such a suggestion. He had always been tough. Or so he believed. It was pathetic and she was glad that she no longer had to submit to his rough, insensitive, selfish so-called love-making.

She wanted no more of it. Yet at times, strange feelings of need came unbidden to secretly torment her. She kept remembering her brief sexual encounter with Alec Jackson. It had taught her what love-making could be like. It could be exciting and thrilling and tender and gentle.

Sometimes she could hardly look Madge in the eye in case her friend could read her thoughts. She fought to banish Alec from her mind. But it was difficult when she saw him so often – with Madge or with the boys. Sometimes she'd be visiting Madge and, while she was there, Alec would come in from a football match with the boys. Or with Sammy Hunter. Tall, slim and handsome, with the usual twinkle in his eyes and

98

his jaunty sailor's roll, Alec seemed to immediately bring the whole place to mischievous, good-humoured life.

Catriona was even beginning to feel there was something about Sammy too. He had the craggy, broken-nosed face of a fighter, rather similar to Dermot O'Donnel who lived on the top floor. Dermot had a dark, cropped head and a bitter mouth. Sammy had red hair, thoughtful grey eyes and a kindly smile. But mostly the difference between the two men was something about the eyes. Dermot's eyes were hard like marbles and, most of the time, he stared out at the world and everybody in it as if he hated what he saw. Sammy seemed to actually *like* people.

She wondered what Sammy's body would look like naked and then felt terribly ashamed of herself. 'You're having unclean thoughts,' her mother would have said, reminding her of God's wrath and exactly how He would be sure to punish her. When she'd been a very young child, she had been warned of being flung into the 'black burning fire', a somewhat confusing image but a frightening one nevertheless.

Her mother had grown too old and lethargic now for such passionate warnings. She was more or less content to pick on Catriona's father. Hannah and Rab niggled almost constantly at each other. It wouldn't have surprised Catriona, however, if Hannah came out fighting with a dig at Melvin or a message from God if she got the chance.

Catriona struggled to control her wayward thoughts and feelings. She didn't know what was

99

happening to her. All the years before Melvin had become impotent, she'd hated sex. Now she could hardly look at a man – any man – without experiencing shameful arousal.

She wondered if there was some sort of herb or homeopathic potion she could take for her condition. She knew quite a lot about alternative therapies now. At least, she'd collected many books on the subject and had read most of them.

Melvin kept saying, 'Is that more of that cranky stuff you're reading? You're getting to be a right hypochondriac.'

'My arnica cream got rid of your bruising double quick, didn't it?' she'd reply. Arnica as a cream was magic for bruising, and taken internally as tablets was an excellent first-aid treatment for shock.

After Melvin had hit his finger whilst hammering a nail into something, she'd massaged on some of the cream for him and it had helped.

'It would have cleared up double quick without your arnica,' he insisted. 'I'm a quick healer because I've a naturally tough constitution.'

Compared with Sammy or Alec, Melvin was a weakling. At one time, he'd had a tough, muscular physique but not any more. He still tried to do his 'physical jerks', as he called them, but he got sweaty and out of breath very quickly and had to give up. He'd never admit it but the war had ruined his health and strength.

She remembered – how long ago it seemed now – how he had gloried in beating people at arm wrestling. He'd sit opposite one of the other bakers or customers, elbows on the table or the counter, hands poised and locked, straining this way and that. When Melvin eventually managed to thump his opponent's hand down, his face would light up with joyous triumph. He'd even beaten Baldy Fowler once.

He'd been a different man since he'd come back from the war. There was still much of his old bravado but he never carried anything through. If he had to take a turn of serving in the shop, however, he could be as rude to customers as his father had once been. Recently, she'd spoken to him about that.

'Look, Melvin, it's time you learned to be more businesslike and diplomatic if you want to keep the business afloat. The customer is always right, remember?'

'Me? Unbusinesslike?' he'd roared incredulously. 'I've run a successful business all my life. What do you know about business or anything else?'

'I'm only trying to help. We'll have to start trying to keep up with the times. Have you not heard about how that Co-op in London – Royal Arsenal, it's called – converted three shops into one and let customers help themselves, instead of needing to ask the shop assistants to fetch things for them.'

'Help themselves?' Melvin's eyes bulged. 'You're mad. You'd ruin me and my business if you had your way.'

'But it seems to be the coming thing, Melvin. You see, you stock up lots of shelves all around the place and the customers walk about with a basket or a…'

'Aw, shut up!'

One of these days, she thought, I'm going to murder him. That's the only thing that'll shut him up.

Melvin seemed stuck in a time warp. It was as if it was still wartime, with all the war-time restrictions and food rationing, when some shopkeepers behaved like little Hitlers. The weekly ration of bread had been two loaves for each adult and one for each child. Now, when anybody could buy what they liked, where they liked, he still acted as if he was doing the customers a favour selling them anything at all. Catriona felt sure that, if it hadn't been for the fact that he employed excellent bakers – indeed that Melvin himself was still a good baker – the customers would have deserted the shop by now. But, for now at least, despite everything, there was no disputing the fact that they were still the best breadmakers in Glasgow.

All the same, if this London Co-op idea spread, customers might find it more convenient just to pick up a loaf at the same time as they were going around helping themselves to other items off shelves. She also thought McNair's should diversify. After all, they'd once been a grocery shop as well as a baker's. In Dessie Street, the corner shop had, in fact, sold everything. She remembered the travellers' monotone chants, echoing down through the years:

Aboline, Askits, blades, bleach, Brasso, bandages, castor oil, zinc, cough mixture, notepaper, pipe clay, sanitary towels, safety pins, Snowfire Cream…

102

Now it was just a baker's shop with the bakehouse at the back. They made cakes and biscuits as well, of course, but they weren't as good as the ones their last confectioner used to make. There had been a bit of genius about Jimmy the confectioner. Not only could he conjure up mouth-watering cakes but he was a wonderful pianist as well and such a handsome and sensitive young man. His death had been one of the worst tragedies of Dessie Street.

Catriona had felt a strong attraction to him and now she wished she'd succumbed to that attraction. She could vividly imagine what heaven it would have been to be made love to by him.

She thought a lot of being made love to these days – and nights. Especially sleepless nights lying beside a snoring Melvin. A recklessness was beginning to grow inside her. She wished she could confide in someone. She needed help. However, when she'd needed help before, when she'd been in a truly desperate situation, no one she'd turned to understood or offered the help she needed. Not even her GP. She had eventually collapsed and nearly died.

Thinking of dying reminded her of an experience she'd had in the hospital. She'd felt, during the hysterectomy operation, that she'd floated outside of her body, and hovered up near the ceiling looking down on herself. She remembered every detail of the scene, of her prone body, of the doctors and nurses in their masks and gowns. She had never told anyone about this, knowing that no one would believe her. She could just imagine

Madge's hoot of laughter. 'I always knew you had a terrible imagination, hen,' she'd say.

Sometimes Catriona wondered if she could mention it to Sammy. Probably he wouldn't laugh. But he might take it as some sort of religious or spiritual experience. She couldn't believe that, didn't want to believe it. Something must have happened to her brain during the operation. She must have had a dream, that was all. Yet it was so real that every detail remained crystal clear in her mind's eye, even now, years later.

She wanted to talk to somebody about the turmoil of her innermost thoughts and desires. But there was no one. Except perhaps Sammy. Some things she might be able to talk to him about, but how could she talk to any man about her sexual fantasies? No, no. She cringed with embarrassment at the thought.

She concentrated on other things. Making herbal creams and potions for friends and relatives took up time and attention. Even her mother had been grateful to be helped by her treatment for haemorrhoids. And a friend of her mother's had been generous in her praise of how *carbo veg* alternating with *rhus tox* had successfully banished her exhaustion.

She'd offered some medicine to Sandra McKechnie but Sandra had refused, saying, 'What's the use?' The poor girl was obviously depressed.

She began to treat herself with valerian, passiflower, hops and lemon balm for stress, tension and sleeplessness. The concoction did help but deep down she knew that only freeing herself of Melvin and finding someone else would cure her.

12

Her father had lied. More than that, he had actually looked hurt and offended. But he forgave her, he said. Her mother remained cold and hard-looking and, although Sandra heard no harsh words pass between her parents, she could see that any love her mother had ever had for her father was gone. It had been frozen away. Sometimes Sandra thought it would have been better, more bearable, if they had shouted at each other. But there was only coldness, bitterness and silence.

The journey to Kingdom Hall and the meeting with the elders had been like going to hell and back. Her mother had done all the talking. Sandra wished yet again that she had died in the hospital. Her poor mother, sitting so erect in an attempt to remain dignified, had been too painful to witness. Her greying hair was pinned back in its usual neat bun at the nape of her neck and topped by her black felt hat. Her long black coat had been neatly pressed and her black wool gloves were clasped tightly on her lap.

Her mother was suffering and it was only the first ordeal to be faced, she had warned Sandra. The brothers would want to do the right thing and inform the police. It had not come to that, however. The brothers had insisted that nothing more should be said or done. They must leave everything in the loving hands of Jehovah. Sandra had been relieved in a way but it had only increased her mother's bitterness.

'After this,' she said, 'I'll sleep with you.'

'Oh, but...'

'No buts about it, Sandra. And another thing, you and I are never going to set foot in the Hall again.'

'Oh, Mummy...'

She had not only been the cause of spoiling her mother's love for her father, she'd taken away her faith. A nightmare was rampaging out of control. She wished she could disappear as if she'd never existed. She was still going to work and somehow getting through each day without knowing what she was doing. At home, the atmosphere, the lack of love, was unendurable. She felt isolated by her father and her brother. Even her mother seemed withdrawn and far away from her now.

Once her father had caught her on her own, after one of the many occasions when he'd tried to speak to her mother. As usual, she had ignored him and walked away. He had cornered her as soon as her mother had left the room.

'See what you've done,' he said but in a sorrowful tone, not an angry, bitter one. The sad sigh that had softened his words made her feel a hundred times worse. She had always loved him before. Now her confused, unhappy feelings were peppered with disgust. But part of her disgust was always levelled at herself.

Catriona McNair kept asking her how she was and, in reply, she just shrugged and said, 'All right.'

Catriona had even offered her medicine.

106

'What for?' she'd asked.

'Well, you look to me as if you're suffering from depression, Sandra. I think you should see a doctor but, if you won't do that and providing you're not already on any other anti-depressants, then St John's Wort will help you. It won't do you any harm.'

Or any good either. What could some herbal medicine or any other kind of tablets do to help her and her family? Catriona meant well but she didn't understand. She knew nothing of how she felt and why. As long as she continued to serve in the bakery shop and not make any mistakes there, that's all Catriona need worry about.

Melvin McNair, of course, wasn't so tactful. He kept saying, 'What's wrong with your face? If it gets any longer, it'll be hitting the floor.' But Melvin was never tactful. No one paid any attention to him.

At home there was only silence. Silent accusations. Her father and Peter now attended Kingdom Hall even more devotedly. Some of the brothers had come to the house to speak to her and her mother, but her mother would have none of it. Once she said to them, 'How many others have you turned away, I wonder? How many other men have you protected?'

But they still patiently, forgivingly, insisted that everything was in Jehovah's loving hands. The elders wanted her to go to the Hall with her father and brother but she couldn't and not just out of loyalty to her mother. She had developed a fear of men, any men. If she couldn't trust her father who could she trust?

Everything had been so good before. They had all enjoyed going to the Hall three times a week and studying the Bible and the *Watchtower*. Learning the answers to all the questions. It had given them such a feeling of rightness and security. They were special, God's chosen people, Jehovah's Witnesses.

Now everything was spoiled. Everything had gone. Nothing was left except confusion, shame, guilt and emptiness. Every day she walked down Wellfield Hill and boarded the train in Springburn. Every day she got off the train at Queen Street Station and got the Underground to Byres Road, spent the day automatically working in the shop, and then travelled back on the train again. As she stood on the platform, she began to feel a strange impulse. It was detached from logical thought, purely a physical thing. She had a growing compulsion to hurl herself from the platform on to the rails as the train came thundering into the station.

Every night as she left the shop, she felt a recklessness start to build up inside her. One part of her was terrified by the strength of her feelings and fought to control them. She'd stand well back from the edge of the platform. She'd stand behind someone. Nothing helped. She could easily push anyone aside. There were only a few feet from the edge of the platform, no matter where she stood. One sudden rush. That was all it would take. The impulse was so real, so strong, she knew beyond all doubt that one day it would be too strong. It would suddenly push her over.

And one day it did.

'Well,' Melvin said, 'at least it's been good for business. The shop's been going like a fair with nosy customers and reporters. Great publicity. The name of McNair's bakery has been in all the papers.'

Catriona was shocked.

'How can you speak like that about such a tragedy? I really thought that even you would be able to feel at least some pity. But all it means to you is more money. You really are...' she was lost for words, '...dreadful,' she managed at last.

'Aw, shut up.'

'The poor girl had no life at all and now, to end it like that! I knew she was depressed but I never dreamt...' Catriona shook her head. She couldn't get over it. 'So horribly violent.'

'Will you shut up about it? You'll be making me bloody depressed.'

No chance of him throwing himself under a train though, she thought bitterly. His insensitivity never ceased to amaze her. His first reaction to the tragedy was that he'd been made short-staffed on one of his busiest days. He'd put on a suitable act for the customers and the reporters, of course. To the reporters especially he was the good, caring, indeed grief-stricken, employer. He was shocked, devastated. She had been 'such a nice wee girl. She was like a daughter to me.'

It sickened Catriona, and she hated him more than she'd ever hated him before. To think he'd never had a good word to say about Sandra. He'd once called her 'a right ugly wee cow'. Poor Sandra, with her straight, greasy hair and pale face, and National Health spectacles. She had been a gentle soul and a good worker, but what a wretched home life she must have had in such a fanatically religious family. The McKechnies were enough to put anyone off religion for life. Any kind of religion. The funeral had certainly put *her* off – all that talk of hell and damnation. It made her feel so angry. Poor, weak, unhappy Sandra. How dare they speak about her like that! Miserable and unhappy though she was herself, Catriona couldn't imagine resorting to suicide. She'd rather commit bloody murder.

For the hundredth time, she recalled Baldy Fowler's wife and how she'd silenced her mother-in-law forever with a kitchen knife. Oh, she understood exactly how and why Sarah had committed the violent act. Sometimes she believed that one day her own feelings would get the better of her and she'd silence Melvin with equal violence. If she could think of a way to get away with it, that is, without the law catching up with her, she believed that she would do it.

At other times, she felt shocked and horrified at herself. She'd tell herself that she must not allow Melvin to degrade her by causing her to harbour such thoughts and she'd banish them from her mind. But the hatred remained as strong as ever.

13

Sammy could not believe his eyes when he saw his mother. It wasn't her shopping day. The shops would be long shut anyway. She didn't have her handbag with her. She wasn't even wearing a coat.

'Mother, come in.' He put one arm around her shoulders and led her into the house. 'What's wrong? What's happened?'

'I've been to the police.'

'Wait, I'll pour you a wee sherry.' He kept a bottle especially for her. She always said it strengthened her.

She sipped at the golden liquid but Sammy had to hold the glass to steady it, her hands were shaking so much.

'Better?'

She nodded.

'Now, just relax, Mother. You're perfectly safe here.'

'I went to the police. They brought me to the close but I didn't let them come up the stairs, in case they gave you a fright.'

'Mother, what's wrong? What's happened?'

He knew it must have something to do with his father. He didn't need to ask. But she'd never gone to the police before, nor had she come to him for shelter or help like this.

'Patch.' Her lips trembled and tears splashed

down over her cheeks. 'Patch had never done him a moment's harm. It was to upset me, you see. It was to get the better of me.' She gulped the remains of her sherry. 'He'd threatened me with his open razor, dangled it in front of me. Patch barked at him. He kicked poor wee Patch aside. Patch was trying to protect me, you see. I suddenly felt so angry, Sammy. I was so angry I spoke up to him. I said...' She gazed wide-eyed up at Sammy. 'I said to him, "What would all your important friends say if they saw you now? What would your lawyer friend do if he saw you threaten me with a razor? Maybe it's time I told him."'

'Good for you, Mother,' Sammy said with genuine pride and enthusiasm. 'Good for you!'

'He was furious then. I've never seen him so angry. I'd never spoken up to him before, you see. And then Patch rushed at him again, barking as loud as he could. And then... Oh, Sammy...'

He put the sherry glass aside and gathered her into his arms.

'Just calm down. You're going to be all right. You'll stay safe here with me from now on. And Patch will stay too. I'll go and fetch him as soon as you calm down.'

'It's my fault,' his mother sobbed. 'That's what I should have done long ago. Brought Patch here. Stayed here where we both would have been safe. But I didn't want to be a burden to you, son. And he would have come after me, you know. He would never have let either of us have a minute's peace.'

'Well, never mind, you've come now and don't

ever think you'll be a burden to me. I know you mean well but it was just foolish to think that. I'll enjoy having you here with me. I really will, Mother. That's the honest truth. And you know how fond I am of Patch.'

'I ran out of the garden and along the path until I got to Broomknowes Road. I thought I'd have to run all the way to the police station and it would be too late. But then I saw Constable Campbell,' she said, ignoring Sammy. 'I thought how lucky I was. He's been walking that beat along by the park for years. I called out to him and he ran back with me. We saw your father flattening the earth with his spade, then stamping on it.'

Sammy closed his eyes. 'Mother, he didn't?'

But he knew the reply already.

'Constable Campbell grabbed the spade and dug as fast as he could, and I helped. I scrabbled at the earth with my bare hands, Sammy. We got Patch up eventually and he was unconscious but still breathing. Constable Campbell lifted him and said to me, "It's all right. We'll get him to the vet" and he pushed your father aside and said, "I'll deal with you later."'

'What a bastard,' Sammy managed. 'I hope they lock him up and throw away the key.'

'But by the time we got to the vet, it was too late. Patch was dead. And he was only trying to protect me, Sammy.'

'Oh, Mother...'

'He did that to Patch to intimidate me as he always has done. I'd never spoken up like that, you see – actually threatened him. He knew that

113

hurting Patch, giving Patch that horrible death, was the worst punishment he could give me. If I hadn't threatened your father, Sammy, Patch would still be all right.'

'He would have found some other excuse, some other time, Mother. He hated the dog. Don't for pity's sake blame yourself. Patch wouldn't blame you. You did the right thing. Now you're free of that evil bastard for good. I'll put the kettle on.'

Different emotions careered about inside him as he brought the brown crock teapot down from the shelf and the tin tea caddy with the Japanese scene painted on it.

'After we have a cup of tea, I'll go up to the back road and collect your things. You'll be comfortable in the front room here. You know I never use it. I sleep here in the kitchen bed. Unless you'd prefer here, Mother,' he added hastily. 'Yes, come to think of it, you'd be much cosier in here. You know how you feel the cold. Here, you could make a cup of tea to heat you up whenever you fancied it, even if it was in the middle of the night.'

'Oh, I don't want to put you out, son.'

'I'd prefer the front room and it's time it was used more. No, that's what we'll do. You'll have the kitchen and I'll have the room.'

'I don't know what I'd do without you, son. You've always been a good lad to me.'

'It'll be great having a bit of company, Mother. I'll enjoy having you here, believe me!'

'Poor Patch.' Tears suddenly glistened in her eyes again. 'When I think of what he must have suffered.'

'You mustn't think about it, Mother. You'll only keep upsetting yourself. If you do, that evil old bastard will win. He'll keep on making you miserable. For Patch's sake, as well as your own, you've got to be happy. You show him, Mother. Be brave and be happy, for my sake as well.'

He poured them both a cup of tea and they soon felt better for the comforting brew. But he wasn't looking forward to going up the back road to face his father in the isolated cottage opposite the hospital mortuary. The place held so many terrifying memories for him. But he was going to be all right. There was so much gladness and relief in his heart that at last his mother would be safe and he would now have a real opportunity to make her remaining years happy and contented. Maybe he could take her with him to a meeting. That might help give her peace of mind. Of course, he could buy her another dog, but no doubt she would need a little time to recover from the shock of losing one pet before being able to give any love to another.

He could do all sorts of things for her. He would spoil her because she deserved to be spoiled. He thanked God or Good or whatever or whoever in the spirit world, if there was such a place, for helping his mother. They'd taken an awful long time to do it, but still...

'Do you think you should, son?' his mother was saying now.

'Go up for your things, you mean? Why shouldn't I?'

'He might be there and you know what he's always been like with you.'

115

Oh, didn't he just!

'I'll be fine, Mother. Don't worry. He doesn't bother me.'

So much for his Quaker honesty. He took his coat from the hook behind the door, keeping his back to his mother. Just before he left the room, he turned towards her.

'I won't be long.'

She gazed back at him.

'Oh, son!'

The two words expressed volumes. He hurried away but was forced to slow down the moment he reached the close. A dense fog lay heavy and yellow tinged over the whole city. He'd already felt it filling his nostrils as he'd been coming down the stairs. Now he saw that it had reduced the street lamps to ghostly quivers, hardly visible at all. There were no lights at all up the back road.

His gut churned with fear. Round on to Well-field Street. Past the cinema without seeing it. Up the Wellfield hill. On to Broomknowes Road. He was ashamed of his fear. He had thought he had conquered it but it was still there. It would never go away. Determination quickened his stride. He was not a child any more. His father could not intimidate or frighten him.

The houses with their foggy blotches of windows shrank into nothing. He could hear the rustling of the trees in the park. Along the back road now. How deathly quiet it always was here. The garden gate creaked. His feet groped along the path. His hands felt for the cottage door.

'Father,' he called out. No reply. Was he sitting on his big chair in the dark, hands gripping his

116

heavy walking stick, waiting?

The evil old bastard.

So much for the Quaker belief that God was in everyone. Maybe that was the true reason he had never fully committed himself to them. He couldn't accept all of their beliefs. Where was the good in his father?

He wasn't crouched in his big chair waiting in the dark.

'Father!'

The house was empty. Except for the ghosts of a thousand terrible memories.

After lighting a lamp, he began packing two large suitcases with clothes and toiletries and everything he could lay his hands on that his mother might need or want.

His father, no doubt, would still be at the police station. He was halfway back to his own place in Springburn when he saw the old man or rather heard him – feet stomping, stick thumping. Then his big hunched-shouldered form loomed up through the billowing fog.

Sammy stopped in front of him. 'Mother is with me and she's staying with me from now on. I've collected all her things. Don't you ever dare come near her again, do you hear? If you put a foot near my house or if you make any attempt to contact her in any way, I'll make sure you'll regret it. I'll tell the newspapers. I'll tell everybody. I'll shout from the rooftops, if necessary, everything you've ever done. I'll ruin you. Do you hear me, Father?'

Then, before his father could say or do anything, Sammy pushed roughly past him and was swallowed up by the fog.

117

14

The Springburn library was a darkly weathered sandstone building which had been built with money provided by Andrew Carnegie, the millionaire philanthropist. As a regular reader in the library, Chrissie already knew that it contained a large stock of engineering books and shelves full of left-wing novels. The American writer, Upton Sinclair, was one of the most popular authors.

The children had a separate department and Miss Cruikshanks, the head librarian there, was a stickler for silence and clean hands. Children would have their hands examined on arrival and, if they did not pass inspection, they would be sent out. Chrissie had often seen children hunkered around puddles outside trying to wash their hands before trooping back in.

If speaking was absolutely necessary, it had to be done in hoarse whispers, even in the adult department. In the staff room at the back, conversation over a cup of tea and a biscuit or lunchtime sandwiches had also to be conducted in hushed tones. Miss Cruikshanks, tiny and hunchbacked, was severe in her reprimands if she heard any voice raised. Although, due to her strange eating habits, she could make a surprising amount of noise over her tea break or her lunch. A pear could make quite a riot as her teeth eagerly squelched and chomped at it. She could even make a baked potato sound as if it had a life of its own. No one had the nerve to comment on any of this. At least not to her face. Miss Cruikshanks, despite her small stature, ruled the place with a conscientiousness that gave no quarter.

As Betty Paterson said, 'She could throw you out on your ear without a blink of the eye.'

Behind her back and at a safe distance, the young library assistants often enjoyed a giggle at her expense. Betty Paterson was a bit of a mimic and could do an impersonation of Miss Cruikshanks that was a little bit too cruel for Chrissie's liking. The poor woman couldn't help being a hunchback and maybe she suffered from deformed teeth as well. One thing was certain, she knew about books and Chrissie admired Miss Cruikshanks's knowledge. What Miss Cruikshanks didn't know about books and authors wasn't worth knowing.

The worst of it was that Chrissie, as a library assistant, had hardly any time to spend on the bookshelves. She and the other assistants had to spend most of their time on what was called 'ruling the books'. Everything was recorded in these large notebooks. Everything. And there were particular record books, or rule books as they were more usually called, for each thing. Each of them had to be ruled in a certain way. Columns had to be carefully drawn up with a ruler and pen and ink. Coloured ink. If you didn't rule it properly, you had to start all over again. Even the amount of toilet rolls had to be recorded. Old newspapers had to be kept and folded neatly and added to monstrous piles in the storeroom with equally important bits of string. Nothing was thrown away. Each light bulb had to have a date scratched on it and had to be entered into a book. When the bulb was finished, the brass part was broken off and stored. There were thousands of these bits of numbered brass in the store.

Books had to be ruled to record meter readings. One book had to be ruled for pencils and pens, another for dusting – the whole place had to be dusted every morning and the dusting carefully recorded. Every receipt from firms, for instance who supplied soap for the toilet, had to be recorded, as did every penny that was charged for the public toilet. There were also statistics to be noted of the number of readers who came in and the number of books borrowed and which particular book each reader had borrowed.

Chrissie had begun to rule books in her dreams. Once she had quite a frightening nightmare about being lost among the piles of yellowed newspapers and oceans of string in the basement storeroom and being unable to make her escape back upstairs.

Chrissie had never imagined being a librarian would be like this. All right, the Corporation paid for everything and had to know where every penny of their money was going. 'But come on,' Betty Paterson said, 'who's to know how many toilet rolls and elastic bands we use? Nobody comes to check, do they? Have you ever seen a councillor come here to check how we rule the books or anything else?'

The main thing should be, everyone agreed, that libraries and librarians, and councillors for

120

that matter, should concentrate more on seeing that the public bookshelves were always well supplied with good books to read.

Fair enough, there was already a pretty good stock on the shelves. But it was Miss Cruikshanks's obsession with storing everything and never throwing anything away that ruled the roost. Once old and much-borrowed books had begun to fall to bits or had to be removed from the public domain, they were entered in the record book and stored.

Betty always rolled her eyes at this. 'Who's to know if we burned the lot of them? What use are they to anyone now?'

The other assistants, including Chrissie, were shocked at this idea – it seemed too reminiscent of Adolf Hitler's orgy of book burning. Anyway, Chrissie for one loved them too much, not only for their fascinating contents, but as physical objects as well. Sometimes she took interesting ones home to read – after first asking Miss Cruikshanks's permission, of course, and following her order to mark in the appropriate rule book the titles and date of borrowing. Chrissie would add the return date when she brought them back. Glasgow Corporation might not bother to check up on anything but Miss Cruikshanks's beady eye certainly made up for them.

Big Aggie Stoddart, even many months later, could still be heard to say to friends and acquaintances, 'Fancy, she gave up a good job at the Co-op to bury hersel' doon in that Springburn library wi' that wee hunchback wumman.'

Chrissie had been well warned that she'd live to

regret the day she took the job. She didn't really. What kept her going through the constant 'ruling of the books' was her ambition, and her dearest hope of one day getting to the Mitchell.

As it turned out, there was indeed hope. The Mitchell had always been staffed by men. Women were the ones relegated to the local libraries. Men could be head librarian at a local library but only if it had a separate toilet. Only recently, a male librarian had been transferred back to the Mitchell when it had been discovered that the local library in question did not have male toilet facilities. Shades of 'ruling the books'?

Since men were called up for National Service, the Mitchell had been getting shorter and shorter of staff and requests kept going out to local libraries for volunteers to go and fill the vacancies. To Chrissie's surprise, she'd heard they were having difficulty in finding volunteers. Let them come to me, she thought. They won't have to ask me twice.

Eventually, they did approach Springburn and again, to her surprise, no one wanted to go.

'I'll go,' she told Miss Cruikshanks.

Miss Cruikshanks eyed her suspiciously. 'Why?'

'I've always wanted to work in the Mitchell. It's a marvellous big place.'

'Big is the operative word, Miss Stoddart. You obviously don't realise the amount of work that is entailed in such a place.'

'I don't mind, Miss Cruikshanks. Honestly.'

'Very well.'

Chrissie could hardly contain her excitement. As soon as her father came in from his shift, she cried out to him, 'Daddy, they're sending me to the Mitchell. I'm starting in the Mitchell on Monday.'

'Good for you, hen,' Jimmy said, without much enthusiasm. He was always exhausted after a shift. 'It's a rare big building, that.'

Aggie groaned. 'Whit's up wi' you? Always goin' on about buildings. What do buildings matter? It's what's in them. That's what I say.'

'Millions of pounds' worth of books and archives and manuscripts,' Chrissie burst out excitedly. 'They have a whole collection of books about Robert Burns, and books and letters written by him. They're priceless, Mammy.'

'Aye. Aw right. Eat yer fish supper before it gets cold.'

Aggie had been out buying the fish suppers when Chrissie had arrived home. She was still in her headscarf and voluminous swagger coat. She tugged off her coat, flung it aside, then dumped the suppers onto the waiting plates.

Sixteen-year-old Maimie, who had triumphed in getting a good job at the Co-op, was as unimpressed as Aggie at Chrissie's news.

'I bet they don't pay as good as the Co-op,' she managed, despite cheeks bulging with chips.

'Money's not everything,' Chrissie said.

Aggie let out a derisive howl. 'Would you listen to that. Talk about comin' up the Clyde in a banana boat!' She splashed tarry-looking tea into the cups. 'Ah don't know what we're goin' tae dae wi' her.'

'For goodness' sake!' Chrissie said.

Sometimes she wondered if she really belonged in this family. She fantasised that she'd been adopted or found on the Stoddarts' doorstep when an infant and one day her real parents would arrive and claim her. Parents who wouldn't mind one bit about her working in a library or having Catholic friends. She remembered how she'd been given a right walloping by her mother when it had been discovered that not only had she been consorting with girls from the Catholic school on her way home from her Protestant school every day but she'd actually set foot in a chapel with some of them. This had been an unforgivable sin in both her mother and her father's eyes. Her father was normally not as aggressive as her mother and seldom resorted to physical violence. On that occasion, he'd bawled at her and, although not hitting her himself, he had approved of the battering her mother had meted out.

'What's wrong with being friendly with the girls at that school?' Chrissie had asked plaintively.

'You know fine they're aw Papes.'

'What's wrong with being friendly with Catholics?'

The severity of the battering had at least taught her to keep her mouth shut on the subject and also to be more discreet as far as her friendships were concerned. Ailish O'Donnel was her best friend. Sometimes she even had secret thoughts about Ailish's brother, Sean. Well, quite often, in fact. She had never let on to Ailish about that. She could just imagine the shock and horror it would cause in her house, and probably at the O'Donnels' as well, if she and Sean ever got together in a romantic way. She could never understand what

124

all the fuss was about. What good was religion when it made people hate each other? Ailish and she sometimes spoke about this. Ailish didn't see why it was necessary either. Why didn't both sides just let each other be?

'Makes me mad,' Chrissie said.

'Me too,' Ailish agreed.

But mostly they never mentioned religion. They just enjoyed being best friends. Chrissie wanted to keep it that way. So she didn't risk doing anything about her crush on Ailish's brother – because that was what it was becoming. She no longer thought about how she and Sean had once gone to the pictures together because they had only been children then. Now she thought of him in a different way altogether. She was beginning to fantasise about him. It was difficult to ignore him when she saw him so often – just in passing, on the stairs or in the street. He was two years older than her and rather good-looking. Clever too, she bet, with his good, steady job in an office. And he dressed every day in a collar and tie instead of a muffler like most of the other blokes she knew. His hair was smooth and a rich, glossy black, like his father's. Although his father's hair was now going grey.

Chrissie sighed every time she thought of Sean. His eyes were so dark and sexy. She could not get him out of her mind. She wondered if she dared stop him one day and speak to him. Not just to say 'Hello' or 'It's a nice day', but to really have a conversation with him.

She began to think about how she could do it. She could perhaps get him talking about books, as Ailish said he was a great reader. She imagined what she would say. Then what he would say. In her imagination, one thing led to another.

Her fantasies were beginning to become more vivid. Sometimes they made her blush. Sean just needed to look at her now and she blushed.

It was terrible!

15

Word was spreading about her knowledge of herbs and other remedies. It surprised Catriona. She had helped her mother's piles, so perhaps it was Hannah who was telling everyone – at least in the Band of Jesus, where she still ruled the roost.

Certainly quite a few of the ladies from that particular organisation had come to Botanic Crescent asking for help. There had been Mrs Dawson, who had been bothered with constipation, and Mrs Green with her varicose veins. Catriona hadn't been confident enough to risk doing anything with the varicose veins, which had been like big bunches of black grapes. She'd given Mrs Green willow herb for the pain but advised her to go to her doctor. Mrs McGurk had been miserable with diarrhoea and a stomach upset, and Catriona had given her *arsen alb* and told her to alternate it with *carbo veg* every hour for a day, then every two hours the second day.

'Ye're a right wee stoater,' Mrs McGurk had

assured Catriona afterwards. 'Ma runs stopped. Nae bother.'

Mrs McDougal had brought her wee boy to be treated for eczema. 'While I'm here, hen, could you give me something for my cough?' *Bryonia* and *drosera* did the trick for her.

Then a lady from the West End had called. She also suffered from an upset digestive system but she had added, to Catriona's surprise, 'I'll pay you, of course. Just tell me what your fee is.'

Catriona was taken aback but not so much that she needed to confess that she had never charged anyone before.

'We'll leave that until your next visit, shall we?' she said. 'I think I'd better see you again to check if the medicine I give you has had the desired effect. If it doesn't, we can try something else.'

Afterwards, she thought with gathering excitement, 'Why not?' She decided on a consultation fee, plus whatever it cost for the medicine. The medicine she would prescribe could be either herbal or homeopathic, although she'd come to prefer homeopathic. These were the medicines she was having most success with. Already she had a small stock of herbs, creams and ointments in the house, as well as homeopathic powders and tablets. She lost no time in stocking up with more of everything. For the first time in a long time, she felt happy. Excited too. For the first time, she actually felt glad to be living in such a large house. What was to stop her using one of the downstairs rooms as a kind of surgery? Maybe one of the rooms at the back that they never used? How about putting a bench in the

127

passageway and using it as a waiting area?

Hallelujah! The back door would be of real use at last. She and the family always used the imposing front entrance. Customers – or should they be called patients? – could go along the back lane and enter by the back door. That way they could be completely private and separate from the rest of the house. In her excitement and enthusiasm, she could hardly wait to tell Melvin.

'What?' His voice shot up an octave with incredulity. 'Have strangers traipsing in and out of my house? Have you gone mad or something?'

She quickly switched to what might appeal to him more. 'Think of the money, Melvin.' She had been babbling on about how she could help people. 'I could make – we could make...' she hastily corrected herself, '...we could make a fortune at that. And no one would be traipsing through the house. Anyone coming would go along the lane and just knock at the back door. I'd take them in and keep them in that back room until I showed them out that way again. You'd never see anybody, Melvin. You'd never know and we'd make a fortune.'

'How could we make a fortune? Don't be daft.'

'Well, there would be no extra overheads, for a start. I wouldn't need shop premises and the medicines are so cheap. You wouldn't believe how cheap – especially if we bought in bulk. You'd have nothing to worry about, Melvin. As I've said, you wouldn't even see anybody. You could just forget about it and leave it to me.'

She adopted a wheedling tone. 'I know you always want to do your best for me, Melvin, and

128

make me happy, and I'd be so grateful if you'd let me do this – even just as a wee hobby.'

'That's all it would be – a wee hobby.' He laughed uproariously. 'Make a fortune – you? What a joke! OK, have your wee hobby if that's what'll keep you happy.'

She rushed at him to hug and kiss him. 'Oh, Melvin, thank you.'

He puffed up with pleasure. 'Aye, well, don't you ever say I'm not good to you.'

'No, Melvin. You *are* good to me. I know you are.'

She knew nothing of the kind. But she did feel a surge of happiness. It gave the previous intensity of her emotions a different focus. She'd always suffered from intense emotions – usually guilt and regret, fear and hatred of Melvin and, more recently, shame at the intensity of her sexual feelings for just about everybody else. The sheer intensity of her emotions would exhaust her and they'd fizzle out and be replaced by lack of confidence in herself. Suddenly she felt that again. What on earth was she thinking about? A fortune? For goodness' sake, wasn't that just like her? A few of her mother's friends had come to ask for a bit of advice. Only one woman had offered to pay. Melvin had been right to laugh. One woman and she had immediately gone over the top and imagined herself making a fortune. She felt depressed then.

Fortunately that didn't last for too long. She began to think – well, surely it's worth a try? Even if she didn't make a fortune, maybe she would find satisfaction in being somebody in her own right, doing something she wanted to do, just for herself. All her life, she had never been allowed to be herself. Or get to know herself.

All her life, she had been forced, first of all, to do what her mother told her and to accept her mother's view of what she was or should be, and what she had to do. Then it had been Melvin's turn.

All right, even if it did prove to be no more than a hobby, at least she would be doing something she enjoyed and perhaps she could actually help a few people at the same time. Then it occurred to her that it would be a good idea to advertise. After all, if people didn't know about the service she provided, how could they come? Word of mouth was all right, but postcards in a few shop windows wouldn't do any harm. She spent some time concentrating on writing the postcards or, rather, printing them for the sake of clarity.

'Herbal or Homeopathic Treatment can help when all else fails. Homeopathic treatment especially is a gentle, natural way with no side effects. Phone this number for an appointment.'

She put the postcards in various windows in the Great Western Road shops. Then she gave a few to Madge to put in some of the shops in the Balornock and Springburn area. Madge thought it was a great laugh. But somehow her laughter was not hurtful or demeaning like Melvin's. 'Good luck to you, hen.' She gave Catriona a slap on the back that nearly knocked her off her feet. 'You'll probably make a bloody fortune with the kind of luck you have. I wish I'd thought of something like that. See me? I'll still be a slave to

130

these weans and that big useless article I'm married to when I'm ninety – if I last that long.'

When Catriona had asked her to help distribute the postcards, Madge hadn't hesitated. 'Sure, hen. Give me as many as you like.'

She was a good friend. Catriona did feel lucky in that respect. She nearly gave some to Julie as well, knowing that she too would not hesitate to help all she could. But then she thought, what if too many patients turned up, too many for her to cope with? It wasn't something that was very likely to happen, but still.

She worried about the treatment – herbal or homeopathic? Again she thought that although herbal treatment could be marvellously successful, it could be a bit unpleasant to take. Some mixtures could have quite a vile taste. But that wasn't as important as the actual mixing of it. People could cope with the taste if it helped them but could she cope with the dispensing of it? The more she thought of it, the more she wished she'd left the word 'herbal' out of the postcards.

She could use the big unused walk-in larder opposite the treatment room as a dispensary but another problem was that herbs could be strong-smelling and powerful odours could spoil homeo-pathic medicines. The latter had to be stored safely away from anything like eucalyptus, men-thol or peppermint. Indeed, she would have to warn anyone taking homeopathic treatments not to use any rubs, creams or ointments or take any pastilles, cough mixtures or indigestion tablets containing these pungent ingredients. Otherwise the homeopathic treatments just wouldn't work.

131

She'd have to tell people too not to touch the homeopathic tablets or powders. Powders had to be tipped straight from their special paper wrappers into the mouth. Tablets had to be tipped from their bottles or phials on to the lid and, from the lid, straight into the mouth. That way the medicine was kept sterile.

It would be awkward storing all the medicines separately. It would mean having the homeopathic medicines on shelves and in cupboards in the consulting room. There weren't any shelves or cupboards there and she didn't think the housekeeping money would stretch to paying a joiner to do the necessary work.

No use asking Melvin. He would only start cataloguing all the money he'd spent on her, especially in recent years. The television was one of his favourite examples, although it was he who watched it most of the time and it was always programmes that he liked, never the ones she'd prefer. She never watched it at all, except when he was there and she had to sit with him. He never liked doing anything on his own. He was a family man through and through, he always said.

'You like them as well,' he'd say. It was one of his most infuriating habits. He had never even given a moment's thought to her point of view. He always took it for granted or insisted that her taste was exactly the same as his.

The new refrigerator would be dragged up and the washing machine, of course. Not to mention the various gadgets he'd bought for her. He liked gadgets.

No, safer not to mention anything about the

'wee hobby' or the room in which it was to be conducted. He'd never mentioned it again. No doubt he'd completely forgotten about it. It was fortunate that he was working less and less at night – hardly at all now. Like his father before him, as he got older, the night shift became too much for him. He could only cope with the day shift. In fact, more and more, he wasn't even doing his usual work baking the bread. Instead, he was selling it behind the counter in the front shop.

'There's enough bakers on the job and Baldy knows to keep things going the way I like them. I'm more needed to keep my eye on the shop these days.'

He would never admit that he was no longer fit enough for the hard work of baking. Catriona began to realise that life was starting to go her way. She had several hours a day completely free of Melvin. She didn't need to tiptoe about and try to ensure silence while he slept during the day. She no longer needed to be at his beck and call and suffer the brunt of his bad temper when he couldn't sleep. Nowadays, she didn't even need to go down and help in the shop. Between Melvin and the three girls in the shop, it was ticking over very nicely. Often, after his studies or at the weekends, Andrew helped out if one or more of the girls was off sick or on holiday. He made a bit of extra pocket money doing that.

Catriona had to admit that Melvin wasn't mean with the boys. Although he did grumble to her about still having to keep Fergus 'in the lap of luxury' while he 'loafed about playing a guitar and enjoying himself,' prolonging his time at the

Aberdeen College of Music and Drama by doing yet another course.

She found herself in the situation now of having to constantly defend Fergus. Changed days. It used to be that she had to defend both herself and especially Andrew from Fergus.

Melvin, however, seldom criticised Fergus to his face. He just nagged at her about him. Fergus was still his favourite because Melvin could never forget that Fergus was the son of his perfect first wife. Not that he spoke about the poor woman any more. Gone were the days – thank God – when he spoke about nothing else. Catriona had long since come to the conclusion that in fact his first marriage had been far from perfect and his first wife, far from adoring him, had felt much the same way as his second – or worse. Maybe he talked the way he did because he felt guilty. Or he just wasn't able to face the truth.

'Fergus doesn't loaf about. He works hard.'

'Work?' Melvin sneered. 'What kind of work's that?'

He'd say the same thing if she brought up the subject of her 'wee hobby' as a therapist. No, better to forget the joinery work needed. Better to wait until she had made enough money to pay for it herself. Meantime, she'd just keep her homeopathic medicines in a box and a suitcase in the consulting room.

Then it occurred to her that she could start a bank account in her own name.

Now there was a thought!

16

Christmas cards were sent all round. It was the season of good will after all. Big Aggie, however, felt insulted by the card received from the O'Donnels on which there was a picture of the Virgin Mary. Chrissie couldn't understand why. As she said to Ailish, 'Christmas is supposed to be about Jesus and she's his mother. Beats me what Mammy sees wrong in that.'

'My mammy felt the same about your mammy's card.'

'What one did she get again?'

'The one with a snowman with a carrot for a nose.'

'Oh, yes.' They both giggled, remembering it.

'Awful, aren't they?'

'I know.'

Suddenly, Chrissie remembered something else. Serious again, she rolled her eyes heavenwards. 'Next thing it'll be the Old Firm game. I hate that.'

'Me too.'

'It'll even spoil us going to the pictures – especially when it's in the town. Wouldn't be so bad if it was on in the Princes.' They planned to go and see Marlon Brando. They adored Marlon Brando.

'Och, I don't suppose it would make much difference.'

'But the stupid drunks'll be fighting and carrying on all over the place. Nowhere's safe.'

'It's terrible, so it is. I'm hoping Dermot'll be on duty at the pub and not in the middle of all the carry-on at the match.'

'I can't understand what they all see in football. It's stupid getting so worked up about kicking a wee ball around.'

'Even Sean's daft about football.'

'And bringing religion into it.'

'Sean doesn't but so many of them do, right enough.'

Chrissie groaned. 'I know.' Then more cheerfully, 'I like what you've done to your hair.'

'It took me ages brushing it and plastering it down with Sean's Brylcreem before I could tie it back. I was determined, Shirley Temple curls or not, that I was going to have a pony tail. As I keep telling you, you're lucky with your straight hair. You've never any bother getting a great pony tail. You even get a fringe no bother. Every time I try a fringe, it keeps curling up.'

'You look great. Honestly.'

'Thanks.' Ailish hugged Chrissie's arm closer and they walked along in silence for a few minutes as if joined at the hip. Then Ailish said, 'Still liking the Mitchell as much, then?'

They hadn't seen each other for what seemed like ages. At least, not to get together and talk. It wasn't easy to avoid being seen together. Especially in Balornock and Springburn. They'd had a few narrow escapes. Today, however, they had managed to meet in town while doing some Christmas shopping. Surely, they felt, in such crowded city streets, no one would notice them.

'Oh here,' Chrissie creased forward in a fit of giggles, 'I made an awful mistake the other day.'

'Oh, go on, tell me.'

'Difficult to explain when you don't know the place. I mean, the kind of work. It was difficult enough for me. There are three catalogues, you see. When you catalogue books, you've to do catalogues and several different slips for each catalogue. Different colours as well. One is white, one yellow, one red and each of these slips is in three parts with perforations. When they are typed and finished with, they're torn up into the strips, and then they are put in their place in the catalogue.'

Ailish looked a bit puzzled but she murmured a cautious 'Yes.'

Chrissie went on, 'So here, one day, I had nothing much to do, so I asked Miss Andrews – she's in charge of catalogues – if I could do anything to help her. And she said, "Yes, you could tear up these slips" and she gave me a box.'

Ailish began to laugh as light dawned.

'You didn't!'

'I did. Tore up every one of them.'

'What happened? Did you get an awful row?'

'No, and that was worse. It turned out that Miss Andrews is one of these quiet, long-suffering martyr types. She stuck them all together again and wouldn't let me help. It took her ages as well. I felt terrible.'

'I can imagine.'

'But something else happened – another crisis but more of an excitement than mine. Pauline

Winters poured a bottle of perfume over Mr McKay's head. A big bottle, as well. She'd just bought it in Boots as a Christmas present for her sister.'

'Why on earth did she do that? Had he made a pass at her or something?'

'We don't know. It's the talk of the place. He stank to high heavens for ages afterwards as well.'

'He must have done something.'

'That's what we all say. And he's a funny wee man. I mean funny strange. Not funny ha ha. He doesn't walk around between the stacks. He kind of creeps.'

'For goodness' sake!'

'But he always seemed pretty harmless. Just a quiet wee man, you know.'

'But he must have done something,' Ailish repeated, 'to what was her name?'

'Pauline Winters. She's a nervous kind of girl, right enough. A bit jumpy at the best of times. Usually chatters away no bother, but she's clammed up about this. It's driving us all mad, not being able to find out.'

'Do you still like the place then?'

'Oh yes. We still have to rule the books but there's more of us and lots of other interesting things going on.'

'Not half, by the sound of it.'

They both enjoyed another bout of giggles before parting at the arranged place.

All the library staff worked split shifts – nine till twelve, then one-thirty till six. Or nine to one-thirty and six till nine. Chrissie was on the later shift and so had to be back by six.

Being with Ailish had made her think of Sean again. They had spoken a little more than their previous 'Good morning' or 'Good evening' or 'Nice day'. One day Sean had unexpectedly said, 'I hear you've changed your job.'

'Well, not exactly changed.' Silly ass that she was, she'd begun to blush and stutter. 'I mean, I'm still a library assistant. But I've moved to the Mitchell.'

'Great place,' Sean said. 'The biggest reference library in Europe, I believe. I'd love to have a really good browse through their Burns collection. I'm a great admirer of Burns.'

Instead of giving an opinion of the poet – and she could have because she knew his work so well – she just stood blushing and unable to articulate another word. Oh, how she hated her stupid self afterwards. She could have impressed Sean by quoting some of Burns's poetry. That had been her big chance and she'd let it pass without doing or saying a thing. She had determined never to make that mistake again. She rehearsed what she'd say to him next time. Then what he'd say to her. And what she'd reply. Something very witty and knowledgeable, of course, because it was obvious that Sean was impressively knowledgeable about many things. Ailish said he'd even read Proust. Fancy! Proust! Her admiration for him knew no bounds.

Yet the next time he'd spoken to her, instead of telling him that she'd also read Proust – she'd hastily whizzed through it after Ailish had told her that Sean had read him – she'd been just as tongue-tied as before. Sean had said, 'Still liking the Mitchell?'

She'd had to clear her throat before even being able to croak out, 'Yes, thanks.' And that was it.

After escaping into the house, she'd stood in front of the bedroom mirror and peered furiously at the flushed face reflected there. She hated its baby roundness under the dark, straight fringe and the rest of the hair dragged back into its pony tail. She'd actually said out loud, 'Stupid idiot!' She was wearing her fashionable mohair sweater and stylish shoes.

She returned to the Mitchell with a heavy heart, even though she'd enjoyed the afternoon with Ailish. She wondered, for the umpteenth time, if she should pluck up courage and confess to her friend what she felt for Sean. After all, it wasn't as if Ailish was bigoted in any way. Ailish was nothing like Mr and Mrs O'Donnel or Dermot. But, to say the least, it would give Ailish an awful shock and would be embarrassing for both of them. It would probably cause Ailish a lot of anxiety as well. The danger of starting a serious relationship with Sean could, if it was found out, trigger a terrible feud up the close. Her mother and father, not to mention her sister Maimie, would be every bit as bad as the O'Donnels.

Once back on duty and after ruling the time book, Chrissie noticed an old man snoozing behind one of the stacks in the newspaper room. Originally, the working classes who used the libraries had little or no access to newspapers, so one of the first things every library had installed was a reading room which was usually as big as, if not bigger than, the lending department and every reading room took everything from the *Morning Star* to the London *Times*. Janitors were normally on duty in the reading room, not librarians. These janitors were equipped with a long stick with a roller on the end, which they rubbed on an ink pad and then ran up the columns of racing results in the newspapers until the results were illegible. This extraordinary procedure was undertaken because Glasgow Corporation couldn't be seen to approve of gambling. It certainly kept the janitors busy because it had to be done each day with every single edition of every newspaper. If a janitor wasn't there, one of the library staff had to do it. The result was that not only the janitors but also the librarians were regularly covered in ink.

The main problem, however, was not hordes of inveterate gamblers, desperate to see the racing results, it was sad old men looking for somewhere to sleep. For the homeless and destitute, the reading room was a warm and peaceful shelter.

It was usually the janitor's job to eject them. In the Mitchell, on this occasion, the job fell to Bob Lightfoot. A tall, hefty man who carried his big stomach proudly before him, he was anything but light-footed. Striding up to the old man, he grabbed him by the frayed lapels of his shabby jacket.

The old man spluttered awake, making spittle spray over Bob's hands.

'You dirty old devil!' Bob's cry reverberated all round the room. 'Get out of here before I fling you out.'

Chrissie got a whiff of the stench of the old man as he shuffled past her. She screwed up her face.

'Makes you sick, doesn't it?' Bob whispered to her as he ushered the old man away, 'I'm off to wash my hands.'

Chrissie nodded. But, as usual, she couldn't help feeling sorry for the old men whose lives consisted of wandering from one library reading room to another, only to keep being banished to the streets to face every extreme of weather.

That was the trouble with her. She was too emotional. And she had too vivid an imagination. Knowing this didn't stop her from fantasising about Sean again. She would have to *do* something. She'd been suffering like this for what felt like years. She would have to do something or she'd explode!

17

At first, Sean and Dermot had tried to get tickets for the big match without success. They had devoured the papers to see where tickets were being sold and discovered that some were to be had at Albion Rovers' ground in Coatbridge. They immediately got a bus to the station and then another one to Coatbridge and joined the queue. They had been only fifth from the front when a voice said, 'All sold.'

They travelled in silence all the way home, struck dumb with the acuteness of their disappointment. Dermot was especially cast down, as he'd managed to get enough time off work to be

142

at the match. Then the big announcement came that the Scottish Football Association were selling tickets at Hampden Park. Both Sean and Dermot were beside themselves with excitement. They *had* to get tickets and get into that match at Hampden. They got up at four in the morning and walked all the way from Springburn to Hampden Park. They didn't know about short cuts so they followed the bus and tram routes. This meant that it took them hours to get there.

Once there, the police, for some unknown reason, wouldn't allow them or the thousands of others there to queue up. Instead, everyone was forced to keep marching all round the district. It soon became more of a stagger, they were so tired. Eventually the police stopped the march and linked arms to cordon everyone off. Then suddenly they dropped their arms and it was a free-for-all. Thousands raced down the road to get their tickets. Sean noticed, running in front of him, what looked like a wee insurance man, complete with trench coat, soft hat and briefcase. He fell and no one stopped to help. Everyone, including Dermot and himself, just ran across him.

An enormous queue formed once Hampden was reached and, hallelujah, they got tickets. Sean's heart thumped with relief and excitement. It didn't matter what game it was, every time he came to Hampden, every time he turned the corner at Prospecthill Road, his heart skipped a beat. He always felt the same magic. His heart thumped and he kept thinking, 'I'm nearly there.' Excitement reached fever pitch once the game began. A shot on goal, a near miss or the ball hitting the back of the net could trigger off an unbelievable response – exaggerated groans, curses and cries of despair if it wasn't a goal, an incredible wall of sound and frenzied rejoicing if it was. If he was standing at the back of the crowd – sometimes of thirty-five thousand or more – and his team scored a goal, the crowd would surge forward like a tidal wave. By the time everything had calmed down again, he often found himself coming up for air more than halfway down the terracing. Submerged in that heaving mass of screaming fans as they had surged forward, he never knew how he ended up where he did.

ugh

It was the same at Ibrox. The best day of his life was when Celtic had beaten Rangers seven–one. Dermot had been absolutely over the moon, in a sheer ecstasy of delight. He had even danced a jig of joy. The huge dark-coated, black-booted tide of men thundering along the streets after the game swept them along and into their favourite pub. There they celebrated until their money ran out. They had only coppers left for the bus fare to Springburn. Finally, they raced each other up the Wellfield hill and round into Broomknowes Road. Then up the stairs two at a time to the top flat where they collapsed, utterly exhausted but still happy, on to the living-room settee.

'Seven–one,' Dermot gasped, 'Can you believe it?'

Their mother was setting the table for their tea. 'You're both as red as a couple of beetroots. What have you been doin' wi' yersels?'

'Ma, Celtic won seven–one,' Dermot repeated.

'Great, son. That's great, so it is.' Teresa's thin, sallow face creased into a smile. The asthma and anaemia she suffered from drained her energy. She often sounded breathless and tired. 'Big Aggie'll no' like that.'

'Aye, we'll not see much of the Stoddarts today or the Paters.'

'Will I pour your tea?' She addressed both of her sons.

'Thanks, Ma.' Sean struggled up from the settee. 'Sorry we're so late.'

'At least you can keep your feet. Dear knows what your da'll be like.'

'I thought he was working today.'

'He should have been, son, but he took the day off. Just before he was leaving this morning, old Kate Gogarty came to the door and said her Joe had a ticket but had taken one of his bad turns and wasn't able to go to the match and could Michael use the ticket.' Teresa shook her head. 'He got me to phone his work and say he'd fallen down the stairs and couldn't move. I felt terrible, so I did.'

Both Sean and Dermot laughed as they got stuck into their plates of spam and beans.

'He'll still be celebrating, Ma,' Dermot said. 'There was such a mob in all the pubs, it was taking ages to get served. We gave up eventually.'

'Oh, he'll no' give up,' Teresa said, sinking on to a chair beside them at the table. 'He'll come rolling in here after ten at night, what do you bet?' She sipped a cup of strong, sweet tea. She drank endless cups of tea. It helped strengthen her.

'Och, well, Ma,' Sean said, 'it'll be one of the

145

happiest days of his life. You can't blame him for wanting to celebrate.'

'Son, if they'd lost seven–one, it would have been just the same. Only then he'd say he'd been drowning his sorrows.'

Dermot laughed. 'Och, well, he works hard, Ma. He deserves a bit of pleasure.'

She had to concede that Michael did work hard. But all the same, it was really no excuse for his regular weekend drinking bouts. During the week, he had always been fine. A good father and a good husband. Come Saturday, he became a drunken pest, to say the least. He wasn't violent to any of them but he was a pest, staggering around, roaring out sectarian songs aimed at infuriating the Stoddarts and any other Protestant family or Rangers supporter for miles around.

Nothing Teresa said or did ever succeeded in shutting him up. Dermot was usually out either with pals or embroiled in some fight or other. Now he was more often than not working in the pub. So he was of no help. Sean occasionally stayed in to see what he could do but Teresa insisted, 'There's no use you spoiling your Saturday night, son. Away you go to the pictures or the dancing or wherever and enjoy yourself. I can manage your daddy all right. It's no' as if he does any harm.'

It was enough to put anybody off drink, especially drinking to excess. It had certainly cured Sean of any desire to do so. Now and then, he enjoyed a few pints but that was all. To give Dermot his due, he too only ever had a few pints – he said it was because he had to keep fit. Dermot had always been a great one for fitness and exercise. Sean couldn't quite agree with his mother that his father never did any harm. He knew what she meant. Unlike many another drunken man, he'd never raised a finger against her. But he did a lot of harm, in Sean's opinion, by provoking their Protestant neighbours at every opportunity, as aggressively as he could. There was no need for that.

Sean personally had quite a few friends who were Protestants or Rangers supporters and he had no problem with any of them. He would often go to a match with them. Like everyone else, they'd separate at the turnstiles. He would go to the Celtic end of the ground and his mates would automatically make for the Rangers end. They'd sometimes meet up afterwards for a drink if they could find one another. Funnily enough, when Celtic lost, his Rangers pals always seemed to find him no bother. But he could live with that. Often they went together to international matches and just appreciated the skilful football, all the usual poisonous sectarian divisions forgotten – for ninety minutes at least. If it was a Scotland versus England match, they always formed a solid united front. England was the Auld Enemy, after all.

Although Ailish never mentioned her friendship with Chrissie Stoddart, he had known about it for years. Ailish was no more bigoted than he was. She also shared his love of books. As far as fiction was concerned, he was a Dickens man. And of course, he admired Upton Sinclair. In their own ways, what great social reformers both

147

authors had been. Then there was Robert Burns. What a genius! Sean was a great fan of the poet and could recite the whole of 'Tam o' Shanter' off by heart.

Sean had gone to his first Burns Supper recently and thoroughly enjoyed it. Except for the over-enthusiastic consumption of whisky. Like Burns, too much (or even a little) of the hard stuff upset his stomach. Most people didn't know that about Burns. Alcohol didn't agree with the poet, it upset his stomach. Ailish had made Sean laugh by stating with much feeling – which was unusual for her – that, if Burns were alive today or if she had been alive in his time, she'd be queuing up for him. Ailish was usually such a quiet wee soul. As far as he knew, she hadn't even gone out with a boy. Time she did and he'd told her that more than once. She always replied that she was perfectly happy the way she was. That was all very well but she was in her twenties now. Most girls of her age were married and having families. It surely wasn't natural to be happy and single and content with just working and going out with a girlfriend. The same applied to Chrissie. A couple of times, Sean had nearly said this to Ailish but her friendship with Chrissie, he guessed, was regarded by both girls as such a big secret that it added a welcome bit of excitement to their lives. Still, having boyfriends would have been a much better and more natural way of spicing up their lives.

Sean didn't see why not. They were both pretty in their own ways. Ailish was also well read and intelligent. So was Chrissie. Or so Ailish said. He occasionally dropped into their conversation a discreet question about Chrissie.

'How is Chrissie these days?' he'd say carefully. 'Do you ever see her?'

Or 'What's Chrissie up to these days? Any idea?'

And Ailish would say something about bumping into her on the stairs or in the library. Or she'd say she'd just happened to serve Chrissie in Copeland & Lye's.

He knew Chrissie was now working in the Mitchell. You didn't get in there as an assistant librarian without being very intelligent. Sean often remembered, always with embarrassment and intense fury at himself, how he'd once taken her to the pictures and behaved like a right idiot. He had been really keen on her and desperate to make a good impression. And what did he do? He'd halved the bar of chocolate he'd bought for the occasion, instead of presenting the whole of it to her. He'd sat beside her in the hall as stiff as a poker with nerves and never even plucked up the courage to hold her hand. OK, he was only a young lad at the time and she was only a wee lassie. But, all the same, what must she have thought of him? She had turned out a very presentable young woman. Not all skin and bone like some but with nice feminine curves. Nice glossy dark hair too and big, soft brown eyes gazing up from under her fringe.

He liked that. Sometimes a thought would come to him. Maybe he could... Then he'd remember, and the same old embarrassment would sweep over him. He wasn't going to risk making a fool of himself like that again.

18

Whistling cheerily, Baldy Fowler carried the bread board packed with freshly baked loaves through to the busy front shop and dumped it on the counter in a warm haze of floury dust. Gone were the days when they had employed Sandy, the giant beanpole of a van man, to deliver bread all around the district in his van drawn by frisky Billy, the horse.

'I'm off then,' Baldy announced to Melvin as he untied his white apron. 'The others knocked off about half an hour ago.'

'It's a wonder they stayed that long,' Melvin said.

'Och, you know fine they did their full shift. They're good lads.'

'Are you seeing your lady friend tonight then?'

Baldy's big roar of laughter startled some of the queue of customers who weren't used to his exuberant ways.

'She's making my tea at her place and then we're going to the pictures.'

One of the customers said, 'When's the big day going to be then, Baldy? We're all waiting on an invitation.'

'What big day?'

The customer turned to the woman standing behind her. 'He thinks we're daft.'

Still laughing, Baldy strode back into the bakehouse to hang up his apron and to collect his coat and bunnet. There was a door from there that led out to the close.

The daily queues in the shop that stretched out on to Byres Road always reassured Melvin that the business continued to be successful. After all, what other bakery, or shop of any kind, could attract such queues? The suicide sensation was long past and, for most people, forgotten.

'You don't know what you're talking about,' he told Catriona when she spoke about a new kind of store that was 'bound to come', as she'd put it. Indeed, they were already proliferating all over Britain, according to her. Supermarkets, she called them. Even if they did come to the West End, or anywhere else in Glasgow, how could they compete with McNair's delicious, freshly baked bread, cakes and biscuits?

'But people are lazy,' Catriona tried to explain.

'Aye, you for a start.'

'When they're in the supermarket for other things and they see bread or packets of biscuits or boxes of cakes, the chances are they'll just pick them up while they're there, rather than bother going to any other shop.'

'We're not just any other shop. We're McNair's,' Melvin said proudly. 'No one'll find better bakers in the whole of Glasgow than McNair's.'

'I know that but what I'm saying is...'

'Aw, shut up.'

Catriona began to worry about Melvin. She could still feel surges of hatred for him, but such intensity of emotion quickly fizzled out nowadays. Maybe the strength needed to keep hating

151

was becoming too much for her. Or maybe it was all the herbal sedatives she was taking. Sometimes she even felt sorry for Melvin. He didn't look well. He was a mere shell of the man he used to be. He smoked too much and it was giving him a chesty cough. She tried to persuade him to take some of the herbal cough mixture she'd made up.

'Stop fussing, woman.' Angrily he pushed her aside. 'There's nothing wrong with me.'

She tried to make him cut down on cigarettes. All to no avail.

'Mum, I wish you'd stop nagging at Dad,' Andrew said eventually. 'After all, he leaves you to do whatever you want without complaining.'

She felt so hurt by this she couldn't speak. When she thought of how Melvin had nagged at her for years! Not in front of the boys, of course. Certainly not since they'd grown up. It was not the fact that film stars, footballers and every other popular icon smoked and even doctors recommended smoking to calm the nerves that Andrew was pointing out. He was just taking his father's part against her. Was it because he loved Melvin more than her? Andrew's love was what had always made up for everything else in her life. For him, she had suffered a terrible marriage. It was the only way she believed she could give him – and Fergus for that matter – a secure and happy home life. As far as she was able, she had hidden her own unhappiness so that the boys could be happy. She had never said a word to the boys against their father. Never complained to them about anything. When she thought of the lie she had lived, she realised she had made a terrible mistake. She ought to have left Melvin years ago. And told the boys why. But where could she have gone? Especially with young children and without a penny to her name. How could they have understood then any more than they would understand now?

She began to realise, remembering little things, an occasional word or look, that Andrew did indeed favour his father and viewed her with increasing criticism. She couldn't bear it. But she didn't know what to do. Life went on. She tried to be as good as possible to both boys but especially to Andrew. Fergus was a grown man now and seemed perfectly happy in Aberdeen and with the music he had become so absorbed in. His father didn't approve of any of it. 'That stupid skiffle rubbish,' Melvin called it.

She quite enjoyed Lonnie Donegan, the famous skiffle player, herself. Most of his music had a catchy, cheeky rhythm to it. Fergus had explained that it was 'folk songs with a beat'. Melvin disapproved of young people in general but specially of those who were slightly younger than Fergus, not yet in their twenties. 'Teenagers' was the latest word for them. She believed Melvin had a point in a way when he said that this new category was being pandered to at every turn. Certainly many businesses were aiming to attract the younger customer. Concentrating on them, in fact. Young people had more earning power now and were happy to spend all they earned. They were completely taking over, it seemed, from the society or generation who believed in being thrifty. Earnest discussions on the 'youth question' took up much space in newspapers. Nineteen-year-old dramatists appeared and seventeen-year-old singers were becoming stars. Before the war, the stars had been in their thirties, or older. Men like Johnny Rae or Donald 'Babbling Brook' Peers. Now youths like Tommy Hicks, or Tommy Steele as he'd become, were grabbing the limelight. If a young man was described as 'angry', he was listened to with almost reverential attention.

Youth, everyone was told, was in revolt. Youth, Catriona believed, had always been in revolt – the difference was that now, for the first time, they were becoming economically independent. She had read somewhere that teenage earnings were now more than fifty per cent higher than before the war. The few shillings of spending money before the war had now become pounds.

Andrew had not been swept up in this kind of revolt. He didn't wear Teddy boy clothes or dash about on a motorbike or indulge in 'blow-waves' or Tony Curtis hairdos. Nor did he go to the other extreme of sporting the fringe, beard, bold, checked, open-necked shirts and nostalgic melancholy of the skiffle groups. He was more interested in sport, regularly going to football matches, but also playing football himself. Recently he'd taken up karate. He had done well at school, got the necessary qualifications and was now studying to become a physiotherapist. As part of his training, he was getting experience in hospitals and all sorts of places. It was all very exciting. What he hoped to do eventually, once he finished his course, was to work with football teams. Catriona had been thrilled and touched at first when he'd spoken of training as a physiotherapist. She'd thought that it was because she was interested in therapies and he admired what she was trying to do. She'd even had secret dreams of Andrew working in one of the other back rooms, treating patients. She had lovely visions of them working together, being partners. She struggled to be firm with herself and forget her disappointment, though. Physiotherapy was a good profession and he would be especially happy working with sportsmen. She was glad for him. As long as he was healthy and happy, that was all that really mattered.

She hardly ever saw either of the boys now that Fergus was in Aberdeen and evenings during the week were devoted to Andrew's karate club. At weekends, he would be off to see some team or other. His favourites, she gathered, were Rangers and Partick Thistle.

If Fergus was home at weekends or during the summer holidays, he would spend most of his time playing skiffle with some of his odd-looking friends. Even the girls he went out with looked strange with their loose sweaters, black stockings and longish, carefully disordered hair. They seemed unaware of the new trends in music – rock 'n' roll was all the rage and now there was this new band from Liverpool, The Beatles, that everyone was going mad about. But it was still skiffle with Fergus.

Melvin's main interest was television. They never went to the cinema together any more.

'Why should we go out and spend good money

on seeing a picture when we can watch one on the television, in the comfort of our own home?'

It was always money with Melvin. Even on television, his favourite programme was *Double your Money* with Hughie Green. If she went out to the cinema, or anywhere at all, it was with Madge or Julie. She didn't mind so much now that she had her work – and of course she never stopped reading and studying, especially books on homeopathy. Quite a few people had seen her postcards and phoned up for an initial appointment. They in turn told others. What impressed everyone on their first visit was the time she took to listen to them and talk to them compared with their doctor. At the doctor's surgery, you were in and out in double-quick time.

Homeopathic prescribing depended upon which 'constitutional type' the patient belonged to and so a lot of time had to be spent during the first consultation to try to find this out. It meant building up a complete physical, mental and emotional picture of the patient – likes and dislikes, hopes and fears, general health and sleeping patterns.

Herbalism also required a detailed history of the patient to be taken before anything could be prescribed. It was the oldest kind of medicine, of course, and many modern drugs were based on traditional herbal remedies. Catriona had found that aspirin, for instance, was originally processed from the bark of the willow tree and digitalis – which was used to treat heart problems – came from foxgloves.

Catriona blessed the day she had found out about both therapies, for her own as well as other people's benefit. She only wished she'd found out about them years earlier. Years ago was when she'd needed help most, especially when she'd been worn out nursing Melvin's father.

She didn't like the term 'alternative' medicine, though. She preferred 'complementary'. There were many medical conditions and ailments for which surgery was the only answer and no herbalist or homoeopath was qualified to give advice or offer treatment in that particular field.

She began to get herself organised. The walk-in larder was already shelved and proved an excellent storeroom and dispensary for all her herbs. Eventually she was able to afford to get a joiner to come and make cupboards behind her desk in her consulting room for her homeopathic medicines.

The big flat-topped desk had been purchased at a second-hand shop. She painted the walls of her room a soft lavender colour which felt soothing and relaxing. Just sitting in that room by herself, or listening and talking to patients, was the nearest thing she had felt to happiness in years. There she could be herself and people seemed to respect her, be grateful to her even.

The only worry she had while there was that one day Melvin would burst in and spoil everything. It was easy to imagine him making a fool of her and belittling her in front of everybody. He'd done it so often in the past.

She would never forgive him if he behaved like that in front of her patients. That would be too much. Far too much.

19

Julie had gone through all the legal channels and had met with nothing but frustration and failure. She'd become depressed. She'd given up. But the longing had never gone away. She could not believe, could not accept, that she would never see her child, never know where she was or how she was, never know what she looked like, never be able to hold her again.

All she had was the fuzzy memory of a tiny rose-petal face. She was terrified that one day the memory would fade completely. The memory of what it felt like to hold her was already fading. She remembered dressing her and lying on the bed gazing at her as the baby slept in the cot beside her. She'd resented the nurse coming in and interrupting those precious moments. Her fingers had traced the tiny face, felt the warm, silky softness of it. Over and over again, she strained to bring the feeling back, to keep it alive and real. But what was the use? There was no new-born baby any more. Somewhere out there was a girl who was a teenager now.

Julie eventually confessed her feelings to Madge and Catriona. For years, pride had forced her to put on a brave front and continue with her usual perky, 'Sure, I'm OK' attitude.

They lavished sympathy and support on her. But there was nothing practical they could do.

They had even clubbed together to help her pay to hire a private detective for a short time – too short, as it turned out. There had been a few rays of hope from him over the long months but nothing came of it in the end. He'd never even found out the address of the foster parents the baby had been given to for the first six weeks of her life. He'd need a lot more time. Or so he said. Everyone said the chances were the detective was angling for more money. But the money had soon run out and Julie could not bring herself to accept another penny from Madge and Catriona. She felt guilty and ashamed enough as it was for accepting so much already.

'Some help you are, as usual,' Madge told Alec.

As it turned out, Alec was the one that might prove to be the most helpful of them all.

'You know how Sammy's in the Red Cross now?' he said to Julie. 'Well, among other things, he's had to do nursing training in hospital. He's been to the Royal. Now he's doing a stint at Rottenrow. Wasn't that where they took you?'

Flushed with sudden, painful hope, Julie nodded.

'Well, I was thinking…'

Before Alec could say anything else, Madge bawled, 'You never think. You just open your big mouth and put your foot in it. It was nearly thirteen years ago. What could Sammy or anybody else possibly do now? We've all been trying for months. Julie's been trying for years.'

'No, Madge,' Julie pleaded. 'Let him go on.'

'I just don't want your hopes to be raised, hen, just to be disappointed again. You know what it's been like. And I know how you've suffered.'

'I was thinking,' Alec tried again. 'There's always a weak link...'

'Aye, you're a weak link,' Madge said.

'And in this case the weak link might be the nurse.'

'The nurse?' Julie echoed faintly.

'The nurse who took the baby away.'

'Yes, but ... I don't get you, Alec.'

'Aye, and you're lucky you haven't got him, believe me.'

'There was more than one nurse,' Julie said. 'I mean, there were different shifts of nurses attending the wards during the time I was in there.'

'Yes, but that particular one. Do you remember her?'

Julie hesitated. All her attention had been on the baby, not the nurse. And it was so long ago.

'I think so. But why do you ask?'

'Well, she must have met the couple who have your wee girl. They'll have come to the hospital to collect her and that nurse...'

'Oh yes,' Julie cried out, crimson now with excitement. 'You're right, Alec. Why didn't the detective think of that? Oh, thank you, Alec.'

Madge cut in. 'Now, just a minute, hen. Even if what he says is true, it's thirteen years ago. That nurse is probably dead by now or married with a family of her own, living dear knows where. She could have emigrated for all you know and, even if by some miracle you find her, do you think she'd remember every patient or one baby among the thousands that's gone through her hands? And, even if she did remember, do you think

160

she'd tell you anything? She'd be breaking the law for a start. See him and his mad ideas! I could murder the silly ass.'

'I was only trying to help, Madge. And if Sammy agrees to help as well, he's in a better situation than any of us.'

'Alec's right,' Julie said. 'Oh, Madge, it's worth a try. Have you asked Sammy, Alec?'

'No, I thought I'd speak to you first. Even though he's always known about what happened. Anyway, I don't see him as often as I used to since his mother moved in with him. There was a time when he used to come here for his tea quite a lot but he doesn't like leaving his mother and she always has his tea ready for him.'

'Don't worry, Alec. I'll talk to him myself.'

'I hope I haven't raised your hopes too much, Julie. As Madge says, it would be a bit of a miracle if anything comes of it. But it just occurred to me that, if anything or anybody's going to be able to help you in all this, it might just be that nurse.'

'You're right, Alec. You're right,' Julie said. 'And it's definitely worth a try. It's very kind of you to think about me and try to help me like this.'

'Listen,' Madge said, 'you'd better watch yourself, hen. I know his way of helping women. He helped Catriona, I remember.'

'For God's sake, Madge,' Alec growled, 'will you never forget that?'

'No, I will not, so just you watch it. I'm keeping an eye on you, remember.'

Julie laughed. 'Oh, Madge, I feel really cheered up. Don't be angry with Alec.'

'Aye, he's good at cheering the girls up.'

'I'm good at cheering you up.' In a sudden switch to his normal good humour – Alec could never be serious for long – he grabbed Madge and began tickling her. She screeched and tried to push him away but she was in good spirits now as well. Eventually, having succeeded in fighting him off, she said breathlessly, 'See that big midden, one of these days I'll give him a right doin'.'

Lighting a cigarette, his eyes at their sexiest, Alec groaned, 'I can't wait. Make it soon!'

Madge rolled her eyes but she laughed and so did Julie. Then, turning serious again, Julie said, 'I think I'll walk down the road and go and see Sammy tonight. Right now, in fact. It'll save me having to travel from the Gorbals to Springburn.'

'Aye, OK, hen. But try not to get your hopes up too much.'

'Madge's right, Julie. There's another thing – you never know with Sammy...'

Julie looked puzzled. 'How do you mean? I've known him for years.'

'Well, you know what he's like. He has a knack of making life complicated at times when he thinks he's just being straightforward. What do you bet he'll think about the couple who have adopted your wee girl, as well as about you? And what's best for the wean?' He cast his eyes heavenwards. 'God, the more I think of Sammy, the more I think I shouldn't have said anything to you.'

'Now he worries,' Madge said. 'When it's too late and the damage has been done. That's so like him, the stupid big midden.'

'It's all right, Madge. I can cope with Sammy. And I still say it's worth a try. I'm glad you told me what you thought, Alec. I really am. Even if nothing comes of it.'

Before leaving, she hugged and kissed Madge and blew a kiss to Alec.

'Watch it, you,' Madge warned but pleasantly.

Julie hurried down the stone stairs, stiletto heels making a fast, echoing tattoo. Out in the street, she turned to give her usual wave up at Madge's window. Then along Broomknowes Road, round the corner, past the Co-op grocery and across the road at the Wellfield school. Down the hill now, all the time concentrating and praying that Sammy would be on her side and would agree to try his best to help her. She knew exactly what Alec meant. She liked Sammy very much but he could be very awkward at times. Look how he'd been during the war. And his father a sergeant major and a real patriotic type as well. She fleetingly wondered why his mother had left the old man and was now living with Sammy. She'd heard rumours right enough – but surely they couldn't be true – about the old man burying a dog alive. The old man had maintained that the dog was ill and he'd believed it to be dead when he'd buried it. Sammy couldn't have believed him. That must be why he had taken his mother to live in Springburn Road with him.

The old man was a respected member of the Masons and very well thought of by outsiders. He'd always been very polite when he'd passed her in the street, lifting his hat and saying good afternoon or good evening. But she had never liked the sound of his voice. It had a coarse, gravelly edge to it as if he needed to, or was about to, spit.

She didn't hesitate when she reached Sammy's close. She hurried through the shadowy tunnel, which smelled of cats' urine, and up the stairs. It was Sammy who opened the door. He looked surprised. She'd never appeared at his door before. Quickly he recovered and asked her in. The flat was spotlessly clean, cosy and attractive. Sammy's elderly mother was fussing with pots at the cooker.

'Oh, I'm sorry,' Julie said. 'I've come in the middle of your meal.'

'No, no, dear,' Mrs Hunter said. 'This is soup and stew I'm making for tomorrow. I like to have as much as I can done in advance. Tomorrow I'll just have to prepare the potatoes and vegetables and the pudding.'

Sammy laughed. 'You'd think she was feeding the whole of Springburn. I'll be getting as fat as a beer barrel.'

'It was just something I wanted to talk to you about, Sammy. I wondered, you see, if you could help me.'

'Sure,' Sammy said, 'if there's anything I can do, you only have to ask. Now, why don't you sit yourself down and tell me all about it. Any chance of a cup of tea, Ma?

'Of course, son. Of course.' Mrs Hunter happily bustled over to the sink and filled the kettle.

20

'Have you thought this through?' Sammy asked.

'For years. I've been thinking about it for years. Deep down, I've never stopped thinking about it.'

Mrs Hunter said, 'You poor thing.' It was about the third or fourth time she'd repeated it.

Julie paid no attention to her. She was concentrating on Sammy's worried stare. 'It's not that I'd try to take her back. I know I'd have no legal right to do that. I just want to see her and make sure she's all right, that she's well and happy. Right from the moment she was born, Sammy, I've only wanted what's best for her.'

There was silence for a long minute, broken eventually by Mrs Hunter getting up and fetching the teapot. 'Have another cup, dear.'

Then Sammy said, 'I can't really see how I could be of any help, Julie.'

'Doesn't the Red Cross do things like that? Find people? You're working in the hospital. You could enquire about that nurse. If she's still there or, if not, find out where she is. I could take over then. I could talk to her.' Julie thought it safer not to say that he might be in a position to get access to records.

'It's a long time ago, Julie. She could be long retired. Dead even.'

'No, no, she was just a young woman. I can remember her. Her name was Webster. Nurse Webster. She was just a girl. Only in her early twenties at most. There's a very good chance she's still there. If she was in her early twenties she'll just be in her thirties now.'

'If she married, she won't be there and she'll have a different name.'

'Oh please, at least try, Sammy. I can't bear to go on like this for the rest of my life. I can't bear it.'

'You poor thing. Drink your tea, dear.'

'Please, Sammy.'

'All right, Julie. I'll do what I can but it's better not to get your hopes up. At the moment I can't really see...'

'Oh thank you, Sammy.' She lunged over at him, flung her arms around his neck and caused his cup and saucer to fly from his hand.

'Oh, I'm so sorry.' She withdrew, flushing bright scarlet with embarrassment. It was unlike her to be so demonstrative or indeed to show her feelings at all.

Sammy laughed. 'Never mind the dishes. You're welcome to hug me again if you like!'

'It's all right, dear.' Mrs Hunter retrieved the cup and saucer from the floor. 'Nothing's broken.'

'I'm so sorry. I've been an awful nuisance. Coming so late. Bothering you like this.'

Sammy got to his feet. 'Nonsense. You're welcome any time. Isn't she, Ma?'

'Of course, dear. Of course.'

'Come on. I'll see you home.'

'No, no, Sammy. I can't allow you to go all the way to the Gorbals and back.'

'Just do as you're told and get your coat on. I'm not letting you trail away down to the Gorbals by yourself.'

'It's really very kind of you.'

'Here you are.' He helped her into her coat.

'Thank you.' Then, remembering Mrs Hunter, she turned to the old woman, hesitated and then went over to kiss the loose parchment cheek. 'You've been very kind. Thank you.' Mrs Hunter looked pleased. 'Come again, dear. Any time. I'd be glad of the company.'

On the way home with Sammy by her side, Julie was desperately trying to swim through a stormy sea of emotion. Excitement frothed to the surface. She was going to be reunited with her daughter. Despite Sammy's doubts, she felt sure it was going to happen. It *must* happen. And, if anyone could make it happen, it would be Sammy. Everyone knew what a determined character he was and always had been. Once he made up his mind to do something – from refusing to put on an army uniform to helping the Quakers in their work with violent prisoners in Barlinnie Prison – he never gave up. Never accepted defeat. He kept doggedly on. That's what he'd do until he found Nurse Webster. Julie felt sure of it.

They chatted about this and that on the way to Gorbals Cross. His work at McHendry's. Her work at Copeland & Lye's. Their friendship with Madge and Alec Jackson. How the Jackson offspring were doing. The twins were at the Glasgow Art School and shocking Madge but delighting Alec with their nude drawings.

Sammy laughed. 'They wanted me to volun-

167

teer to be a male model in my spare time. Apparently they're short of men in the Art School. I turned them down. I'm not the right shape, I told them.'

It occurred to Julie then that, in fact, he was in very good shape.

'Didn't Catriona tell me that her Andrew had seen you at karate?'

'Sitting in an office all day can make you stiffen up if you're not careful. One of the clerks persuaded me to go along for a few lessons. He's a bit of a keep-fit fanatic.'

'I was quite surprised.'

'Why?'

She shrugged. 'It's not the kind of sport I'd expect you to take up.'

'What did you think I'd be more likely to take up? Tiddlywinks?'

She laughed. 'Not exactly. But you being a pacifist and a Quaker and all that...'

'Being a pacifist doesn't mean I have to be gutless. In the First World War, they shot conscientious objectors. They knew they were going to be killed but it didn't frighten them into changing their beliefs. It was the same with the Quakers in the old days. They were persecuted for having the courage to uphold their beliefs. They suffered worse deaths than anyone in any war. It would make your hair stand on end if I told you some of the terrible things they had to suffer. And just for speaking out against the injustices of the time. Not being violent about anything. Just for speaking the truth as they saw it. Man's inhumanity to man, as Burns said, makes countless thousands mourn!'

Julie didn't know what to say to that and so didn't say anything. In silence they reached her close.

'Here you are.' Sammy smiled down at her. 'Delivered safe and sound.'

'Thank you, Sammy. I really appreciate what you're doing for me.'

'I haven't done anything yet – except see you home.'

'You know what I mean.' Impulsively she reached up to kiss his cheek but somehow their lips met. She was astonished at the floodgates of passion that immediately opened up. The shock of it made her turn and run through the shadowy close and up the stairs. Once safely in the house, she leaned against the door, breathless, heart racing. After all the excitement of what Alec had said to raise her hopes and then of Sammy agreeing to help, this new and unexpected emotion was too much.

It brought back painful memories long since locked away and forgotten. Or so she'd thought. She remembered the sexual passion she'd felt with her husband. It was so long ago now. She'd thought she'd never feel anything like it again. She didn't want to. She belonged to Reggie and always would. That's what she'd believed.

Suddenly, it all came back to her now and she wept. All the claustrophobic years with Reggie's mother weighed unbearably down on her. She and Reggie's mother had never let Reggie go. They shared him in a secret, private world they'd created. They kept him as a real but invisible presence between them, carefully cherishing his memory.

Now she didn't know what to think. She went to the front-room window and stood half-hidden by the curtains, staring out at the street below. At first she didn't see Sammy. Then she caught sight of the stocky figure striding away into the distance.

She'd known Sammy Hunter for years. Why should she suddenly feel like this about him? She could only think that, with one thing and another today, she'd just got herself into an emotional state. She began to feel acutely embarrassed. How could she face him again? What must he think of her? But then, he probably hadn't thought or felt anything unusual about the kissing incident. As for her racing away from him, what of that? It was late and she had reached home. He wouldn't have expected her to hang about in the draughty close chatting to him. They had been chatting all the way from Springburn. No, it was perfectly all right. She dried the tears from her face, went through to the kitchen and put the kettle on. She made a cup of Horlick's and took two aspirins to help her to go to sleep.

She was all right the next day. Copeland's was busier than usual, so busy, in fact, that she was run off her feet. She was quite glad in a way that she had promised to visit Mrs Vincent after work. Her mother-in-law would have a delicious tea ready for her. Better that than having to go back to the Gorbals and start cooking a meal for herself. Then having to do the washing up. Even the

170

thought exhausted her.

It was only when she reached Botanic Crescent and saw Mrs Vincent glued eagerly to the window as usual and giving her usual delighted wave of expectancy that the depression and the claustrophobia returned.

Inside the flat now. Mrs Vincent's grateful embrace. Reggie's photos all around. Reggie on the mantelpiece, looking handsome in his RAF pilot's uniform. Reggie on the coffee table as a university student in his cricket whites. Reggie on the sideboard as a schoolboy in his blue school blazer and cap and as a toddler, clutching his teddy. Reggie as an infant, held in his mother's loving arms.

Mrs Vincent looked as elegant as always and the table was beautifully set, as usual, with lace-edged cloth and napkins to match. The gold-edged china looked too delicate to hold hot tea. The silver cake stand, and the silver cream jug and sugar bowl, gleamed. Julie suddenly felt too sick and tired to eat. But she made an effort for Mrs Vincent's sake. She'd gone to so much trouble.

After the meal, they settled down for a chat in which, as usual, Reggie was never far away.

'You look so tired, my dear. You know, Reggie wouldn't want you to be overworking like this.'

'Do you remember that time when Reggie...'

'I said to Reggie...'

'Reggie said to me ... I'll never forget it... "I love her, Mother," he said. "Look after her for me." That's why I keep asking you to come and live with me, Julie. I want to look after you. For

171

Reggie's sake.'

Julie couldn't bear it any longer. Not for one more day. Not for one more moment.

'I'm sorry. I've met someone else,' she said abruptly.

'What?' Mrs Vincent looked confused.

'I've fallen in love with someone else. You must have known it was bound to happen sometime. Reggie has been dead for years and I'm still a young woman.'

Horror mixed with terror in Mrs Vincent's eyes. Then she glanced away, straightened her back and said very politely, 'Yes, of course.'

'I'd better go,' Julie said, rising and picking up her handbag. 'Perhaps after this, we could meet in town for tea. All you need to do is drop me a note or ring me at work.'

'Yes, of course,' Mrs Vincent repeated, also rising, then following Julie to the door.

'All the best,' Julie said once outside on the landing. 'And thanks for everything.'

She couldn't get away quick enough, she felt so awful. Remembering to turn in the Crescent and wave up at the window, she wasn't surprised to find that Mrs Vincent was not there as usual to wave back.

21

Hullo! Hullo! We are the Billy Boys.
Hullo! Hullo! We are the Billy Boys.
Up tae the knees in Fenian blood, surrender or ye'll
  die,
For we are the Balornock Billy Boys!

The fiery-faced leader of the Balornock Lodge was well out in front and thoroughly enjoying himself – elbows out, four prancing steps forward, four prancing steps back, as if he was doing a barn dance. Big white gauntlet gloves swallowed up the sleeves of his jacket and the long pole of the standard he carried was secured in a white leather holster strapped round his waist. Other people were waving flags and banners. One orange silk banner stretched the whole width of the parade and was held aloft by a man at either end.

The Balornock Lodge had massed together with all the other lodges from all over the city who were making a huge, riotous, drum-beating, flute-tooting, accordion-squeezing, bagpipe-screaming, high-stepping, swaggering parade to Springburn Park.

Every time they passed a chapel – and they made a point of passing as many chapels as possible, even if it meant taking a long and convoluted detour – the beating of the drums became louder, more strident and menacing.

Wee Jimmy Stoddard, resplendent in his bowler hat and Sunday suit draped with an orange sash, belted heavenwards,

I'm a loyal Ulster Orange Man just come across the sea,
For dancing sure I know I will please thee.
I can sing and dance like any man,
As I did in the days of yore.
And it's on the Twelfth I love to wear
The sash my father wore.
For it's old but it's beautiful
And its colours they are fine.
It was worn at Derry Okrim,
Enniskillen and the Boyne.
My father wore it as a youth
And the bygone days of yore.
For it's on the Twelfth I love to wear
The sash my father wore!

Big Aggie, walking behind with the women, all wearing their orange sashes, joined in with great gusto. Children followed silently at a slower pace. It'd been a long walk and although they'd started off with as much bounce as their parents, if not more, and they'd enjoyed the noise and excitement, exhaustion was now dragging at their feet.

The leader's standard was of royal-blue velvet fringed with gold and he sported a fancy purple and orange sash. In the middle of the standard, an orange-cheeked picture of King William curled and furled and flapped about in the breeze. The flute band was giving a high-pitched, tinny rendition of 'Marching through Georgia'.

The drummers followed, giving their drums big licks as they passed the Chapel of St Teresa. Teeth gritted with the effort, muscles ached and sweat poured faster. Tum-tari-tum-tari-tum-tum-tum-tumt, louder and louder until heads reeled and swelled with the noise. Tum-tari-tum-tari-tuma-tum-tum!

Wee Michael sang,

King Billy slew the Fenian crew,
At the Battle o' Boyne Watter;
A pail o' tripe came over the dyke
An' hit the Pope on the napper.

Someone bawled, 'The Twelfth of July, the Papes'll die!'

Afterwards, enjoying the picnic and innumerable bottles of beer in the park, Michael said, 'The Paters weren't on the walk. At least I haven't seen them. Have you?'

'They never came.' Aggie flung him a disgusted look. 'Always some excuse. If it's no' his bad heart, it's her varicose veins. And them in their prime as well.'

'What's to stop their boys?'

'That's what I said and she said they're shy fellas. Shy, my arse, I said. I've seen John Pater in the back close.'

'Is John winchin'?' Maimie asked, with some concern. She fancied him herself.

'Well, he must be in his twenties now an' he's no' a monk.'

Feeling somewhat in the huff now, Maimie muttered, 'Our Chrissie didn't come.'

'Well, you know where she is. Why she sticks that place, I'll never know. The hours are diabolical. Worse than yer daddy's. That's nae life for a lassie. Here, huv one of them sandwiches. They're salmon. I'm no' wantin' tae humph them aw back. There's chocolate digestives and a Victoria sponge as well.'

Maimie was thinking that either John Pater or his younger brother Brian would have suited her fine. They both attended the Springburn karate club and it gave her a terrific thrill to see them occasionally practise sparring with each other in the back green. She loved to watch how their loose white tops could hang open to reveal naked, muscly chests and the way their legs could twist into fierce high kicks. Sometimes she was glued to the living-room or scullery window for an hour or more. Sometimes she'd pretend she had to go and put something into the bin. She'd backcomb her hair and plump it up high. She'd put on her best and widest skirt with the stiff petticoats that made it rustle and stick out, wear high heels, mascara and bright red lipstick. All in the hope that one or other of the boys would notice her. They never did. At least not while they were doing their karate.

Her mother would say, 'What the hell are you playin' at? Goin' out tae empty the bucket dressed like something aff the top o' a Christmas tree.'

Maimie had been hoping and praying that the Paters would be at the Orange Walk. The only time she'd seen anything much of them was when they'd all attended the Albert School. Even there

176

it hadn't been easy because they were both in classes above her. Now, John was at Glasgow University and she'd heard that Brian had recently got a place at Edinburgh University.

So, after September or October, she would probably never see him at all. Except maybe at Christmas and summer holidays. Although students seemed to be travelling all over the place these days, Mr Pater said they never did that in his young day. Not that he'd been to university. Nor his father before him. But, nowadays, people you'd never think of were going. Working-class people, he meant. And why not, he said. Parents now wanted their offspring to have the best possible chance in life and that meant a good education. University used to be just for the middle classes or the toffs. But not any more, he said.

Mr Pater had talked to her far more than his sons ever had. The boys had even talked to Chrissie more than her. Apparently they did some studying in the Mitchell and had spoken to her there. Probably they were snobs. Chrissie was all right, of course, because she'd stayed on and got a lot of Highers and then passed library exams and knew about books. Someone who just worked in the Co-op wasn't good enough for them. Well, to hell with them. She couldn't care less about them.

But she still kept glued to the living-room or the scullery window if the Pater boys were practising their karate. And she sighed with admiration and desire, exactly the same as she always had.

Chrissie had laughed at her. This made her feel

bitter. What right had she to laugh? Chrissie thought she was clever because she'd got a few Highers and had read a few books. Well, she wasn't so clever. She had a thing about Sean O'Donnel. Sean O'Donnel of all people! Chrissie thought no one knew but Maimie had seen the way she'd been ogling Sean and trying to bump into him 'by accident'. She'd seen the way Chrissie blushed scarlet any time Sean spoke to her or even just looked at her. Her mother and father would have a fit if they knew. Talk about a battering? They'd soon knock the stuffing out of Chrissie.

Maimie toyed with the idea of telling them but thought it best to give Chrissie enough rope to hang herself with. At the moment, she'd no proof. They'd never been out together. They didn't have any intimate, telltale look. She decided to keep a watchful eye peeled. If Chrissie got the chance, she would go out with him, Pape or no. And Maimie could bet her last halfpenny that, one of these days, Chrissie and Sean *would* go out together. It was just a matter of time. Chrissie wasn't that smart. Even without any Highers, Maimie knew that marriage was difficult enough without complicating it with different religions. Her mother always said, 'Even if the Protestant one doesn't "turn", the Papes make sure they get the children. The children are always brought up as Papes.'

What a sensation it would cause once her parents found out that Chrissie was serious about Sean. They'd never forgive Chrissie. And quite right too. Miss High and Mighty needed taken down a peg or two. She'd even criticised Maimie's eating habits.

'For goodness' sake, Maimie, stop stuffing food into your mouth like that. It's a repulsive habit and it's not good for your digestion. No wonder you're overweight and have spots.'

Damn cheek! Who did she think she was? Lady Muck? Chrissie wouldn't feel so superior once she was flung out on her ear. That's what would happen if she started courting with Sean O'Donnel. She'd be chucked out on the street. Maimie bet her last halfpenny she would. And what then, m'lady?

22

Sammy tried his best. He asked around as many people and places as he could. Even in other hospitals. All to no avail. At last he discovered a nurse who vaguely remembered a Nurse Webster and told him that she had married a GI she'd met during the war and gone to the States to live. The nurse didn't know where in the States, or even what Nurse Webster's married name was.

However, during his enquiries, he did find out the name of the people who had temporarily fostered Julie's baby and where they lived now. It turned out they'd only moved to a bigger house along the same road they'd always lived on. He had gone to see them in his Red Cross uniform and, probably because of that, the Cliffords thought it was an official request when he asked about the adoptive parents and their whereabouts. Mrs Clifford was a well-organised person and had kept records of all the children she had fostered. After some careful checking, she found the answers to his questions.

He was in two minds about telling Julie. He felt acutely worried about what he might be unleashing. Julie had assured him more than once that all she wanted was a glimpse of the girl, just to see how she had turned out, what she looked like and to reassure herself that she was all right. Sammy couldn't believe that. He couldn't imagine her skulking about, then, after managing to get a glimpse of her daughter, just leaving it at that. Maybe at the moment that was her genuine intention but, once she saw her daughter, she would want to go further. She'd want to get to know her. She might even introduce herself. There could be no end of complication, trouble and heartache for all concerned.

He tried to tell Julie this. But she immediately sensed that he'd found something out and became almost hysterical. Ignoring his warnings, she gripped her hands together and shouted, 'Sammy! You've found out where she is. You have, haven't you?'

'You haven't been paying a bit of attention to what I've been saying.'

'Tell me, Sammy. For pity's sake.'

'Julie, I'm sorry, but I regret having anything to do with this. It's not a good idea. You'll just end up with more heartache and you're liable to cause unhappiness to the couple and the girl.'

'Sammy, for God's sake! I keep telling you...'

'I know but, once you saw her, Julie, it wouldn't stop there.'

'Sammy, you promised me. I'll never forgive you if you don't put me out of my misery right now.'

Sammy sighed. 'They live in Kirkintilloch Road in Bishopbriggs.'

'Oh, Sammy, thank you. Thank you.'

'Calm down, Julie.'

He watched her make the effort. She tipped up her chin, her mouth firmed. Then she nodded.

'You're quite right, Sammy. I must be calm and sensible.'

But her green eyes were still sparkling with excitement. Sammy had always regarded her as a good-looking woman, with her proud, perky features and glossy hair in a neat pageboy style. A subtle aura of sadness always clung to her, however. Not now. Flushed and happy, she looked beautiful. He remembered the time they had kissed. She, of course, had intended to give him a friendly goodnight peck on the cheek but he had not been able to resist the opportunity to kiss her properly. He had been overwhelmed by the passion it had aroused in him.

He had gone out with a few women over the years, since his wife's death, but the friendships had never lasted, never come to anything. When the women wanted more than friendship, he could not respond with any warmth or sincerity. They had all found someone else who could.

Julie was different. He had always been fond of her and felt genuinely sympathetic towards her.

She had lost her loving husband. He had lost his loving wife.

Now he felt more than just friendship. Much more. That one kiss had unleashed a passion in him that he had forgotten he was capable of experiencing. Julie no doubt had been shocked. She had jerked away from him and run.

He was afraid that would be the end of their friendship. He had momentarily forgotten that the most important thing in her life was to find her child. She needed him for that. Or thought she did. She would forgive his passionate kiss for her child's sake. And she had. There was a passion shining from her but it wasn't for him.

They eventually went together to Bishopbriggs. It was on the north side of Glasgow, like Springburn, but further out. Now fast becoming known as 'a highly desirable commuter town', it was a place that had lost some of its former close-knit community spirit as a result. The village or central part had changed little, though, and was still recognisable as being much the same as it had been a hundred years ago. Quinn's pub had been there at one corner and across the road at the opposite corner there had always been a bank. The countryside outside the village that had once been open fields, however, was fast becoming one big, sprawling housing scheme – like so many others around Glasgow.

'I'll make some excuse,' Julie said breathlessly. 'I'll go up and knock on the door and pretend I'm ... a social work visitor, anything.'

'I knew this would happen,' Sammy said. 'I knew it. You're going to cause nothing but trouble.'

'No, no...'

'Yes, yes, Julie.'

'Oh, Sammy, please try to understand.'

'I understand only too well.'

'I saw so little of her when she was a baby.'

At least he managed in the end to stop her going into the close and knocking on the door. But they loitered about outside in the street for what seemed an eternity. Then suddenly the street filled with youngsters. The nearby school was emptying and crowds of uniformed girls and boys came chattering past.

'Oh, Sammy,' Julie whispered, 'there she is.' A tall leggy girl had entered the close nearby. They only caught a glimpse of her but it was enough for Sammy to see the unmistakable likeness to Julie. He had to drag Julie away. He knew, of course, that she had every intention of returning. She wouldn't let things rest now. They caught the bus back to Springburn. It had previously been arranged that she would join Sammy and his mother for tea. Julie could hardly wait to describe her daughter to Mrs Hunter.

'Oh, she was really lovely, Mrs Hunter. Wasn't she, Sammy?'

Sammy smiled. 'The picture of her mother!'

'Flatterer!' Julie laughed. Then, 'Oh, I can't settle to just going home now and sitting on my own twiddling my thumbs.'

'Do you fancy making a day of it and going to the pictures?'

'I'd love to, Sammy.'

'Fine. Finish up your tea and we'll go.'

'I'll help your mum to wash up first.'

183

'No, no, dear,' Mrs Hunter said. 'I've nothing better to do. Away you go, the pair of you, and enjoy yourselves.'

Sammy felt tense. He was wondering if he dared make another move on Julie. Should he take advantage of the back row in the Princes and put his arm around her? The mere thought made him sweat. Yet he was beginning to realise that he could not go on as he had been. It had become too much of a strain to be in her company so often, to be so close to her and yet so far away. He was beginning to have wet dreams about her. He had made passionate love to her a hundred times in his imagination. If she pushed him away again, so be it. But their relationship had to change one way or another.

They walked along Springburn Road cheerily, arm in arm. Feeling her body so near to his made him ache inside, he wanted her so painfully.

In the cinema, the usherette showed them to seats in the back row and, after they settled down, he stretched his arm along the back of her seat. Then he tightened it around her shoulders. She smiled up at him.

'Oh Julie,' he said. Then before he could say or do anything else, she kissed him.

23

'If I go on like this,' Catriona confided to Madge, 'I'll have to employ a full-time assistant.'

'See what I've always said? The luck of the Irish. I bet you're making a fortune. You are, aren't you, hen?'

'Well, not a fortune exactly but I'm doing surprisingly well.'

'What's Melvin saying to it? Proud as punch of you, I bet, eh?'

Catriona immediately regretted saying anything about her business to Madge.

'I don't tell him anything about it and I don't want you to mention it either.'

'Why ever not?'

'He's not interested. He doesn't want to know. Now, promise me, Madge.'

'Here, I know what you're up to. You're coining it and stacking it all up for yourself. Och, well, good luck to you, hen.'

'Thanks, Madge.'

'I'd do the same myself if I could. But what chance have I got with seven weans and that big useless midden I'm married to?'

'You know fine that you wouldn't want it any other way. You love the lot of them, including Alec. Especially Alec.'

'Listen, hen, I could murder the lot of them. First they were screaming at Elvis and hopping

185

about like maniacs at that Bill Hayley, now it's The Beatles and see these wee pelmets of skirts – it's not decent. Girls are the worst. That's another thing you're lucky with – you haven't got girls.'

Catriona gave up. Her mind turned again to the success of her business or complementary therapy practice as it was known. She didn't need to advertise now. She had built up quite a reputation. Even a few men came to her for help, mostly for sports injuries. She had got to know a young physiotherapist called Patricia Brown through Andrew, who had worked with her during one of his hospital placements. Quite often, she would suggest physiotherapy as well as her medicines, and Patricia would treat these patients in the next room. It only happened occasionally but, still, it could be a possibility to let out that other room to somebody like Patricia. Although it probably wouldn't be her, because it looked as if Patricia was going to get married and move to Inverness. But there would be plenty of other physios or osteopaths who might be glad of a room. Osteopathy was becoming more and more acceptable. It might be tricky, though, to have someone else working regularly without Melvin knowing. He would definitely object to that if he found out.

Her 'little hobby' was one thing and he had long since happily accepted it. He never bothered to ask her how she was getting on or even go through to the back to see what was happening. As long as the house was kept clean and polished, his meal was ready for him when he arrived home in the evening and the television was switched on and as long as she was outwardly the quiet, acquiescent little wife, he was happy and content. Or at least as happy and content as a man of his temperament was able to be. He complained about the customers. He complained about the bakers and the girls in the shop. Even the cleaner, it seemed, didn't do her job as well as she should. He always found something to grumble about. If it wasn't people, it was the state of the nation or the weather. Everything accentuated the sour downward twist of his mouth. He even grumbled about the television, although he watched it avidly every night. Grumbling had just become a habit with him. He used to read the newspapers in the evenings but now he read them during his morning tea break in the bakehouse. That way he didn't miss a moment's TV. He now had a tray attached to the arm of his easy chair so that he could watch the screen while he ate. He even watched the adverts.

It would have driven Catriona mad if she hadn't been able to enjoy a secret life of her own while he was at the bakery during the day. She was even attending a course on homeopathic treatment at the university without Melvin knowing. Once she got a certificate she would have it framed and hung on the wall of her consulting room. Although she had been doing exceptionally well without any certificate. Her bank account – in a different bank from the one where Melvin had his account – was amazingly healthy. She had even increased her fees and no one had objected. Money was pouring in. If Madge had known exactly how much she was 'coining' and 'stacking

187

away' for herself, she would have gone on and on ad nauseam about how lucky Catriona was. Madge's mind was closed to all but her own problems. She could be very kind and supportive but she had this fixed idea that her friend Catriona was the luckiest woman on the planet.

She did work hard, whether Madge believed it or not. And there was always the element of underlying stress and fear that Melvin would find out how successful she was and put a stop to all her efforts. He would be furious. He wouldn't be able to cope with a successful woman. Especially now that his business was not nearly as successful as it used to be. Supermarkets had arrived in a big way and, on their shelves, was the magical wrapped and sliced white bread.

Most housewives, mothers especially, regarded it as the best invention since the wheel. No more hacking at a loaf with a half-blunt knife. Now children's sandwiches would be made with ease No more crumbs on the kitchen floor. The children could even help themselves.

These days there was a huge range of food offered on supermarket shelves, all attractively packaged. Now that refrigeration was the thing in shops and most homes, the supermarkets had fresh fish on display. There were cheeses and beautiful fruit from all round the world. It was like a whole new, magic world. Also, because of home refrigerators, shopping was no longer a daily necessity. Weekly shopping was becoming more convenient. It suited Catriona very well. As did all the new convenience food, like tinned soup and rice pudding. Rice pudding especially was a godsend. Previously it had seemed to take all morning in the kitchen making it. Now there were ready-made meals and even 'boil in the bag' foods. She could whip up a meal for Melvin, and Fergus and Andrew if they were there, in no time at all. All this helped her to cover up her other activities – Melvin still thought she had been busy all day in the kitchen as well as cleaning and polishing the house.

But what with the washing machine, the Hoover and all the other gadgets she had, and the cleaning lady a couple of mornings a week, she never thought about housework. She never wasted any time on the house.

In the evenings, Melvin liked her to sit with him with a tray on her knee and watch television. Once a week, she managed to get out to visit Madge or Julie without too much fuss. He grumbled of course, but then something on the box would catch his eye and he'd burst out in exasperation, 'Away you go before you make me miss *Opportunity Knocks*.' Or whatever programme it happened to be.

Now she didn't see so much of Julie because she had started going out with Sammy Hunter. Catriona was glad for them both. At the same time it made her feel sad. She longed to love and be loved as they had been and were again. Most of the time, though, she was able to concentrate on her job and feel fulfilled in that. It was only at times when she saw Julie and Sammy strolling happily along, arm in arm, that she felt the pangs of longing. Even visiting Madge could trigger off emotional pain. Madge was the happy centre of her brood and, despite all the names she called him, she had a loving husband. Not just loving either but handsome and sexy. Madge was the lucky one.

To counteract these feelings of desperate unhappiness, Catriona would seek comfort from examining her bank book like a miser nursing a secret hoard of gold. It gave her some sense of worth and self-confidence to have the proof of her success in facts and figures before her eyes. Here was the proof that she was not the useless, hopeless, laughable idiot that Melvin had always made her out to be.

Even with the facts and figures, though, she still took a lot of convincing. For so long, first with her mother and then with Melvin, she had been brainwashed to believe that she was not only helpless and hopeless but wicked. Deep down, she still believed it. And because she still believed it, she continued to try her best to please her mother and to be nice to her. For the same reason, she continued to try to please Melvin and see to his every need and comfort. She also worried about the shop. She could never be cruel enough to say, 'I told you so', or 'I warned you ages ago but you just told me to shut up.' But the supermarkets were affecting Melvin's trade and the trade of many small corner shops, just as she'd feared they would. Now she hardly dared to think what would happen to the bakery if trade continued to decline in the way that it seemed to be going.

Melvin hadn't said anything. He would never be able to admit failure. She had taken a look at the books, however, and had spoken to Baldy. They were losing customers, all right. Baldy was planning to get married and had confided in Catriona that he was worried about losing his job. She had assured him that there could be no danger of that. He was the most valuable and necessary worker in McNair's.

She wasn't so sure herself that there was no danger, though. The prospect of Melvin losing the shop was too awful to contemplate. Every time anything went wrong, he always blamed her. She couldn't quite see how he could blame her for the shop failing but no doubt he'd find some way. Then the vision came to her of Melvin being in the house all day. She couldn't bear to dwell on such a terrible prospect and hastily banished it from her mind.

Sammy's father had been ill, she'd heard, and Mrs Hunter wanted to go back to look after him but Sammy wouldn't let her. Quite a few people thought this was terrible of Sammy.

Mrs Pater said, 'And him supposed to be a Christian. Of course, he's some queer sect. Quakers, I think they call themselves. What kind of Christians are they supposed to be?'

Mrs Pater lived up the same close in Broomknowes Road as the McKechnies, who belonged to the Jehovah's Witnesses. Apparently, she and Mrs McKechnie had crossed swords more than once and, as a result, Mrs Pater had no time for what she called 'queer sects'.

Madge also lived up that close and never, it seemed, had any problem with the McKechnies. But then Madge thought about everybody in a friendly, good-natured, trusting kind of way. Except about Alec, of course. Catriona thought how wise Sammy was in protecting his mother from the grim fate of nursing that awful old man. She'd never liked Hodge Hunter. The fact that Melvin liked him was enough to put her off. He and Melvin had their army days in common. A couple of times Mr Hunter had visited them in the past and they had spoken in loud, aggressive, boasting voices about nothing else and both had treated her like a servant and one of the lower orders at that. Firstly, Melvin had showed Mr Hunter around the house. That was soon after he'd first met the old man and when they'd not long moved in to Botanic Crescent. Melvin had just wanted to show off his big house.

Hunter, apart from reminiscing about the army, had wanted to make Melvin see the advantages of joining the Masons. But Melvin was not a social kind of person. Catriona couldn't imagine him just going out for a drink with friends for a laugh and a blether about football, for instance. She wasn't sure what men did or talked about at Masonic meetings. Very secretive - - - -

Anyway, she hoped for Mrs Hunter's sake that Sammy's way would prevail and the old woman would never again be trapped and isolated in that eerie house with that horrible old man.

At least Melvin's father hadn't been that bad. Then Catriona suddenly remembered what age Melvin was. Already he looked like an old man.

'Oh, God,' she thought. 'Oh, my God!'

24

Sammy knew perfectly well what Julie was up to. She did not want to get a house in Bishopbriggs simply because, as she insisted, 'It's such a lovely place. So near the Campsie Hills. Yet it's only fifteen or twenty minutes away from the centre of town in the bus. And there's the railway station as well. There's even a nice wee cinema. What could be handier?'

What indeed? But handier for seeing her daughter was what she really meant.

He had no personal objection to looking for a house in Bishopbriggs and starting a new life there with Julie. But there were problems and not just of Julie forever hanging about trying to catch a glimpse of Alice. (She'd found out her daughter's name when she heard one of the other schoolgirls call it out.) There was the problem with his mother as well. If he and Julie got a house in Bishopbriggs, he wanted his mother to come with them. Julie assured him that she wouldn't mind. She was fond of his mother and got on very well with her. His mother, however, was refusing to leave the Springburn flat.

'I'll be fine here, son. It's such a cheery wee house, being on the main road like this. I'm never lonely sitting at the front-room window looking at all that's going on in Springburn Road. There's never a dull moment.'

There certainly wouldn't be if his father turned up. He could just hear him wheezing up the stairs – probably spitting on the stairs as well. He'd arrive at the door and put on a dying swan act for his mother to play on her pity. He'd allow her to help him into the house. His stick would thump noisily on the floor, no doubt, alarming the downstairs neighbours. He'd crash into a chair and wait for a glass of whisky to be administered to him.

Then he'd take either of two tactics. He'd either adopt his usual bullying, snarling style: 'Get your coat on, woman. You're coming back with me.' Or he'd wheeze and cough and splutter and eventually manage, 'You're my wife. In sickness and health, you vowed before God and the church. Till death us do part. Cherish, you said, but as soon as I'm ill, you scuttle off. Some Christian! The minister came to see me the other day and the reverend gentleman was so shocked, he could hardly credit it...'

His mother would be conned into going back to look after him and would have to endure absolute hell in the process. He would soon be the death of her. But he would determinedly wheeze on for years.

'We could get a flat in the main road in Bishopbriggs, Mother,' he kept telling her. 'It's a busy road – Kirkintilloch Road, it's called. Lots of people doing their shopping there and buses and trams going by. You'd love it. You could sit at the front-room window there and watch everything that's going on.'

Julie tried to persuade her as well. 'And we

could take you for trips to Kirkintilloch and Blanefield. There's lots of lovely country places to visit.'

'I really appreciate it, dear,' Mrs Hunter told Julie. 'You're always so kind to me and I'm so happy that Sammy has found someone as nice as you. But to start married life with your mother-in-law is not the best way. You and Sammy should get a decent start on your own. I'm an old woman. I don't want to be a burden to either of you.'

Nothing either of them could say could make her change her mind. Eventually, Sammy had to agree but on one condition. 'I'm only going to leave you here if you promise me, Mother – promise me – that you'll never go back to Father. Even if he comes pleading with you on bended knee.'

She shook her head. 'Son, can you imagine your father either pleading or bending a knee? To me – or to anybody?'

'Well, no matter what he does to try and persuade you, Mother, you must promise me that for no reason will you ever go back.'

'All right, son.'

'You promise?'

'Yes, I promise.'

He had the telephone installed too and he planned to have one in the flat that he and Julie would rent. 'That way I'll just be on the other end of the phone for you, Mother,' he told her.

It was certainly true what Julie had said about Bishopbriggs being an attractive place. The centre was called the village and had a row of

195

shops, mostly family businesses, on either side of Kirkintilloch road, with grey stone flats above them. Large old villas, a church, a chapel, burgh hall, a library and a leafy park were all nearby. New houses were mushrooming up and, further back, brightly coloured bungalows and semis. But there hadn't been many changes in the village for a hundred years or more.

Along Kirkintilloch Road from the bank was the Kenmure cinema. Sammy knew he and Julie could be very happy in Bishopbriggs. Except for the worries about his mother and about Julie because of her obsession with Alice.

However, he could not bring himself to spoil Julie's happiness by voicing objections to the move. As a result, he agreed to rent the flat they eventually found above one of the shops. It was almost exactly opposite where Alice lived. They could have got a larger flat in far better condition in Springfield Road, but Julie's heart was set on the one in Kirkintilloch Road, for obvious reasons.

It was agreed that the wedding would be held in the Quaker Meeting House in Newton Place in Glasgow. As usual with Quaker weddings, it took place as part of a normal meeting for worship. Everyone sat on rows of benches on three sides of the room. On the fourth side there was only one bench and a table. On the table, as usual, was a Bible, a book of Quaker faith and practice, a copy of *Queries and Advices* and a little bowl of flowers.

Sammy sat at the table waiting for the arrival of Julie. When she did arrive in her wide-brimmed straw hat with its band of turquoise ribbons and matching turquoise suit, she immediately brightened the whole room, and radiated light and colour. A gasp of admiration broke through the silence as, smiling radiantly at Sammy, Julie clipped over on her high-heeled shoes to join him. She settled herself comfortably on the bench, her head held high with pride.

Sammy marvelled at her self-confidence. He remembered how the set-up of the meeting-house benches and the heavy silence had discomfited him the first time he had attended.

After ten or so minutes of silence, the Registry Officer rose and said, 'I am John Richards, Registry Officer for the West of Scotland monthly meeting of the Society of Friends. My sole purpose is to ensure that legal requirements are completed. I do not marry the couple – for they do that themselves.

'The basis of our simple Quaker wedding remains the same as it was in the earliest days of the Society of Friends. For the rite of joining in marriage is the work of God only, not the priests or the magistrates. We marry none – it is God's ordinance and we are but witnesses.

'We *will* settle into a quiet meeting for worship during which Sammy and Julie will commit themselves to each other in the presence of God.

'In their own time, Sammy and Julie will stand up and make their declarations to each other.

'Then, during the worship that follows, in which everyone here is equal in the presence of God, we hope that anyone so moved will give a spoken message or a prayer for the couple. Later

I will ask the couple to sign the Quaker marriage certificate which I am then required to read out.

'The meeting will last approximately an hour, when two elders will close the meeting by shaking hands.

'Then everyone will sign the marriage certificate, which is in the form of a scroll, for you are all witnesses of this joyful occasion and this certificate will also remind Sammy and Julie of our ongoing support in the years to come.'

John Richards sat down and, in the silence that followed, Sammy could have wept with happiness and gratitude. Gratitude for finding Julie. Gratitude for her love and gratitude for finding the Society of Friends. They were his saving grace, his rock. They had come as a light in his dark world and the light had never gone out.

Oh, how lucky he was. Sitting wrapped in the peaceful Quaker silence, he felt he was the luckiest man on earth. After losing Ruth, he had believed he would never love again. Ruth would always have her own special place in his mind and heart and soul. He would never forget her. But life had to go on and he believed that Ruth would not want him to be alone and lonely. She would want him to love and be loved. Julie would have felt the same about Reggie, he felt sure.

It was then that Sammy felt the time was right and he stood up. Julie also stood up.

'Friends,' Sammy said, taking Julie's hand. 'I take this woman, my friend Julie Vincent, to be my wife, promising, with God's help, to be unto her a loving and faithful husband, so long as we both on earth shall live.'

Then Julie said, 'Friends, I take this man, my friend Sammy Hunter, to be my husband, promising, with God's help, to be unto him a loving and faithful wife, so long as we both on earth shall live.'

Then they both sat down and were once more absorbed into the silence. After a time, a woman rose to her feet to speak or 'give ministry' as it was referred to in Quaker terms. And what she said 'spoke to his condition', to use another Quaker phrase.

'It says in Corinthians:

Love is patient, Love is kind.
Love is not jealous or boastful;
It is not arrogant or rude.
Love does not insist on its own way;
It is not irritable or resentful;
It does not rejoice at wrong,
But rejoices in the right.
Love bears all things,
Believes all things,
Hopes all things,
Endures all things,
Love never ends.'

A long period of quietness followed. Then a man rose and said, 'Friends, we hold this couple in the light. May God's love enfold them this day and for the rest of their lives. We have known Sammy for some years and have great respect for his struggles as a conscientious objector. We welcome you, Julie, and know you bring each other

199

great happiness. We pray that, whatever life may bring, your union will be enriched by the Spirit. This Glasgow Meeting will always uphold you.'

Julie felt for Sammy's hand and squeezed it. They kept their fingers entwined in the silence that followed.

Then, unexpectedly, Sammy's mother got up. She said, 'I've not been to a Quaker wedding or service before. I'm not sure if this is all right. I just hope that God will bless our Sammy and Julie and keep them safe. They have had such hard times. Please give them many happy years together.' She sat down again, head lowered.

There was a long, peaceful silence again, before someone else rose and said,

'There is a place for you
Where there is perfect peace.
There is a place for you
Where nothing is impossible.
There is a place for you
Where the strength of God abides.'

And Sammy thought, no matter what fate had in store for him in the future, or where he ended up, he would always remember the place of perfect peace he was in now.

25

Chrissie and Ailish always enjoyed a good gossip. Ailish would tell Chrissie of all the antics of employees and customers in Copeland & Lye's and Chrissie would recount stories about what went on behind the book stacks in the Mitchell. Both girls, especially Chrissie, tended to exaggerate at times but this only made their secret conversations all the more enjoyable. Chrissie assured Ailish, however, that the incident with Mr Farquhar's false teeth happened exactly as she'd related it.

Poor Mr Farquhar – an awfully nice old man, ancient really – was kept upstairs all the time, out of the way. His job was to stand by the hoist and when any customer orders for books came up, he found the books on the stack, brought them to the hoist and pulled the rope to send them down. Chrissie felt sure he had been put upstairs partly because of his false teeth. They were loose and always moving about in his mouth when he spoke. Or even when he didn't speak.

'On this occasion,' Chrissie told Ailish, pausing for a barely suppressed giggle, 'he was leaning over to see why the hoist was taking such a long time to come back up, when his false teeth came out and careered right down the shaft to the bottom. When Miss Thornton went to put the return books in, she was met by a double set of grinning dentures.' Chrissie let out a hoot of laughter to join Ailish's hilarity. 'We all nearly wet ourselves laughing.'

'Poor Mr Farquhar,' Ailish managed. 'He must have been so embarrassed.'

'Not a bit of it. He's such a good-natured old soul. He came downstairs and had a good laugh along with us. Even before he put his teeth back in. A real gumsy laugh, that was.'

'Who would believe there would be such a carry-on in the Mitchell? It's so quiet and dignified in the main hall. I mean, going in there is like entering a cathedral.'

'I know.'

'Did you hear about the wedding?' Ailish said, changing the subject.

'You mean the one the Jacksons went to?'

'Yes. You must have seen that Sammy Hunter. He often visits the Jacksons. Quite a tough-looking guy with a broken nose like our Dermot. But Sammy has red hair.'

'Oh yes, I know who you mean.'

'He's a Quaker, would you believe? No one seems to have heard of them. My mother and father, for instance.'

'Och, mine won't have either. They think they're religious but all they care about is their Orange Lodge and Rangers.'

'Celtic with mine, of course. And you know what Dermot's like.'

'Sean's not bigoted though, is he?'

'Oh no, Sean is angelic. At least to you, he is.'

Chrissie blushed at the unexpectedness of this remark. Even her ears burned and took on a scarlet hue.

'How do you mean?'

Ailish sighed. 'You must think I'm daft, Chrissie. You're always asking about Sean. It's obvious you fancy him.'

Chrissie was so taken aback, she didn't know what to say.

Eventually, Ailish said, 'You do, don't you?'

Chrissie nodded, miserable now.

'No need to look so tragic about it.'

'No?' Chrissie raised a sarcastic brow.

'No.'

'Now I do think you're daft. Even if he did feel the same about me, what future could we have? It's bad enough you and me trying to be friends. Trying always to keep our friendship a secret from your mother and father and my mother and father. I dread to think what would happen if I started going out with Sean.'

Ailish's eyes had gone dreamy. 'I think Peter McKechnie's rather dishy.'

'Peter McKechnie?' Chrissie's voice became shrill with incredulity. 'He's a Jehovah's Witness!'

'Maybe not.'

'How do you mean, maybe not? I'd even get a battering if I went out with him and Jehovah's Witnesses are Protestants.'

'Well, he may feel like us, for all we know. All we know is his parents are stupid bigots, the same as ours.'

'But he's gone to their meetings, or whatever they call them, ever since he was a child. Poor Sandra was the same.'

'You've gone to church and I've gone to chapel.

Anyway, I haven't a crush on him like you have on our Sean.'

It was Chrissie's turn to sigh. 'I don't suppose he ever asks about me.'

'As a matter of fact, he does. You're a right pair of idiots.'

'Does he?' Chrissie brightened, then deflated again. 'But even so. It's hopeless. I hate religion. I really do.'

'Och, ignore it. Do you want me to help you and Sean get together? I could. No bother. Honestly.'

'Ignore it? How can I ignore it? You know what my parents are like. Especially my mother.'

'It's so stupid.'

'I know that. But knowing it doesn't help, does it?'

'Once the pair of you got together, there would be nothing they could do about it. Sean's a grown man. You're not a wee girl any more, Chrissie. Your mother can't batter you now.'

'Oh, no?'

'Stand up to her.'

'You're a fine one to talk. You've never stood up to your mother about our friendship.'

'That's different. My mother doesn't keep well at the best of times. She's half dead with her chest.'

'It would be even worse for her then if she had to face anything going on between Sean and me.'

After a minute's thought, Ailish said, 'It's really damnable.'

'I know.'

'Maybe if we did it kind of gradually. Be subtle, you know. Get them used to our friendship first.'

'How do you mean, exactly?'

'Well, our parents do say hello and pass the time of day with one another. We could start dropping casual remarks like, "I bumped into Chrissie Stoddart in the close. She was saying she likes her job in the Mitchell." Keep dropping in wee remarks like that, plus things like, "She seems nice." Get them used to the idea of us speaking to each other first of all.'

'It's worth a try, I suppose. I could say I went to buy something in Copeland & Lye's and Ailish O'Donnel served me and was terribly helpful.'

'Watch you don't overdo it at first. The idea is to make it gradual.'

'As I say, it's worth a try, Ailish, but you know what they're like. I don't think we should build up our hopes. And, anyway, it would be a big jump between accepting us being friends and Sean and I going out together.'

'One good thing nowadays, nobody needs to be caught out in any other way.'

'The pill, you mean?'

'Yes. The best invention since sliced bread.'

'Have you used it?'

'Good Catholics aren't supposed to. It's a sin, so I'm told.'

'Nobody need know.'

'Our doctor's a Catholic.'

'But surely…'

'Forget it. He'd either refuse to give me it or dish out a sermon instead. Or he'd tell my mother.'

'Oh, surely not.'

'I'm telling you.' Ailish suddenly brightened.

205

'But you could get some from your doctor and pass them on to me.'

'What if my mother found out.'

'It's not against your religion, is it?'

'I don't think so, but sex is taboo before marriage as far as my mother is concerned. The Swinging Sixties haven't swung in her direction yet. She saw a couple lying kissing each other on the grass in Springburn Park the other day and she shouted at them, "You ought to be ashamed of yourselves. Get up out of there, you dirty devils." She told me herself.'

Ailish couldn't help laughing. 'I can just imagine it. They'd get the fright of their lives. Your mother is a formidable sight.'

'I know. Her and Madge Jackson have voices like foghorns. At least your mother's quiet spoken.'

'Poor soul. It's her chest. She can hardly breathe at times, never mind raise her voice. My father makes up for her, though.'

'I wonder what a Quaker wedding's like.' Chrissie's mind began to wander. 'I wish we'd gone along. They don't care what religion you are, apparently.'

'I wish our lot were like that. I mean I wish they'd try to have a bit of respect for what other people believe.'

'In your dreams, Chrissie.'

'Och, there's bound to be lots of people who do.'

'Not up our close.'

Chrissie sighed.

'That's true.'

They continued walking along the street, arm

in arm, in silent sympathy with each other. Then suddenly their path was blocked and a voice said, 'Caught you!'

26

'But how does it work? It was Mrs McAllister's first visit and obviously she was not too sure if she'd done the right thing in coming to see Catriona.

'Well, in the first place, it's from the words *homoios* which means similar and *patheia* which means suffering or feeling. That's the basis of homeopathy – like is cured by like. For instance, it was known that the bark of the cinchona tree, known as quinine, caused fever in a healthy person – shaking, trembling, sweating, hallucinations and vomiting. Then it was discovered that if you gave the quinine to someone already suffering from those symptoms, for instance with malaria, it cured them.'

Mrs McAllister didn't look too convinced. She was tense and anxious, sitting there frowning, hands clenched. Catriona took over an hour to get to know everything about Mrs McAllister's personality, as well as her symptoms. It was important to know about her emotional state and mental symptoms, about which foods she preferred, even whether she liked hot or cold weather. Absolutely everything. Homeopaths treated the whole person and one of the most important aims was to build up and strengthen the body's natural immune system. Catriona tried to explain to Mrs McAllister what she'd been doing and why.

At the end of the session, Mrs McAllister hadn't altogether lost her anxious look, but she was grateful for the opportunity to talk and be listened to with such attention and sympathy. So much so that she was eager to come back for another visit.

'See how you feel after taking the medicine,' Catriona said. But she made an appointment and Mrs McAllister went away hopefully clutching her package of powder and tablets.

Mrs McAllister had just gone when, to Catriona's surprise and consternation, Melvin appeared in the doorway.

'Hello, dear,' she greeted him, hastily getting up from her desk and hurrying over to deflect him from entering the room. She knew he would hate to see her sitting at her desk, a calm, confident figure of authority.

'You're home early. Is there anything wrong?' She steered him into the passageway and shut the consulting-room door behind her.

'Damn weddings!' he complained. 'They must be getting infectious. Now Baldy announces he's getting hitched and wants two weeks off. Two weeks! He wants to go to some fancy place abroad. Can you beat it? Dunoon or Rothesay's not good enough for him any more. It must be that woman he's got mixed up with. It's her that's behind this.'

They were safely out in the hall now. 'I'll make us a cup of tea,' Catriona soothed.

In the kitchen, he was still raging. 'I told him. You'll be the ruination of me, I said. You'll be the ruination of this business, I said, and then where will you all be?'

'Sh, sh, drink your tea. It'll be all right.'

'What do you know? The man's gone off his head. Flying. Flying to some foreign country for two weeks.'

'That's what people are doing nowadays, Melvin. Holidays abroad are all the fashion now.'

She could see his problem. Baldy practically ran the whole place now. Melvin was afraid to be without his right-hand man.

'The place won't fall to bits in two weeks.' She had meant it to be reassuring but immediately the words were out of her mouth, she knew she'd said the wrong thing.

'My business won't "fall to bits", as you put it,' he sneered, 'even if Baldy never came back. My business depends on me. Not him, or anybody else. He couldn't run or manage it any more than you could. I run that business and always have done. Do you hear me?'

'Yes, Melvin.'

She stared at his hollow-cheeked, sallow face. Even his untidy straggle of a moustache was quivering with indignation. He was pathetic. She could read him like the proverbial book now. Yet, despite everything that had passed between them, she genuinely wished she could help him. She knew different homeopathic remedies that she was sure would work. But no way could he be persuaded to take any of her 'stupid rubbish' or listen to her 'mumbo jumbo'.

She had been forced to resign herself to the worst – both in the deterioration of his health and of his business. She had lost count of the times she had tried to persuade him to stop smoking, for instance, without the slightest success. No matter what she said or what warnings she gave him, he continued to smoke and suffer paroxysms of coughing. He preferred to buy cough medicine from the chemist's, ignoring or denying the fact that the medicine upset his stomach.

She had tried, as tactfully as she could, to suggest changes and warn him of the dangers of supermarkets to his business. All to no avail. He hated her 'acting the clever dick'. 'What do you know?' was his usual response.

Oh, how she would have loved to have said to him, 'Obviously a lot more than you.' But she hadn't the heart. Nor did she want to endanger her business by proving her point to him.

Sometimes she could hardly believe herself how successful she had been and was continuing to be. In commercial terms, she had found a niche in the market. People were becoming disenchanted with conventional medicine and were turning more and more to alternative or complementary therapies. Her dream was still to have different therapists under the same roof. She believed, for instance, that massage and osteopathy could work wonders. Even hypnotherapy could have its uses. The Alexander technique was marvellous and there were other treatments she had been reading about that intrigued her.

She was so glad that she had found her place in

life. One grateful patient had remarked to her, 'It must be wonderful being a healer.'

A healer? She supposed she could be called that now. She had helped a great many people. The thought made her feel truly happy. Lucky too.

Then suddenly her happiness was shattered by grief. Word came that her father had collapsed and died of a brain haemorrhage. She immediately cancelled all her appointments for a week and took a taxi to the street in Partick where her mother and father had rented a house. She found Hannah distracted and in a state of collapse.

'Oh, the pity of it, Catriona,' she kept saying. 'Oh, the pity of it.'

Catriona assumed she meant their whole life together, which had been little more than a battleground, as far as she could see. Then her mother gazed up at her with tragic eyes and said, 'Was I not nice to him, Catriona?'

'Of course you were nice to him, Mummy,' Catriona lied in an effort to reassure her. 'He thought the world of you.' Which indeed he had. Her father had loved her mother despite all their differences and disagreements. Of that at least she was sure. And maybe her mother, in her own way, had loved him too.

She gave her some homeopathic ignatia for grief and took some herself. It helped calm and comfort them both.

But her mother said, 'This is an unlucky house. I'm not going to live here any more.'

'You don't need to make any decisions about anything just now, Mummy. It's too soon. Just come home with me for a few days, or a few

211

weeks if you like, until you feel a bit better.'

'It's an unlucky house,' Hannah repeated.

'Daddy's death had nothing to do with this house.'

'We should never have left Farmbank. Neither of us could settle in Partick and your daddy never liked that Byres Road shop. It wasn't the same as the old one he was used to in Govan. He had worked in that bakehouse in Dessie Street all his life. He couldn't settle in that Byres Road shop. It's an unlucky shop and this is an unlucky house.'

Catriona didn't know what to say. She'd never heard her mother talk in these terms before and, as far as Catriona knew, she had never believed in anything like that. Gambling of any sort had always been regarded as a sin by her mother.

'Do you want to come home with me just now, Mummy? I think you should. I'll pack a case for you. All right?'

Her mother nodded, making tears hasten down her cheeks. Catriona worried about what Melvin would say and how he would react to her mother coming to stay – even just for a short period. She would never hear the end of it. He would be so furious. He had always hated her mother.

To her astonishment, when she did return supporting her weeping and trembling mother, who seemed to have shrunk in height in the few hours since the tragedy, Melvin was kind and sympathetic.

'Oh, that's terrible! What a terrible shock!' he said, on being told the news. 'Rab was one of the best. But don't you worry. You're welcome to stay

212

here for as long as you like.'

Catriona could hardly believe her ears. Although of course she felt relieved and grateful. It would have been really terrible if Melvin had been nasty to her mother as he'd so often been in the past. Not even the knowledge that he was now short of one of his oldest and best bakers was making him show any anger – at least not to her mother. Or any other emotion except sympathy. He even went away to put the kettle on and make a cup of tea.

An explanation for his unexpected behaviour came to Catriona eventually. She felt guilty at the thought. After all, she could be misjudging Melvin. But she couldn't help thinking that Melvin only felt happy and came into his own with people he believed to be weaker than himself. Previously her mother had appeared a strong character and a threat to him. Not any more. Her mother was now pathetically grateful for any act of kindness and support anybody gave her.

As days and then weeks passed after the funeral, Catriona was plunged back into the desperate, despairing days when she had nursed her father-in-law. She didn't need to actually nurse her mother, who wasn't physically ill. But her mother had developed a neurosis. She could not bear to be alone. Not even for a few minutes. She even followed Catriona to the toilet. If Catriona went out, her mother had to come too, rather than be left alone in the house.

During the day, she sometimes went down to sit about in the bakehouse or stop to pass the time of day with the bakers, the shop assistants or

213

the customers. If she stayed in the house, she followed Catriona around, stuck to her so close that if Catriona stopped suddenly, they collided.

Catriona struggled to keep seeing her patients but it was very distracting to her, and to waiting patients, to have her mother chatting ceaselessly to them.

After two months, Catriona was getting really desperate and tight-lipped. Eventually, she could hardly utter a word to her mother, as she struggled to control her feelings of frustration and anger. It was an added stress that Melvin continued to be extremely nice to the old woman because it added guilt to all her other emotions.

Then she discovered that her mother had given up her flat in Partick because, 'Melvin agreed with me that it was an unlucky house and he said I was welcome to stay here for the rest of my days. He's such a good man, Catriona. I hope you realise how lucky you are!'

She had exploded then and before she could catch her tongue or her emotions, she cried out, 'No, I'm not bloody lucky. It was the unluckiest day of my life when I set eyes on that pathetic excuse for a man.'

It was just her luck that Melvin had come back from work earlier than usual and had heard her. Her mother burst into tears and Melvin assisted her away to the kitchen to administer tea and sympathy.

'Don't worry about me, Mother.' Mother, he called her! Catriona could hardly credit it. 'I'll be all right. I can cope. I'm used to her.'

27

Everything was all right after Sean caught Chrissie and Ailish together. At least for a time. After their first moment of horror, Sean's burst of laughter at their shocked faces made them relax into laughter as well.

'You're not angry at us being pals, then?' Ailish asked.

'Ailish,' Sean said, shaking his head, 'I thought you knew me better than that. This is Sean not Dermot.'

For the first time, Chrissie was able to chat easily to him. The three of them strolled along laughing and chatting. Ailish said, 'Chrissie, tell Sean that story about Mr Farquhar.'

So Chrissie, in between her own giggles and those of Ailish, related the story of the false teeth. They were all enjoying themselves so much that they were on Broomknowes Road before they knew it.

'I'd better run,' Chrissie said, suddenly agitated. 'In case my mother's at the window.'

Sean put a detaining hand on her arm. 'Don't,' he said. 'It's time we put a stop to all this nonsense.'

'I know you mean well, Sean,' Chrissie said. 'But you don't understand.'

'What are you talking about, Chrissie? My parents, not to mention my brother, are every bit

215

as bigoted as yours, if not worse.'

'I know, but I've had a right battering from my mother before over this sort of thing and I don't want a repeat performance.'

'Not since you've been a grown woman, surely?'

'Well, no. But that's because over the years I've learned to be more careful. Not to let her know about Ailish and me, for instance.'

'You don't want to go through your whole life like this, do you?'

'No, but...'

'She's dying to go out with you for a start,' Ailish interrupted, much to Chrissie's horror. When she saw Sean's face light up with boyish delight and joy, her feelings for him immediately changed to love. Not the dreamy crush spiced with sexual fantasies she'd had for him before. This was serious, heart-melting love.

'Oh Chrissie,' Sean said. 'I've wanted to ask you out but I was too embarrassed after making such a fool of myself the last time.'

'I was just a wee schoolgirl then. And you were just a wee boy. We've both grown up and it's different now.'

'I've always felt the same about you.'

'And I've always felt the same about you.

Ailish gave an impatient groan. 'OK. Is that it all settled then? The pair of you are both crazy about each other and are going to start courting – to use an old-fashioned word.'

Chrissie blushed but she had never felt so happy before in her life. Sean said, 'Definitely!'

Laughing, Chrissie echoed, 'Definitely!'

216

Then, remembering the realities of the situation, she became worried again. 'It still doesn't change our parents though. My mother and my father will have a fit if they find out. Let's keep it a secret – at least for a wee while, Sean, until we see how we get on.'

'We'll get on just great.'

'You know what I mean. Maybe if we take things gradually, they'll change.'

'Huh, you don't really believe that, Chrissie, any more than I do. But OK. I'll go along with the secrecy ploy for a wee while at least, if that'll make you feel any better.'

Ailish said, 'Well, thank goodness we've got something worked out at last. I thought the pair of you were going to go on being a couple of idiots to the end of your days.'

Chrissie laughed with relief now and Sean, his dark eyes mischievous, said, 'Let's meet tomorrow night round the corner at the Co-op and then go down to the Princes. I promise to give you the whole bar of Fry's Cream this time.'

And so it was arranged. Chrissie couldn't sleep that night for excitement and for planning what she was going to wear. Eventually, she decided on a navy mini skirt with a striped top and white buckled belt. Before she set out next evening, she made up her eyes with lots of black mascara so that they looked as large as possible. Carefully she backcombed her hair into a beehive at the top but with the ends flicked out – she'd long since abandoned her childish pony tail.

As soon as she met Sean, they linked arms and strolled across the road and down the Wellfield hill to Springburn, chatting easily and happily. They both liked the Bee Gees and The Beatles but they both agreed that John Lennon should not have said, 'The Beatles are more popular than Jesus Christ right now.'

'That jarred with me,' Sean said.

'It really put me off him as a person,' Chrissie said, 'but I still like the music.'

'Me too,' Sean agreed.

They sat in the back row in the Princes just as they had done when they were children. Now, however, there was no shyness or hesitancy about Sean. He immediately put his arm around Chrissie's shoulders and within moments, they were kissing. After they emerged from the hall, they were both in a kind of dream. Neither could have said what the film was about.

Chrissie felt ecstatic. All problems were banished from her mind. Until they reached the top of the hill.

'We'd better say goodnight here, Sean.'

'This is ridiculous, Chrissie.'

'You promised.' Panic heightened her words.

'All right. All right. When can I see you again?'

'Saturday?'

'After the match?'

Wasn't that so typical of a man, Chrissie couldn't help thinking, but not with the slightest annoyance. Football had to come first. That was just how it was with men.

'Yes, fine.'

'Same place, same time?'

She nodded then, before he could kiss her goodnight, she turned and hurried away towards

Broomknowes Road. She was still savouring the kisses they had enjoyed in the back row of the Princes. She didn't want to spoil the memory by a quick peck laced with fear. From her side at least. No doubt Sean would have tried to repeat their long, passionate embraces. But she was much too fearful to risk such a thing in the middle of the street and so near to home.

She was flustered and breathless when she arrived home after running along the street and into the flat.

'What's up wi' you?' her mother asked.

'Nothing.'

'You're going wi' a boy.'

'What on earth makes you think that?' Chrissie widened her now smudged, mascaraed eyes and tried to look completely innocent.

'Ah'm no' daft. Look at ye. Ye've lipstick all over yer face, for a start.'

Chrissie hastily, guiltily, fumbled for her hanky. Her mother burst out laughing.

'Ah wondered when on earth ye'd start winchin'. I was beginnin' tae think ye were goin' tae end up a right auld maid. Who's the unlucky fella?'

Chrissie avoided her eyes. 'Och, just somebody at work.'

'Oh God!' Her mother cast her eyes heavenwards. 'Another bore o' a librarian!'

'He's not a bore. He's a well-read, intelligent man.'

'Aye, Ah can jist imagine, hen. A pale-faced, specky bloke wi' his nose never out o' a book.'

The image of Sean's handsome features and

219

dark, glowing eyes was still fresh in her mind and out of loyalty to him, she almost burst out with an indignant and accurate description. Only in the nick of time did she stop herself. What Big Aggie looked like was enough to put anyone off risking the slightest confrontation. With the hunched shoulders of a bull and an aggressive, head-jutting, wide-legged stance, Chrissie's mother was taller and stronger than her and could still fell her with one blow. It would not matter at all that she was not a child any more but a grown woman, as Sean had put it. His mother hated 'Proddies' as much as her mother hated 'Papes' but Sean's mother was thin and delicate and could barely struggle about. His father would be the physical threat. She often saw Michael O'Donnel coming along the road after his work in greasy railway cap and dungarees, his face streaked with dirt. He was heftily built, but with a beer belly, so maybe he wasn't all that fit either. Dermot was, though. She felt a shiver of fear on Sean's behalf. Dermot could and would hurt Sean if he found out.

It was true what Sean had said – it was all so ridiculous. She and Ailish had been saying that to each other for years. It did not change the facts though or the hatred. Her mother would batter her and Dermot would batter Sean. It didn't bear thinking about. She didn't care half as much for herself now as she did for Sean. The thought of him getting hurt was unendurable. He wasn't heavily built like Dermot. He had a good physique, of course – it was just that he was slimmer, more elegant, more thoughtful, more intelligent-looking than his rough-looking brother.

Dermot had found his proper niche in life as a barman in one of the toughest pubs in Glasgow. He swaggered proudly about now, looking even more confident, bigger and tougher than ever.

No, they must never let anyone in either her family or Sean's (apart from Ailish) know about their growing closeness and love for one another. Yet something had to happen. Neither of them could go on as they were doing, just existing on a few kisses in the back row of cinemas.

'Chrissie,' Sean said, losing his patience one night, 'I want to be with you all the time and not care who knows it. I can't go on like this.'

She persuaded him that maybe the next stage was to have a few days and nights somewhere. A weekend away perhaps. She could say that there was a cycling trip that the staff from various libraries had organised and it was planned that all the cyclists would stay overnight in a youth hostel. Her mother was always nagging on at her for not getting enough fresh air, 'shut up all the time in that stuffy old Mitchell'. This cycling idea would please her. Sean could perhaps say he was going to a match up in Aberdeen or somewhere that meant he would have to stay overnight.

And so it was arranged. Sean booked a room in a small country-house hotel. Oh, how they both longed for the wonderful time they would feel free and could be lovingly together.

28

At first Maimie hadn't twigged. Chrissie had always been over-enthusiastic about the Mitchell Library. They were all fed up listening to her rabbiting on about it. So no one paid any attention to her announcement about the Mitchell's cycling weekend. It wasn't until Maimie happened to find out that Sean had also disappeared for the weekend that she thought, 'Oh, aye, you think we're all daft but I know what you're up to, m'lady.'

She phoned the Mitchell to enquire about the cycling trip and, of course, there was no such thing. She wondered if snooty, blonde Ailish O'Donnel was in on this. Meeting her on the stairs, she asked her point blank. 'Where's Sean disappeared to? He's usually around at weekends.'

Thinking about it later, Maimie realised that Ailish had acquired a furtive look. She'd glanced away when answering and her voice was a bit too casual. 'Oh, he's away to some match up in Aberdeen.'

Of course, Ailish might just have been taken aback at being accosted on the stairs like that. They didn't usually talk to each other. A brief nod in passing was usually the best either of them could muster. But no, Ailish was a two-faced little madam, just like Chrissie. She knew what the pair of them were up to all right. Oh, just wait till she told Mammy and Daddy! She ran back into the house.

'Mammy! Daddy!' she gasped breathlessly as soon as she burst into the living room. 'You'll never guess what's happened!'

Aggie was enjoying a cup of tea. She took another swig. 'Johnny Pater has asked you to marry him?'

'Och, you're always tormenting me about him. I'm fed up with it, so I am. I couldn't care less about John Pater.'

'Aye, that'll be right.'

Wee Jimmy lit a Woodbine. 'OK, spit it out, hen. We're aw ears.'

'Our Chrissie and Sean O'Donnel have gone away for the weekend. Together!'

'What?' Aggie and Jimmy cried in unison. Then Aggie said, 'I'll murder her. I'll batter the living daylights out of her.'

'Are you sure, hen?' Jimmy's voice became disbelieving. 'I mean, just because she's gone away on the Mitchell's cycling weekend...'

'He's away as well, Daddy. I've just been speaking to Ailish O'Donnel.'

Aggie said, 'I told you not to speak to them Papes.'

'You speak to them on the stairs.'

'Just to say hello in the passing, no' tae stand and blether. You'll be getting as bad as Chrissie if you're no' careful. Mind how some Papes got her into the chapel one time? Ah battered that out of her and Ah'll do the same with you if you're no' careful.'

223

'For goodness' sake!' Maimie rolled her eyes in exasperation. 'I asked her where Sean was because he's usually around at weekends. And...' Her voice hastened on before her mother could interrupt again. 'I only asked because I suspected what they were up to, and I was right. Sean's away for the weekend as well.'

Jimmy shook his head and managed a half-hearted laugh. 'But hen, that doesn't mean...'

'There's no cycling weekend. I phoned the Mitchell. There never was any cycling weekend,' Maimie ended triumphantly.

There was silence for a few seconds as Aggie and Jimmy struggled to get over their incredulity. Aggie was first to recover. 'See her!' she bawled. 'Lying like a trooper as well. I'll bloody murder her when she gets back.' Her big fists punched the air. 'She'll no' forget this in a hurry. Fancy her sleeping wi' a Pape! What's the world coming to?'

Maimie was overjoyed. Her fat cheeks quivered with anticipation. 'They must have been going out for ages.'

'Fancy! Behind ma back! Just you wait until Ah get ma hands on her.'

Maimie could hardly wait, she was so excited and delighted. She prayed that her daddy wouldn't be out working when Chrissie returned so that he could have a go at her as well. He often worked on Sundays because, for one thing it meant extra pay. But anyway, it would be her mammy who would do all the battering. All her daddy would get the chance to do would be to bawl and shout.

224

What a carry-on. Marvellous! Oh boy, oh boy!

It was while they were in bed in the hotel that Sean asked Chrissie to marry him. Everything had been so beautiful in the oak-beamed country house, where they seemed to be the only guests. How quiet and peaceful it had been, sitting together in front of the big log fire sipping their nightcap of whisky. The bedroom had an old-fashioned brass bed with a mountainous mattress, piles of feather pillows and a beautiful patchwork quilt. There had been a fire in the bedroom too and they had undressed by its soft light. They took their time, admiring each other, gently exploring and caressing each other. Eventually, when they were both naked, Sean scooped her up into his arms and carried her over to the bed. How tender and loving and passionate he had been! They told each other how much they loved one another and Chrissie wished they could stay there forever, warm and safe in each other's arms. She didn't want to sleep and miss the wonderful awareness of a single moment. She had never felt so happy and content.

Sean had told her that he felt exactly the same and added, 'We could be together like this forever. We could get married. Will you marry me, Chrissie?'

For that magic moment, all difficulties were forgotten and she had gladly said, 'Yes.' It wasn't until they were on their way back to Glasgow and Balornock that the realisation of all the difficulties returned.

'We can't just walk in together like this. Not just

now. For one thing, it would make everything a thousand times worse if our families thought we'd lied to them and been away for the weekend together. We need more time to think of the best way to approach them. We need to make lots of plans and preparations first, Sean.'

Sean sighed. 'Yes, you're right. We'll have to meet again soon and talk about the practicalities, like exactly when we can get married and where we're going to live.'

'Right. We'll separate at the corner as usual. Give me a minute or two to reach my house before you start for yours.'

He nodded. Then, as she was about to hurry away, he put a hand on her arm and said, 'I love you, Chrissie, and, no matter what opposition and difficulties we have to face, we'll overcome them together. We will be married.'

She gave him a loving smile and left him standing at the top of the Wellfield hill, a tall, elegant-looking young man with a black shock of hair she loved to stroke, a handsome, intelligent face and serious dark eyes that could burn with so much passion. She felt as if she was melting with love for him. She was so happy.

29

Melvin had always enjoyed being a martyr. A long-suffering, brave and courageous one, of course. Now, he had found not only a partner in suffering but someone who was dependent on him, some-one who was truly grateful to him. Someone who shared the same opinion of Catriona.

Melvin and her mother had ganged up against her. When Melvin had showed concern that the old woman was struggling down to the bakery in all sorts of terrible weather to spend most of her time there, Hannah had explained that Catriona was so busy all day with her patients that she didn't want to be disturbed by her mother. Melvin was furious and returned early one day to see for himself.

There were several people waiting on the bench in the passageway and Catriona was busy with a patient in the consulting room. It didn't help that this particular patient happened to be a man.

Melvin hadn't the courage to say anything then and there. He waited until they were safely away before he boiled over.

'Fancy banishing your poor old mother from my house and making her struggle through the wind and rain to get some shelter at the bakery...'

'I did nothing of the kind, Melvin.'

'...while you carry on with men in that back room.'

'Don't be ridiculous…'

'Aw, shut up! That's it. There's to be no more of this. You're an absolute disgrace. That back door is going to be locked and barred from now on. And, if you don't get rid of all that rubbish that you call medicine, I'll get rid of it myself. If I see any of it still there by the weekend, I'll throw it all in the bin.'

Something else suddenly occurred to him. 'And another thing. There's too many rooms in this place for you to play around in and you know far too many people around here. I'm going to look for another house – up in Aberdeen. Yes, Aberdeen. I can keep an eye on Fergus there as well.'

'Don't be ridiculous, Melvin,' Catriona repeated. It seemed the only appropriate thing to say. It was all getting beyond her. 'How could you get to work every day?'

'I'm going to retire. I'm past the age when everybody else does. Why should I keep slaving my life away just to keep you in the lap of luxury? No, that's what I'm going to do. I've been thinking of doing just that for a while.'

Catriona could see he'd just that minute thought of it. It was simply another way to get the better of her. To isolate her as he'd isolated his first wife, Betty, to have her completely to himself, to own her, to lord it over her, to make himself feel big. Well, she wasn't Betty.

For a moment she didn't say anything. Maybe what he was threatening was no more than empty bluster. Yet she was afraid that he would at least carry out his threat of locking the back door and destroying her stock of medicines. Destroying her therapy business.

After Melvin had gone to have one of his sympathetic heart-to-heart talks with her mother, Catriona sat thinking of what she could do. She knew what her life would be like without her business. It didn't bear thinking about. She couldn't live like that any more. No, no, God no! Definitely not.

Eventually she thought of a way, the only way in the circumstances. She would get digs somewhere while she looked for a place to stay permanently and suitable shop premises near to where she would live. Springburn would be the best place. For one thing, it was a very busy area, so chances were there would be plenty of customers and patients. Springburn was also on the same side of Glasgow as Madge and Julie. Melvin would not succeed in separating her from her business, from her patients or from her friends.

She hesitated in going to Madge at this stage because Madge seemed to think that Melvin was the world's best husband. Madge would support her but would tell her she was 'a daft wee midden' all the same. Julie and Sammy would be more sympathetic and understanding and willing to give practical help. She immediately set off to see them and her belief that they would be understanding and helpful proved true. Sammy even said, 'I've often wondered why you put up with him for so long. Of course we'll help you all we can. I've passed one or two empty shops in Springburn on my way to work. I'll find out who's letting them, if you like.'

'Oh, thanks, Sammy, and as soon as possible,

please. I want to be out of Botanic Crescent right away if I possibly can. I might even book into a hotel in town until I find digs or some place to rent.'

It was Julie who said, 'I've got an idea. You know how you worry about your mother, Sammy. How about Catriona going to stay with her until she gets a place of her own? That way she can keep an eye on your mother, in case your father turns up.'

'Great!' Sammy enthused. 'That's the answer, Catriona. And you'd be on the spot to watch out for anything to let exactly where you want it.'

'Are you sure you don't mind, Sammy? What about your mother?'

'Not a bit. She'll love the company. And you'll be doing me a favour.'

They went right away and within the hour it was settled. She would go back to Botanic Crescent only to pack up her medicines, her medical books and patient records. Three separate tea chests would hold everything. One for the herbs, one for the homeopathic medicines and one for all her medical books and records. Sammy was going to get Alec Jackson to collect them in one of McHendry's vans and keep them in the storeroom at McHendry's until Catriona found her new premises. The van would also lift a couple of suitcases filled with her clothes and personal belongings and drop them off at the flat in Springburn Road. She wasn't going to take anything else from the house – not even a teaspoon. Melvin was welcome to his precious house and everything in it.

Something had to be done about her mother, of course. She spoke to her first.

'Mother, I'm leaving Melvin.'

'What do you mean you're leaving Melvin?' She sounded just like Melvin. It was exactly the sort of thing Melvin would have said.

'You were right in the first place, Mother. I should never have married him.'

'Don't you dare blame me for anything, you wicked girl!'

Here it comes, Catriona thought.

'God will punish you for your wickedness. Melvin McNair is a good man, I see that now. If you desert a man like that, you'll be punished, just as you were punished for putting your poor innocent child in danger. You were the death of poor wee Robert and you'll be the death of Melvin yet.'

'I'm leaving Melvin,' Catriona repeated. 'I've always been unhappy with him. Maybe it's not his fault. Maybe we're just not suited to each other. Maybe with different people, we would both have behaved differently.'

'You've got another man!' Her mother was suddenly electrified with horror. 'You're going to commit, or already have committed, the sin of adultery. You wicked, wicked girl.'

'No, I have not, Mother. There is no other man. What I need to talk to you about is what you want to do. I'm going to lodge with Sammy Hunter's mother just now until I find a place to rent. I can look for a place with an extra room. I can't afford a big house like this, but I hope to find a nice flat in Springburn. Maybe even a three-room and kitchen – two bedrooms, a sitting room and a kitchen, a bathroom too if possible. I don't think there's anything as big as that in the main road but I'll see...'

'I forbid you to leave your good husband. You obviously don't realise how lucky you are.'

'Mother, I'm not a child any more. You can't forbid me to do anything. Nor will it work to threaten me with God's wrath or any of his punishments. I don't believe in any of that any more.'

Horror returned to her mother's face. Her eyes bulged with disbelief. 'You don't believe in God? You are rejecting your Maker?'

Catriona decided it would be a complete waste of time to try to explain. 'Yes.'

'You are wicked. Truly wicked. I don't want anything more to do with you.'

'You don't mean that, Mother.'

Hannah turned and walked away. Catriona followed.

'All right, you can stay on here with Melvin if that's what you'd prefer. But I just want you to know that I'll get a place with an extra room in case you change your mind.'

Her mother glanced round with a look of disgust. 'I am not like you. I am a decent, good-living woman. I would not live under the same roof as a man who is not my husband.'

Catriona struggled to continue speaking calmly.

'I'm not going to live with another man, Mother, and there would be nothing indecent about you living here along with your son-in-law. If you won't come with me and you won't stay here, what will you do?'

'I'll go into a home.'

'Now, there's absolutely no need for that.'

'Little did I think the day would come when my own flesh and blood would see me go into a home.'

Oh God, two martyrs now!

'Believe me, Catriona, God will punish you. One day, someone you love will be taken away from you...'

Catriona wondered if she would ever be able to forgive her for that.

30

Alice looked happy. There she was, an ordinary teenager. No, not ordinary – beautiful. That's what Alice was – really beautiful. She was tall and leggy in her blue school uniform with a school-bag swinging at her side. Usually she was with a group of other girls, chatting happily. When boys passed by, they nudged each other and giggled. Julie longed to stop in front of her and say, 'I'm your real mother.' But, so far at least, she had managed to control the urge.

She wondered about going to the house across the road and speaking to the couple who had adopted Alice. She kept rehearsing what she would say.

'I'm Alice's real mother.' Or 'I live across the road and I have just found out that...' Or 'I don't want to cause any problem but...' Or 'I thought perhaps you ought to know that...'

She tried not to keep looking out of the front-room window or talking about Alice when Sammy came home from work. She knew it worried him. She kept telling him, 'I don't want to cause any trouble for anyone, Sammy. All I want is for Alice to be well and happy.'

'She *is* well and happy, Julie.'

'I know, but don't you think she's entitled to be told the truth about herself and her true background?'

Sammy gave her a long, serious stare. 'Her true background, Julie? Would knowing that really make her happy?'

Julie didn't say any more. If she did speak to Alice about her background, she'd have to lie about who Alice's father was. How could she say, 'You were conceived as a result of drunken copulation with a stranger on VE night'?

No, she would have to lie about that. If Alice asked, she would have to say he was a pilot who was shot down and killed during the war. She would have to pretend the father was Reggie. But what if Alice tried, at some point, to check facts – especially the dates? No, better just to say he had been killed and not give any details of what service he had been in, when he had been killed or anything.

She watched for Alice continuously and, when she wasn't standing waiting at the front-room window, she was constantly thinking about her. Or she was across at the shops or loitering near the school, hoping for a glimpse of the girl.

'Julie,' Sammy said eventually, 'this has to stop. You're making yourself ill.'

She widened her eyes. 'What?'

'I knew we shouldn't have come here.'

'I love it here, Sammy.'

'You're not even aware of the place, the area, this house. I bet you couldn't tell me the names of our neighbours. Or the names of any of the shops. Alice has become an obsession with you, Julie. I'm telling you, it's not healthy.'

'Nonsense. You're exaggerating. All right, I wanted to come here to be near Alice but now I am near her, I'm happy. That's all.'

'No, it's not all and you know it.'

She looked away from him. 'I haven't a clue what you're talking about.'

He sighed. 'Try not to do anything rash, Julie. For the girl's sake. She seems perfectly happy. Don't spoil it for her.'

'How many times must I tell you? All I've ever wanted is her happiness.'

'All right. All right.'

He never mentioned the subject again and she tried all the harder to control her longings. But with not the slightest success. She could not bear a day to pass without at least catching sight of the tall, slim figure.

Then Alice disappeared. One day after another passed without a sight of her. Julie felt distracted with worry. She wondered how she could find out what had happened. Eventually, in desperation, she told Sammy of her concern over the child.

Sammy shook his head. 'Julie, she is not a child any more. She's probably off to university or she has a job somewhere away from Glasgow.'

He was right, of course. In her heart, Alice had

235

always remained the baby she had allowed the nurse to prise from her arms. But Alice was not a child any more. She was a grown woman. This realisation saddened Julie, instead of making her happy. She wanted her baby back.

Time was flying past. She could not let it speed on relentlessly. She needed to be properly reunited with her daughter. Alice was her baby, her child, her grown woman, her own flesh and blood. The only way she could think of was to approach Mr and Mrs Robertson. She'd seen Alice with them one day and she had long since found out their name. She had learned all sorts of devious methods of getting information. She knew, for instance, that Mr Robertson was a clerk in the railway offices. She knew, by watching what Mrs Robertson purchased on Saturday mornings in the butcher's, that the Robertsons' favourite Sunday lunch was steak pie. That was usually followed by steamed apples and custard, judging by what was purchased at the grocer's on the same day. She and Mrs Robertson had got to the stage of smiling at each other in the grocer's and the butcher's. She looked a nice woman, with a kindly, lined face and grey hair. Most women nowadays had their grey hairs dyed as soon as they appeared and favoured a spot of make-up. Not Mrs Robertson.

Julie thought of going to their door. Then it occurred to her that it would be easier to speak to Mrs Robertson, casually at first, in one of the shops. The next day she followed Mrs Robertson into the chemist's, stood behind her, smiled and then said casually, 'I haven't seen your daughter around for a while. She's that tall, dark-haired girl, isn't she? I hope she's keeping all right.'

'Oh yes.' Mrs Robertson's face lit up with pride. 'She's doing very well. She's training to be a doctor, you know.'

'Is she?' Julie too felt pride. 'How wonderful!'

'Yes, her dad and I are very proud of her. She's a born doctor. Ages ago, when I had flu, she insisted on looking after me. She's always been so good to both of us. She's such a loving girl as well. Her dad and I feel really blessed to have her.'

It wasn't fair. Later Julie wept to herself. Her need had become an agony. Alice belonged to her. It was right that Alice, that everybody, should know. She did not care what Sammy or anyone said. She dreamed of their reunion. She saw Alice's surprise and delight. She felt Alice's young body in her arms. She held her close. She vowed never to let her go again.

In her dreams, they spoke for hours. They got on *so* well and they had so much lost time to make up for. She listened eagerly to every detail of Alice's childhood and young womanhood. All her likes and dislikes, every detail she could think of. They laughed together.

Julie told her about the job she had once had in Copeland & Lye's. She told her about Madge and her large brood of children. She described Madge's tall, handsome charmer of a husband and how Madge kept him on a tight rein. She told her about Catriona and her troubles.

She told her about Sammy and how he had been a conscientious objector during the war, served in the Friends' Ambulance Unit and now worked in McHendry's. He also did first-aid work for the Red Cross, helping tend to the injured at football matches as well as other events. She told Alice that Sammy was a Quaker and that she often she went to meetings with him now. She was getting to quite enjoy going there. There was something appealing, genuine and comforting, about them.

Oh, she had so much to tell her beautiful, loving daughter. First of all, she would tell her that she loved her so much and had always loved her. It was important for Alice to know that she hadn't given her baby away because she didn't love her.

Thinking about love made Julie remember her wedding. She'd tell Alice about that too. It was then she remembered what had been said there about love. She looked it up again in Corinthians. She sat alone in the front room with the open Bible in her lap.

Love is patient, Love is kind.
Love is not jealous or boastful;
It is not arrogant or rude.
Love does not insist on its own way;
It is not irritable or resentful;
It does not rejoice at wrong,
But rejoices in the right.
Love bears all things,
Believes all things,
Hopes all things, Endures all things. Love never
  ends.

Julie wept. She could not insist on her own way.

She did love Alice. She would bear all things. She could only pray now that one day Alice, in her own time, would try to find her.

31

Alec and Sammy didn't go to so many matches together now, because of Sammy's Red Cross work. Most of the time, if Sammy went to a match, it was to see to the injured. He also attended other big events. He had been at a ceremony in the City Chambers recently where a procession of councillors was led in by a piper. Sammy had made Alec laugh afterwards by saying, 'I've often seen haggis piped in but never dumplings.'

The last match they went to together turned out to be a bit of a disaster. The section of the Celtic end called 'The Jungle', where the worst of the hooligan mob stood, had erupted as usual with sectarian songs and chanting. The Jungle had been filled with a thunderous rendition of,

Faith of my fathers,
Holy faith we will be true to thee till death.
Faith of our fathers living still
In spite of dungeon, fire and sword.
Oh, how our hearts beat high with joy
When e'er we hear these glorious words,
Faith of our father...

And after it, 'Hail glorious Saint Patrick, dear saint of our isle' was roared out.

Then of course the Rangers end where Alec and Sammy were standing countered with 'The Sash' and 'God Save the Queen', although some other, not so complimentary words had been substituted for the original ones. Then there were the usual obscenities and gestures of hatred.

Sammy had turned on the nearest foul-mouthed man and, before Alec could tell him to ignore all the taunts – after all they weren't aimed at him – Sammy had told the man in no uncertain terms what he thought of him. Unfortunately this particular man didn't ignore Sammy. He started bawling abuse, while grabbing Sammy by the lapels to jerk his face nearer. Alec tried to get in between them, protesting in what he hoped sounded a friendly and good-humoured manner. He said, 'He didn't mean it, pal.'

But Sammy stubbornly insisted, 'I did mean it!'

Alec felt like helping the man throttle Sammy. Instead he jerked Sammy away, at the same time making signs to the man that Sammy was mad and no further attention should be paid to him.

The man wasn't going to be fobbed off, how-ever, and was joined by his immediate com-panions. A real barney developed, with Sammy and Alec in the centre of it. Then a couple of policemen struggled among them. One, reaching Sammy, told him to 'fuck off'. But Sammy, indignant now, refused to budge. The policemen gave him another chance but Sammy was now objecting to the policeman's attitude. The result of all this was that Sammy, Alec and the other men all ended up in court. The other men had pleaded guilty. But Sammy, awkward as ever, pleaded not guilty and told the sheriff that he had been provoked, first by the men and then by the police officer who had twice told him to fuck off.

The sheriff wasted no time. He had the usual heavy after-match quota of cases to get through. 'Guilty,' he told Sammy abruptly, 'because if you'd had any sense at all and fucked off the first time, you wouldn't be standing here now.'

And he gave Sammy a hefty fine. Sammy was furious. He had to be dragged away, protesting loudly.

'Will you never learn to keep your mouth shut?' Alec shouted at him outside the court. He genuinely felt nerve-wracked by the whole incident. He had never been one to get into fights if he could avoid it.

'Talk about a pacifist. I've been through the bloody war and I've still to meet anybody as aggressive and confrontational as you, Sammy. If this is what pacifist Quakers are supposed to be like, give me a military man any day.'

The moment the words were out of his mouth, he regretted them. Sammy's face paled, showing a smattering of freckles that hadn't been noticeable before. His eyes widened with shock, horror, guilt and hurt. Alec felt so terrible, he grabbed Sammy in a bear hug, then immediately let him go in acute embarrassment. Men didn't hug each other in Glasgow.

'Sammy, don't listen to me.'

'Why not?'

Sammy was such a bloody awkward idiot.

'I didn't mean it. What do I know about anything?'

'You know about me, Alec. I never thought... I didn't realise. Do you think I'm just the same as my father, after all?'

'No, no. Definitely not. What a daft thing to say. It's just that there are times when you should keep your mouth shut, Sammy. There are surely better ways to tackle problems than head-on like that.'

'You're right, Alec. You're quite right.'

'Come on, where's your sense of humour?' Alec began to laugh when he remembered what the sheriff had said. He tried an impersonation of him.

'If you had fucked off the first time...'

Sammy began to laugh too.

'Right enough, it was funny when you think about it.'

'Let's go for a drink. To The Titwood,' he added hastily. 'I've had enough excitement for one day.' The Titwood was a neutral pub.

The usual sectarian rivalry could erupt into violence in pubs even quicker than in football grounds. A new pub had recently been scheduled to open, but on the window they'd put an advertisement for staff which read, 'Only Catholics need apply'. After the match that day, the place had been turned over. Not a glass had been left unsmashed, not a chair or table left in one piece. The place never opened.

'You're right,' Sammy repeated after they'd settled in The Titwood. 'It's my quick temper.'

'It goes with your hair.'

242

'I'll have to do something about it.'

'There's no need to make a big drama of it. It's not a life and death situation. Although,' Alec tried to look serious, 'I don't know. We've had a few close shaves.'

'You're right,' Sammy said, taking him seriously.

'Will you stop telling me I'm right? I'm not used to it. Madge has cast me as a villain and always in the wrong for too many years.'

'Yes, you're right.'

'There you go again.'

Sammy relaxed into laughter. 'I think Madge is just scared you'll go off and leave her, Alec. She's daft about you.'

'I've been tempted many a time.'

'Wait till Julie hears about me being found guilty and fined. She'll be tempted to kick me out.'

'More like the Quakers kicking you out.'

Sammy's look turned tragic again, making Alec groan and add, 'Sammy, it was a joke!'

They finished their pints and made for home.

'Did I tell you,' Sammy said eventually, 'that Julie has been taking a typing and secretarial course? She could have gone back to Copeland & Lye's after we got married. I was perfectly happy for her to do that but she fancied a change.'

'Good for her. Here, you'll be well off, Sammy. Two wage packets coming into the house. Even so, I don't think I'd like my wife going out to work.'

'You're behind the times, Alec. This is the '60s. With all the labour-saving gadgets you can get for the house now, more and more women are going out to work.'

'It'll lead to trouble. You mark my words.'

'What kind of trouble?'

Alec shrugged. 'I don't know. But the man's always been the breadwinner, the head of the house.'

Sammy laughed.

Alec said, 'What's so funny about that?'

'Nothing. Sorry. I thought it was another of your jokes.'

'Oh, aye. I know what you're thinking.'

He had been thinking of big, battling Madge, who had always worn the trousers in Alec's household.

Alec got off the tram car at Springburn to walk up to Balornock. Sammy gave him a wave and Alec grinned and waved in return before striding away.

Sammy stayed on until his stop at Bishopbriggs Cross. He was thinking about Julie now and the job she was planning to start. Actually, she had already started working part-time, helping Catriona get her new shop ready in Springburn Road. The premises were very handy for where she was staying with his mother in his old flat. But, as she had expected, there had been a lot of trouble with Melvin and also with her mother, Hannah Munro, who refused to believe her son-in-law could do anything wrong. Sammy had said to Julie, 'Do you think you'll really end up having the job with Catriona? Do you think she'll get things up and running? Especially with Melvin carrying on the way he's doing?'

'Yes, I do. She's a surprisingly spirited wee lady

244

underneath that timid-looking exterior. You'd be surprised if you knew just what a hard time she's had. And the things she's had to put up with over the years.'

'Nothing surprises me any more.'

'Things are looking really promising – she's already got one or two therapists interested in renting rooms from her. We've organised a desk and space for me in the waiting room. The phone's been installed there. I'll answer it, keep the appointment books up to date and type letters for Catriona and the other therapists – ordering stuff, and all that kind of thing. I'm looking forward to working there, it'll be really interesting. And one of the best things about it is that it's not nearly as far to travel to Springburn as it would be into town to Copeland & Lye's.'

'Is Melvin still selling the house?'

'Well, he's still threatening to. His idea is to sell it so that Catriona can't carry on with her therapy work. He plans to drag her off to Aberdeen to live. That's where Fergus has settled. Separate her from her friends. Catriona says he did that to his first wife but he isn't going to do it to her. I'm telling you, Sammy, she's got guts, that one.'

'Well, good for her. I wonder if she could give me some medicine for my quick temper.'

Julie laughed. 'That could prove to be one of her biggest challenges, Sammy. But I'll see what she says.'

'Don't bother. There's no pills or potions that can cure a fault like mine.'

'Oh, you never know. Miracles do happen.'

'Come here, you.' He made a lunge at her and,

dodging him, she ran through to the kitchen laughing. He called after her, 'You're getting too cheeky for your own good.'

'What do you want for your tea?' she called back.

He thanked God that everything seemed all right with Julie now. She never spoke about Alice any more. Or only very occasionally and just to say that, wherever Alice was, she hoped she was happy. He didn't know what had brought about Julie's contentment, what had calmed her previous agitation and obsession with being reunited with her daughter. But whatever it was, he thanked God for it and he prayed that it would last.

32

The moment Chrissie opened the front door, she sensed the atmosphere. The air inside was tense, waiting.

'Oh, so you're back, are ye?' Big Aggie sneered. 'Enjoyed it, did ye – sleeping wi' a bloody Pape?'

Maimie was crouched by the fire, her fat cheeks quivering with excitement.

Her mother strode towards Chrissie. 'Your father says he's gonnae teach you a lesson when he gets back frae work but Ah'm gonnae give you something for starters.'

For a second, Chrissie was paralysed with shock before she could get herself moving and try to escape. Aggie caught her by the hair and Chrissie began to scream and fight. She was no longer the cowed child she had once been, too terrified to protest. She screamed herself hoarse and wildly fought to protect herself, kicking and punching. At one point, her mother lost her balance in the struggle and fell onto the floor. Aggie was enraged and as she struggled up, helped by an eager Maimie, she bawled, 'Ah'm gonnae murder you for this.'

Chrissie turned and ran but Aggie caught her by the hair again. Before the older woman could land a blow, there was a terrific explosion at the front door. The door flew open, kicked in by Sean, who now rushed at Chrissie and jerked her away from Aggie.

'Go and pack a case, Chrissie. You're coming with me right now.'

'What a bloody cheek!' Aggie was genuinely astonished, as well as outraged. 'Who do you think you are?'

'I'm the man Chrissie is going to marry.'

'Over ma dead body. No bloody Tim is going to be part of this family. Get out of ma house before Ah throw ye out.'

'Mammy,' Chrissie protested, 'what does Sean's religion matter? He's a good man and we love each other.'

'Aw, shut up, ya stupid wee cow. What do you know about anything? Ah'll soon knock aw this bloody nonsense out of you.'

'You'll never lay a finger on Chrissie again,' Sean said. 'Go on, Chrissie. Pack a case.'

'Don't you dare act the big man in ma house,'

Aggie bawled. 'Ah'll soon make short work of you.'

She strode menacingly towards him but Sean didn't budge. Instead, he gave Chrissie a push. 'Go on.'

Aggie tried to grapple him aside but failed. In frustration, she screamed obscenities into his face.

'And wait till Ah tell ma Jimmy. He'll murder you. You'll no' get away wi' this.'

'I love Chrissie and I want to take care of her for the rest of our lives together. What on earth's wrong with that?'

'You're a bloody Pape, that's what's wrong,' Aggie bawled.

He shook his head in despair and called to Chrissie, who was now in one of the bedrooms, flinging clothes, shoes, make-up and books into the biggest suitcase she could find.

'Are you ready, Chrissie?'

'Yes.' Chrissie staggered into the lobby, clutching the bulky suitcase in front of her. He took the case and pushed her out of the house, banging the door shut in Big Aggie's face.

'Up the stairs,' he told Chrissie.

'Oh Sean!' Chrissie was near to tears. 'Will your mother be any better?'

'Don't worry. My mother won't have the energy to be aggressive.'

'Your father then?'

'As long as they think you'll "turn", as they call it, and have our children brought up in the faith, they'll probably be OK. And don't worry,' he added, 'we can both end up atheists for all I care, but anything to shut them up at the moment. Just until we get a place of our own to stay. OK?'

'Yes, all right.'

She followed him anxiously up to the top flat. Sean opened the O'Donnel door with his key.

'Now, don't worry,' he repeated as they entered the lobby. 'It'll be all right.'

'What's this?' Teresa O'Donnel asked. Her voice sounded shocked but it lacked the volume of Big Aggie's. Teresa was smaller and thinner, and bent forward as if she was a heavy burden to herself.

'Ma, Chrissie and I are going to get married. She can't stay downstairs, so is it OK if she stays here until after the wedding and we move to a place of our own?'

Michael O'Donnel had been reading his *Daily Herald* and now let it drop down onto his knees. 'How long has this been going on?'

'Long enough,' Sean said.

'And what do the Stoddarts think of it? As if I don't know,' he added with a sneer. 'Turfed her out, did they?'

Chrissie plucked up courage and said, 'I love Sean and he loves me. That's all that matters.'

Dermot gave a howl of laughter at this. 'That's what you think, hen.'

'It's all so silly.' Sheer frustration made her stick to her guns. She really, genuinely could not understand. 'Why should it matter? If we respect each other's right to worship as we want to, there won't be a problem. There needn't be any problem.'

'Is she gonnae turn?' Teresa asked Sean. 'Are

249

yer weans gonnae be brought up in the faith?'

'You've no need to worry, Ma. Chrissie and I have discussed this. If she can just stay here for a week or two – OK?'

Dermot laughed again. 'OK? You're joking. The Stoddarts live in the close, remember. They're going to love her passing their door every day. I don't think! You're daft, you.'

'Well, if you're so clever,' Sean said angrily, 'what do you suggest?'

'Why can't you be content with a good fuck and leave it at that?'

'Shut your filthy mouth!' Sean rushed at Dermot and grabbed him by the lapels of his smart black jacket. 'You ignorant bigot.'

Dermot began to laugh at Sean's unexpected nerve. Not even the toughest ned in Glasgow had enough nerve to attack Dermot O'Donnel. But before his laugh got going and before he had time to dust down his lapels, Sean had head-butted him in the face.

Dermot's head jerked backwards, then, his face livid with rage as well as blood, he landed a savage, scything left hook just above Sean's left ear. Another jabbed into Sean's eye. Sean's knees buckled but he managed to grab Dermot's jacket again. Dermot drove his knee deep into Sean's stomach, then followed up with two more vicious, chopping rights to Sean's face.

Chrissie was screaming and hanging on to Dermot in an effort to drag him off Sean. Teresa, gasping and choking for breath, tried to claw her sons apart. At the same time, Michael was shouting at her, 'Let them settle this their own way,

Teresa. Leave them to it, for God's sake.'

Eventually, Chrissie's scream of 'Look what you're doing to your mother, you maniac!' did stop him, stopped both men.

Dermot hitched at his shoulders and smoothed down his jacket.

'He started it. Are you all right, Ma?'

'Does she look all right?' Chrissie said. 'And Sean didn't start it. You started it with your filthy talk.'

'I'm OK, hen,' Teresa managed, groping for her chair. 'Just give me a minute to get my breath back and I'll pour myself a cup of tea.'

'I'll pour it.' Chrissie hurried over to the table.

'Thanks, hen.'

Sean also sank into a chair. One of his eyes had already begun to swell and turn black.

'I'm sorry, Ma. Sorry for upsetting you but I'm not sorry for wanting to marry Chrissie. We're still going to go ahead with our plans, even if everyone in both families is against it.'

'Aye, well,' Michael said, 'you're no' bringing her here to stay, no' for a day, no' for a week, no'...'

'All right, all right, Da. I get the message. But if she can't stay here, then I can't either. Chrissie and I are together now and we're staying together.'

Teresa had begun to get control of her breathing.

'She's a nice wee lassie, son, but there'll be lots of other nice wee lassies.' She turned towards Chrissie. 'Nae harm tae ye, hen, but mixed marriages cause nothing but grief.'

'It doesn't need to be like that,' Chrissie said.

'Exactly,' Sean agreed.

'Huh!' Michael rolled his eyes. 'Talk about living in cloud cuckoo land.' He jerked his head in Sean's direction. 'He's always been like that, of course. A right idiot. If this is what bloody education does for you, I'm glad I left school when I was twelve.'

'Yes, and think of it.' Sean sounded bitter as well as sarcastic. 'I might have gone to university if you hadn't pulled the plug on that.'

Teresa said, 'Where can you go to stay? I'm sorry, son, but it'll just no' work. As Ah've just said to Chrissie, Ah've seen it happen that often.'

Sean heaved a big sigh. 'Come on, Chrissie. Help me pack my case and then we'll be away.'

Chrissie rose and began to follow him towards the door.

Teresa tried again. 'But, son, where will you go?'

'Don't worry, Ma, we'll get some place.'

Dermot had been mopping up blood from his nose. 'Let him go, Ma,' he said. 'He'll soon find out for himself.'

In no time at all, they were out of the house, out of the close and walking along Broomknowes Road. They walked in silence and with no idea where they were going.

Eventually Sean said, 'There's always Aunty Mary. She might be worth a try.'

'Aunty Mary?'

'She's Ma's unmarried sister. She's just as religious, or even more so than the rest of them, but she's an awful romantic as well. She thrives

252

on Mills and Boon novels. She might think this is more of a romantic situation than anything else and be more easily persuaded to help us. It's worth a try anyway.'

33

'Did you hear about the barney up our stair?' Alec asked Sammy.

'No, what happened?'

'You know the Stoddarts and the O'Donnels?'

'Who doesn't?'

'Sean O'Donnel wants to get hitched to Chrissie Stoddart. Both families have disowned them now. Apparently, Big Aggie started battering Chrissie and Sean hauled her off upstairs. then Dermot tried to give Sean a beating. The Stoddarts went upstairs to try and drag Chrissie down again. It was a right punch-up.'

'I hope you didn't get involved.'

'Listen, mate, I've enough to cope with with you. No, I was at work when it happened. Thank God,' he added with feeling. 'But Madge got stuck into Big Aggie.'

'No!'

'Yeah. Apparently, it was because Teresa had come down the stairs – to try and calm things down, I suppose, and Big Aggie set about her. Well, I mean, poor Teresa and her asthma. I couldn't blame Madge.'

'What a carry on!'

'Yeah, the police carted them all off. Wait for it – Madge as well. I had to go and bail her out of the police station.'

'No!'

Alec laughed. 'I'll never let her live it down. I had the kids in fits about it. We were all falling about.'

Sammy shook his head. 'You're an awful man, Alec.'

They were sitting in the bus the Quakers had hired to take the hillwalkers out to the country where the walk was scheduled to start. It had become a regular outing for Alec. It was a joy for him to get out of his crowded, noisy house for a few hours of freedom and perfect peace. He loved his family but could only take them in small doses. Being with them at weekends, especially all day on a Sunday, could be totally overwhelming.

Usually he stood outside the door of the Quaker Meeting House until all the Friends came out. They always gathered inside for a few minutes' silence before setting off. Friends with a capital F, Sammy called them, to distinguish his Quaker friends from his other friends. Alec always tormented him about this.

'Oh, aye, friends with a capital F are special, are they? Better than friends like me?'

'Och, you know what I mean. It's just to let you know it's Quakers I happen to be talking about. It's just a matter of clarification.'

'Aye, OK, OK.'

'Although they are special in their own way. The salt of the earth, in fact. I can say that

254

because I'm not one of them. I mean, it's not just boasting.'

'Not one of them?' Alec gave an incredulous laugh. 'Of course you're one of them! You're the most Quakerly Quaker I know.'

Sammy laughed. 'You're suddenly an expert, are you?'

'Well, I've met quite a few now, haven't I? I'm sitting at the back of a busload of them right now.'

And a motley-looking bunch they were – both men and women in their woolly hats, shabby anoraks and bulky backpacks. Sometimes Alec wondered what on earth he was doing with such a crowd. It surely wasn't his scene. Yet, more and more, it had become his scene. But soon he felt the incredible beauty of the place, the surrounding green of the hills and mountains, the shadowy villages, the vast blue of the sky, the welcome solitude in a beautiful world. Yet he did not feel cut off. Instead, he had a sense of being at one with the whole universe. He could never have told Madge or anyone about this. They would have thought he was mad. Maybe he was. Yet there was part of him that felt he belonged, mad as it seemed, as he sat on top of a mountain.

These were the moments when he felt perfect peace and happiness. At the end of the silence, the circle joined for a minute by holding hands. Afterwards, looking back, he would feel a secret sadness at the knowledge that he could never be truly one of them. He was a typical Jack the Lad, he had flirted with innumerable women and went

255

further with them when he got the chance. He had committed adultery. He had gone with prostitutes. Sammy didn't know the half of it and he never would. All he could do was to show some respect for Sammy's place of worship, his Quaker Meeting House, by never desecrating it with his presence.

Sometimes they sang songs in the bus or when they were trudging through the countryside – cheerful, rousing tunes. But Sammy said they never sang or had music during their meetings for worship in Meeting House. On other occasions they did have music though. Alec had attended several meetings in Sammy's house. Once there was a group playing guitar music and then they all had tea and home-baked cakes. Another time, a Muslim had been invited to speak about his faith and what it meant to him. Then, on other occasions, a Hindu, a Sikh and a Catholic had come to speak in Sammy's front room. It had proved really interesting. Alec had joked to Sammy, 'My God, Sammy, I'm getting converted to a different religion every couple of months now. I don't know where I am any more!'

Sammy laughed. 'I feel a bit like that myself. It's interesting though, isn't it? If people could just listen to each other more and have a bit of understanding and respect for other people's faith... Hopefully there would be fewer wars. Ignorance just seems to breed fear and aggression.'

'Like the Stoddarts and the O'Donnels?' Alec said. 'You can't get much more ignorant than them.'

'Sean and Ailish aren't like their parents and

Chrissie is very different from hers, so maybe there's hope for the next generation.'

'I wouldn't bank on it,' Alec said. 'There's been wars and fighting since time began. It seems to me that it's an incurable weakness in human nature.'

'Och, don't be so negative, Alec.'

'I know, I know. Friends with a capital F believe there's good or God in every human being but sometimes it's hellish difficult to find, Sammy.'

'True. But that doesn't mean we should give up looking.'

'If only everyone was a Quaker, eh?' He really meant it.

'You're making a big mistake there, Alec.'

'How?'

'Thinking Friends are perfect. They're no more perfect than you or me or anyone else.'

'I don't see any ignorant or aggressive people here,' Alec said. 'Most of them are bloody academics.'

'You think academics are perfect? Don't be daft!'

Alec shrugged. The bus had arrived at its destination and they had all begun to clamber out. It was a crisp autumn day and Alec gratefully took deep breaths of the clean, cool air. One of the good things about living in Glasgow was its proximity to beautiful country areas.

They hitched up their backpacks and started the trek to the hills. At one point, Alec found himself beside a girl wearing a checked shirt and khaki parka, with woolly bobbles swinging from her hat. He began kidding her on and chatting

257

her up. He couldn't help it. Anything for a laugh. He was incorrigible. He never even passed Big Aggie without greeting her with 'Hi, Gorgeous'. Once he'd even nipped her bum.

Big Aggie! He didn't know what to do to cure himself so he just gave up and braced himself for hell.

The girl was called Sarah. She was a good sport and they enjoyed a laugh together. Once they started climbing, however, it was necessary to save one's breath and concentrate. Or at least it was for Alec. He had been on a few climbs now but not as many as the others. They were a hardy bunch and he had quite a bit of training to do in order to reach their level of fitness. He had been toying with the idea of joining the local karate club. The Pater boys across the landing were members and he used to see them practising in the back green. Some of the kicks and throws made him wince. He doubted if he could be as physical as that. Or wanted to be.

Eventually, reaching the top, he stood and gazed admiringly at the grandeur of hills and mountains and distant hollows, some hazed with mist, some sparkling with rays of sunlight. He could see woods – brown, dark, occasionally faintly blue as the light changed.

How beautiful the world was. He had lived most of his life in the slums of Glasgow and never really appreciated the beauty of the wider world. He had been happy enough, though, especially in the Townhead where he'd been brought up and in the Cowlairs Pend in Springburn where he'd lived after getting married. He'd no complaints about Glasgow. He loved the place. But here was a world that was new to him. Indeed, a whole new world on many levels had been opening up to him these past few years.

Thanks mostly to Sammy. His friend with a capital F.

34

In one way, Catriona could hardly credit it. Yet, in another way, she wasn't a bit surprised. First of all, Melvin had tried to make her feel guilty about 'putting her poor mother into an old folks' home'. She countered that by reminding Melvin that she had not *put* her mother there, her mother had insisted on going. She also tried to assuage the guilt that she admittedly felt by visiting Hannah as regularly as she could, even though the visit only lasted half an hour at most and her mother put her through purgatory.

Melvin wanted her to go with him to live in Aberdeen to be near Fergus. It was almost enough to make Fergus move to Timbuktu. But she didn't believe Melvin really meant what he said about that. He wouldn't fit in with Fergus and his crowd of hippy friends any more than she would. Nor did she believe he'd go ahead with selling the house. He was too proud of it. He had always needed something to boast about. All that happened was that he kept knocking on Mrs Hunter's door. Catriona was still staying with Sammy's mother until a suitable flat became available near her shop.

Melvin started by trying to bully her to come back to him. Then he tried making a fool of her. 'You'll never manage on your own. You think you're OK now but that's just because you've got a substitute mother, with Mrs Hunter looking after you. You couldn't run a house, never mind a business.'

He'd retire from the bakery by now and would get a good price for it, he assured her. They'd never be short of 'a bob or two' and he'd always been good to her. 'You know that. So stop all this nonsense.'

He wouldn't listen. That didn't surprise her. It didn't matter how often she told him she was perfectly capable of managing on her own, and that she had already proved she could run a successful business. He refused to believe her.

He wouldn't leave her alone. Every night after work he was on the Hunter doorstep. If she was out when he knocked, Mrs Hunter would be persuaded to let him in and he'd be sitting waiting on Catriona when she arrived back at the house. It was almost worse than living with him. In desperation, she went to a lawyer and began divorce proceedings.

Then he tried to play on her sympathies by making her feel guilty. Except she didn't feel sympathy for him. Nor did she feel guilty about him.

Mrs Hunter became upset though. 'Och, he's a poor soul, Catriona. Yesterday he was so breathless with climbing the stairs, he could hardly say a word to me. He sat there for ages coughing. He's your man, remember, Catriona, and he needs you.'

That was rich coming from her, Catriona thought. She felt bitter at Mrs Hunter's attitude. She wanted to say, 'What about your man? Last I heard he was coughing his lungs out.' But of course, she didn't.

Melvin then tried speaking to Andrew and not just speaking, apparently, but weeping. Andrew was terribly upset and came to plead with her to 'have some decency'. He was still living with Melvin in Botanic Crescent and he couldn't even concentrate on his studies for worrying about his dad.

Now Catriona did feel guilty. But it was about Andrew not Melvin. She didn't even feel guilty about her mother who now seemed settled and happy in the old folks' home. She'd already got the Band of Jesus involved, with regular services and hymn singing being held in the sitting room of the home. Being amongst so many people, and no doubt bossing them mercilessly, was the best thing that had happened to her mother since Catriona's father had died. She had plenty of company day and night now. She never had to be alone.

When Catriona thought of the years she'd wasted living in misery with Melvin, she felt only anger, at herself as well as Melvin. There was no way she could go back to him and his mausoleum of a house. She had to make that clear to Andrew.

'I'm sorry, son, that you've been worried and upset, but I'll never go back to your dad. Never.'

'But he's ill. He could die. How can you be so

selfish and cruel?'

Catriona felt like dying with wretchedness and hurt herself, when Andrew looked at and spoke to her with such lack of love.

'You don't understand, Andrew. Your dad and I haven't been getting on for years. I didn't want to burden you with my problems but I've been so unhappy for so long with him and I just can't bear it any more. I can't. I'm sorry. I'll never go back to him.'

'Dad says you left because he's not making a lot of money to spend on you any more, and so you've found a way to make money for yourself and don't care what happens to him.'

The devious, lying bastard, Catriona thought. But she just said, 'No, that's not true, Andrew.'

'*Are* you making a lot of money for yourself?'

'My business is successful, yes. But whatever money I have made or will make in the future will be used to help you and Fergus in every way I can.'

'I don't want your help. Dad's helping me. And, even if he wasn't, I'd not take a penny from you. I don't want your help.'

He left after that and Catriona felt so completely devastated, she was beyond weeping.

Mrs Hunter had been out doing shopping and when she came back, she found Catriona sitting ashen-faced, staring wide-eyed at the sunken embers of the fire.

'I saw your nice big son on Springburn Road, Catriona. He's awful upset, dear. Can you not go back to your man for his sake? For your boy's sake?'

Catriona gazed round at Mrs Hunter. 'I've got the chance of a suitable flat,' she said. 'It's furnished, but a bit old-fashioned looking. But I've made up my mind. I phoned and it's all arranged. I'll leave here right away. I can move in now and take my time getting it the way I want it.'

Mrs Hunter was taken aback. 'Oh, but there's surely no need...'

'Yes, there is, Mrs Hunter. Thank you for all your kindness.'

'I hope you don't think ... I mean, I didn't mean to interfere. I was just thinking of your own good. I'm fond of you, dear. You're like a daughter to me. I've just been trying to do my best for you.'

'Yes, I appreciate that. Thank you. Now I'd better start my packing.'

'Oh dear!' Mrs Hunter stood wringing her hands. 'What'll I tell poor Melvin?'

Catriona nearly said, 'Tell him to go to hell!' but contained herself in time. She thought that maybe she *was* selfish and cruel. She certainly felt bitter and sad and hurt and unhappy.

But she could not live with Melvin again. She just couldn't. The most selfish thing she had done – and of this she was certain – was marrying Melvin in the first place. She'd agreed to marry him to escape from her mother and her mother's house. All right, she had been a timid wee girl and Melvin had bullied and rushed her into agreeing. All the same, she should have had enough guts to stand up to him. And to her mother.

She hadn't, though. And there it was. Her stupid wasted life. But no! That was what he always said – that she was stupid, she was a waste of time. Well, not any more. She'd show him. A hard core of determination came to her rescue. She would show them all.

She was not stupid.

But at the same time, a river of tears coursed unchecked down her cheeks. She could believe anything, do anything, survive anything, bear anything. Except losing the love of her son.

35

'Aunty Mary's a kindly wee soul and she'll probably let us have her front room no bother. Wait until you see her collection of Mills and Boon and Barbara Cartland romances. Her house is full of them.'

'But she never married?'

'The right man never came along, she says. I think she was looking for a Mills and Boon hero and found they're a bit thin on the ground. Now it's too late.' He grinned. 'Mind you, I don't think she's given up hope.'

They got off the tram at the foot of the High Street and crossed the road. Both Chrissie and Sean had read a great deal about Glasgow's history and so they were well aware that this area and the adjoining streets that met at Glasgow Cross – the Trongate, the Saltmarket and the High Street – were the original part of the city. Chrissie could see in her mind's eye how the very street she was now walking on had once had no street lamps. In the whole of the city, just a very few tallow candle lamps flickered, but these were at long intervals and only intensified the gloom. The only traffic would be the occasional sedan chair, the carriers struggling along unpaved, filthy, rutted roads. There was no police force in those days. Every male citizen between the ages of eighteen and sixty had to take a turn as a city guard. A man had to be at his post at ten o'clock at night and then had to stroll, yawning no doubt, along the Trongate and the High Street and up the pitch-dark lanes, even on winter nights, until three or four in the morning. After that, Glasgow was without any guard at all. It helped, Chrissie supposed, that male and female servants were forbidden to be out on the streets at night 'in companies'. All strangers staying in either private or public houses had to give in their names by ten o'clock at night to the captain of the city guard. Thinking about the history of the area while actually walking through it gave Chrissie an eerie feeling. She'd always had a very vivid imagination.

She clung to Sean's arm as they went into the shadowy close and climbed the stairs. Aunty Mary lived 'one up', a level always regarded as the best. That was because, in the old days, it was above the stench and filth of the street, yet conveniently reached without too steep a climb.

Aunty Mary was a small, slim woman with a surprisingly pretty face. Sean had told Chrissie that his aunt was in her sixties and now, seeing her, Chrissie could hardly believe it. The slim, shapely body, the neat little features and soft, almost unwrinkled skin indicated someone much, much younger. If Sean had told her that Aunty Mary was in her forties and if it hadn't been for her white hair, Chrissie would have believed him.

'Hello, son.' Delight immediately sparkled in the woman's eyes. 'Come in. Come in. And who's this?' Her expression acquired a hint of coyness. 'Do I sense romance in the air?'

Then, noticing Sean's black eye, she went on, 'Have you been in a fight? That's not like you, son. Now, Dermot...'

Sean managed to cut in. 'Chrissie and I are going to get married, Aunty Mary. But Dad and Ma don't approve. Both our families have flung us out and we've nowhere to go.'

'Oh!' Aunty Mary's delight immediately returned. 'Fancy!'

Chrissie could see that, for Aunty Mary, a Mills and Boon plot had come to life at last.

'Well, don't worry, Sean. You've found a safe refuge here and we'll work something out between us. True love always wins in the end. Make yourself at home, Chrissie. Put your case in the front room, son. I'll go and make a pot of tea.' With a spring in her step, she hastened into the kitchen.

Chrissie followed Sean into the front room and was taken aback by the number of religious pictures on the walls. There were pictures of Jesus gazing mournfully upwards and others of him surrounded by lambs or sitting with children kneeling at his feet. Yet another showed a woman washing his feet. There were pictures of the Virgin Mary, with a halo shining above her tragic-looking head, and crosses and rosary beads hanging on hooks.

'Gosh!'

'I did warn you,' Sean said.

'It's all right,' Chrissie assured him, quickly recovering. 'I don't mind really.'

Actually she thought it was not only pathetic and ridiculous but spooky as well. She didn't like the way Jesus was staring at her from every corner. She didn't look forward to undressing under his melancholy gaze. As it turned out, she never got the chance. First off all, they had tea and, encouraged by Aunty Mary who drank in every word with wide-eyed, rapturous attention, went into most of the details of their courtship – not the violence that had forced them to flee but the secret meetings, the furtive goodnights up a close at the top of Wellfield Street. Chrissie would walk the rest of the way to their close on her own. Sean would follow five minutes or so afterwards.

'Oh!' Aunty Mary looked as if she was teetering on the verge of doing a jig of joy. 'How awful romantic.'

Eventually Sean began to yawn widely. Aunty Mary took the hint. But not quite in the way he and Chrissie expected.

'You must be exhausted with all your excitement, son. And you too, Chrissie. I'll fill a hot water bottle for you to take through to the room, Sean. You won't need one, Chrissie. You'll be able to cuddle into me in the nice cosy bed here.'

Chrissie gazed helplessly over at the high 'hole-in-the-wall' bed beside the kitchen range and then at Sean. Sean gazed helplessly back at her.

267

'Right, son.' Aunty Mary was already intent on filling the hot water bottle from the big black kettle that sat simmering on the grate. 'Here you are. There's a po under the bed if you need to perform in the middle of the night. And I've one under this bed that'll do Chrissie and me.' She shook her head in Chrissie's direction. 'That lavvy out there is like the North Pole. Especially in the middle of the night. And you can imagine what it's like juggling with a torch.'

Chrissie could imagine. Nevertheless, she felt she'd rather do the juggling act than perform in Aunty Mary's po. Sean accepted the hot water bottle with a look as tragic as one of the pictures of Jesus.

'Well then...' he said.

'Uh huh.' Aunty Mary was still hanging on his every word.

'Eh, goodnight then.'

'Goodnight, son.'

Chrissie was speechless. She had been looking forward so much to lying in Sean's arms and being lovingly held and reassured.

'Come on, dear.' Aunty Mary was down to her knickers in a flash. She was a real quick mover for an old woman. 'It's long after my bedtime and I'm sure it's the same for you. Get your nightie on and climb up. I'll wait till you're in before I turn off the gas.'

Chrissie began undressing while Aunty Mary donned a voluminous cream flannelette nightdress edged with lace. Then she energetically poked the fire into a cheery blaze.

'Up you go, dear. Can you manage? It's a high

one, that.'

Chrissie was not used to high, hole-in-the-wall beds, indeed any kind of holes in the wall. In Balornock, she slept in a modern, free-standing single bed. She had quite an undignified struggle to clamber up, during which Aunty Mary helped by giving her backside a push. Chrissie was embarrassed and even more so when Aunty Mary cuddled in at her back and clutched her around the waist.

'Isn't this lovely? Goodnight, dear. Sleep tight and don't let the bugs bite.'

It was a horrible image that kept Chrissie awake for some time, as well as longing for Sean. She did sleep eventually, only to be wakened by the tinkling sound of Aunty Mary using the po and then bouncing happily back into bed again. And cuddling her again.

As she told Sean next day while Aunty Mary hurried downstairs to get milk and rolls for their breakfast, 'It was terrible, Sean. I hardly slept a wink.'

'I know. I was the same. But we'll go out today again and look for a wee flat of our own. And we'll get the wedding all organised. We've to put up banns or something first. They'll tell us at the registry office how long it'll all take. It'll be a few weeks at least but that'll give us plenty of time to get organised.'

'You make it sound like a big affair. It'll be only the two of us at the registry office, won't it?'

'Yes. We've no choice about that, Chrissie.'

'I know. It's just – I can't help imagining what it would be like to have a big family celebration

269

with all our folks there and a big cake and everything, and me in a lovely long dress and veil and holding a bouquet of flowers.'

'I'm so sorry, Chrissie.'

'It's not your fault. Me and my silly imagination. As long as we can be together, Sean, that's all that matters.'

He gathered her into his arms and she felt happy then. Grateful too. Sean was not only a kind and loving man, he was tall, dark and handsome, sexy too. She gladly succumbed to his kiss and was just at the point of deep, swooning arousal when she heard the front door open and a cheery voice cry out, 'It's only me, folks.' Into the kitchen bustled Aunty Mary. 'You're going to enjoy this,' she announced. 'That baker down there makes the best rolls for miles around. And I've got plenty of butter so don't stint yourselves.'

It was terribly frustrating and Chrissie could hardly wait to get outside. Sean said, 'She means well.'

'Och, I know. She's really an awful nice wee soul. I suppose we'll just have to try and be patient.'

She was on the afternoon shift at the Mitchell and Sean had arranged for a couple of days off. Chrissie and Sean had thought of inviting Sammy and his wife Julie to their registry office wedding. They'd need witnesses after all. But they'd decided against it eventually. For one thing, it would mean Sammy and Julie taking time off work. For another, it would be an added blow, they supposed, to the family that strangers had been at the ceremony instead of them. Although Sammy and

Julie weren't strangers as such and the family would never have agreed to come. Ailish would be too frightened of 'a doing' or of being flung out of the house if she came. So there it was. All stupid and unnecessary. All the same, Chrissie decided to go to Copeland & Lye's and tell Ailish. At least she would have the chance to come to the wedding ceremony.

Sean said, 'As long as our families don't do anything else to try and stop us.'

'How do you mean?' Chrissie felt suddenly anxious. 'They couldn't, could they?'

'No, no,' Sean said hastily. 'We're both of age. There's nothing in law anybody can do.'

But the anxiety didn't go away.

36

'Are you all right, Julie?' Sammy asked. He had come in from work, gone into the kitchen as usual and, finding it empty and the house unusually quiet, he'd looked into the front room. Julie was standing gazing wistfully out of the window.

'Yes, fine.' She turned towards him, avoiding his eyes.

'You never mention Alice these days, but you're obviously still thinking of her.'

'I've never stopped thinking of her. I never will. I've just decided it would be best for her if I didn't contact her, that's all.'

'She's doing well, isn't she?'

271

'Yes, I've heard Mrs Robertson talking about her a few times. She's been studying to be a doctor. A doctor, Sammy. Isn't it wonderful? She must be almost finished her studies by now. I can just imagine her going around the wards in her white coat, with her stethoscope round her neck.'

Sammy went over and gathered her into his arms.

'You know, Julie, I've been thinking. Now that she's settled in a career, it surely wouldn't do any harm to get in touch with her. No doubt Mrs Robertson has long since told her that she was adopted and it's not as if she's a child any more. There wouldn't be the same risk of her getting a shock or being upset. I really believe it would be all right.'

'Maybe I'm getting old, but I feel too nervous. What if she didn't want to have anything to do with me, didn't like me? Despised me, even, for giving her away?' Julie shook her head. 'And what would she think of me moving here and spying on her and her family?'

'She would be touched that you loved and wanted her so much that you felt you had to be near her.'

'I doubt it, Sammy. It's been so deceitful of me. I've even spoken to Mrs Robertson. What would she think of me if she found out who I really am?'

'She would be touched that you loved Alice and missed her so much that you had to be near her. And she would appreciate how you never tried to interfere or influence Alice or try to get her back when she was a child.'

'I've left it too late.'

'Nonsense. I'm going through to put the kettle on.'

'Oh, Sammy, I'm sorry. I should have had your tea all ready. I don't know what's wrong with me today. Maybe it was overhearing that conversation about Alice in the butcher's. It brought it all back again. There's never a day passes when I don't think of her at some time in some way, but I really believed I had everything, all my feelings, subdued, under control, you know. But now, here I am again...'

'It's perfectly understandable.' Sammy led her away from the window of the room. 'Now, sit down by the fire and I'll make the tea. What'll we have? Scrambled eggs?'

'No, no. I'd rather keep myself busy. I've a couple of meat pies to heat up. That butcher has such good pies. You can set the table if you like. I'll make some chips.'

As she stood cutting the potatoes at the sink, even her back showed her unhappiness, Sammy thought. His heart went out to her and he longed to do something to help banish her misery once and for all.

'It would be such a lovely Christmas present for Alice – to find her real mother and to be reunited with her.'

Julie turned to smile at him. 'There you go again.'

'Well, wouldn't it?'

'Sammy, if she had wanted to be reunited with me, she would have tried to find me long ago.'

'There could be several reasons why she hasn't.'

'Such as?'

'Mrs Robertson might not have told her she's adopted. But I doubt that. Lots of people tell their children that they're adopted as soon as they're able to understand. They usually explain that the child is special – especially chosen and wanted.'

'I agree. OK, the chances are Alice knows. So why hasn't she got in touch?'

'One of the most likely reasons is that she doesn't want to hurt or appear disloyal to the woman who has brought her up and has obviously been so loving and good to her. I've heard of several cases where that has happened. A colleague of mine in the Red Cross and his wife actually told their adopted son that they don't mind if he tries to find his biological mother, but the boy refuses to do so. He insists they have always been his parents and always will be. Loyalty, you see.'

'And love.'

'Yes, of course, and Alice loves Mrs Robertson. You must accept that, Julie.'

Julie nodded. 'I do. And I know that I don't deserve any of Alice's love. I never will.'

'Oh, stop feeling so sorry for yourself and do something about it. I always believed you had more spirit than that.'

'Cheeky devil!' Some of the sparkle flashed back into Julie's eyes. 'I've plenty of spirit, don't you worry.'

'And you'll do something about it?'

She turned away again. 'We'll see.'

He imagined she sounded more positive, more determined, and he felt glad. He had always admired her perky bravado in the face of difficulty and the courage that lay underneath it. He admired her but most of all he loved her and he knew that, no matter what happened, they could face it and get through it together.

He fetched the tablecloth from the dresser drawer and smoothed it over the table. His mother had embroidered the cloth for them as a wedding present. As he set the table with cutlery and china, he experienced an unexpected glow of happiness. How lucky he was to have such a beautiful and loving wife. How wonderful it was to be together in their perfect, homely house. To other eyes, it might only look like an ordinary one-bedroomed, grey stone tenement flat but, to him and Julie, it was perfection. A haven of comfort and privacy and love. Quite apart from what might happen with Alice – and he hoped and prayed that there would be a happy reunion of mother and daughter – they had another Christmas and New Year to look forward to.

They had been invited to a Christmas party at Madge and Alec's house. That would be a really noisy occasion with such a big family but it would be good fun. Catriona was going to be there too. A real happy-go-lucky bloke at heart, Alec usually had them all laughing, even Madge. Alec was always at his best in company. Many another man would have gone under with Madge's overpowering personality – not to mention her voice – and with the house forever packed with so many squabbling offspring. Most young people nowadays were flying the nest, going to college or university and living in halls of residence on

275

university campuses. But not Alec's brood. Madge often said, or bawled more like, 'Am I never going to get rid of you lot?'

She didn't want to, of course. Madge was all mouth. Always had been. But it must be very wearing for poor Alec living under the same roof as her and such a noisy family all the time.

No wonder he was glad to escape to work, or to go to the pub with Sammy after work, and to matches every Saturday afternoon. They were looking forward to the 1971 New Year Old Firm match in a few weeks' time, at Ibrox, although neither of them relished the prospect of all the fighting and trouble usually involved.

Since Sammy had joined the Red Cross, he and Alec had to separate during the match if he was on duty. Then they'd meet up for a drink in a pre-arranged pub afterwards.

This time, with it being such a big match with such a huge potential for trouble and injury, every Red Cross man and St John Ambulance man that could be mustered would be on duty.

But first there was the Christmas party to look forward to. Then, on Hogmanay, Madge and Alec and Catriona were coming to 'first-foot' them. They were going to pick up his mother in Springburn on the way and bring her out to Bishopbriggs with them. So far, thank God, his father had not come after his mother. He had obviously taken the threat to his reputation to heart. Some people might have believed his excuse about burying the dog thinking the animal was already dead. But, if his wife and son spilled the beans about what a monster he'd been behind closed doors for so many years, he really would be finished. Without a friend in the world – if he wasn't in that situation already.

The word 'friend' reminded Sammy of the Society of Friends and he felt a twinge of guilt. He should not, he knew, feel any satisfaction at anyone not having a friend in the world. He tried to banish Friends with a capital F from his mind. He felt suddenly angry at them as well as himself. What could they know about such a man as old Hodge Hunter? Talk about optimists! He felt himself shivering inside with secret fury. If there was anything inside Hodge Hunter, it was the Devil. Evil old bastard!

As Sammy set the table with the cruet and the bottle of HP sauce, the sugar bowl and the milk jug, he felt a terrible confusion in his mind, as well as the anger. He couldn't rid himself of an element of guilt and of the part of himself that, like it or not, was a Quaker. At that moment, he hated Quakerism for making things so impossibly complicated in situations like this.

Deep down he knew that hatred itself was wrong. Hatred, bitterness, all these negative emotions only harmed oneself. It didn't matter who or what was the target of that hatred.

Of one thing he was absolutely certain – according to everything he believed in, to leave his father, now a very old man, alone at Christmas was wrong.

Bloody hell!

37

Despite the danger of being found out, Ailish had volunteered to come to the wedding in the registry office and then for a modest meal at Miss Cranston's Tearoom afterwards. Chrissie and Sean couldn't afford a licensed place – they could only toast each other in cups of tea. They were desperately trying to save up. At first, for a few mad minutes, they had considered inviting their respective parents, and even Maimie and Dermot. They had imagined a last-minute reconciliation at the wedding ceremony but they soon realised that it was only a pipe dream.

'It would have been so nice. If only...' Chrissie sighed.

'Yes,' Ailish interrupted. 'If only ... if only. How many times in our lives have we said that, Chrissie? But we might as well face it. They'll never be any different and, if they came to the registry office, it would only be to fight with each other and spoil what should be a happy day for you.'

'Well, I'm glad at least you're coming, Ailish.'

'Who's to be the other witness or best man or whatever?'

'A pal of Sean's from the office. We thought of inviting Sammy but that would have meant Julie as well and maybe even Catriona and Andrew. Apart from anything else, we just can't afford any more for the tea. We'll need every penny we can scrape together to get a place of our own and buy furniture and everything. I know it sounds awful but...'

'No, it doesn't.'

'We're really desperate to get away from Aunty Mary's. Not that we've anything against her personally,' Chrissie added hastily. 'It's so kind of her to have taken us in the way she did. But we never get a minute to ourselves – not to talk, not to do anything. We're nearly going mad with frustration. The only way she would recognise us getting married is if we tied the knot in the chapel. She never stops trying to talk us into it. I'd have given in for the sake of peace but Sean'll have none of it.'

'Good for Sean. It's the only way to stop all this nonsense carrying on from one generation to the next. We've got to make a stand, beat the bigotry, not let it beat us.'

'Easier said than done.'

'I know, but you and Sean are making a start.'

'Do you think you'll be next?'

'Marrying out of the faith, do you mean? Well, I must admit I won't go looking for trouble and a Protestant lover.' She grinned. 'I'll just look for a lover. If he turns out to be a Catholic, fine. If not, hard luck, Mammy, Daddy and Dermot.'

They had been having a cup of tea together in Copeland's in Ailish's lunch break. They had already tried to decide what to wear at the wedding, without success. Again it was a question of money. Chrissie brought up the subject once more and Ailish said, 'Well, mini skirts are out. I haven't the legs for them. Anyway, midi length is more fashionable now.'

'Yes, I think I'll settle for my navy wool suit. I'll brighten it up with a new blouse and a pretty matching ribbon for my hat. Or a wee posy of flowers, maybe.'

'We're both lucky we still have a hat. Hardly anyone wears them now, except on special occasions.'

'I know. You'll be wearing yours then?'

'Of course. Don't worry. I won't let you down.' Chrissie felt a rush of affection for her friend.

'I know you'd never do that, Ailish.'

It was true what she'd told Ailish about their desperation to get away from Aunty Mary's flat or at least to be able to share a bed there after they were married. Aunty Mary had made it clear that she would not, could not, recognise any marriage other than the one blessed by God at a proper, holy ceremony led by the priest in the chapel. They were welcome to stay on with her after the registry office wedding but only if they were willing to continue with the same sleeping arrangements as before. Aunty Mary still avidly read her romance novels but they were obviously completely devoid of anything of a sexual nature. In Aunty Mary's novels, the story of the happy couple always ended on the outside of the bedroom door.

Now they were afraid that Aunty Mary would accidentally let slip to the family the date of the wedding. She might even, with the best of intentions of course, tell Teresa and Michael so that they could talk them out of it, as she had tried to do.

As Sean kept saying, 'She doesn't mean any harm.'

But a great deal of harm could be caused if the family found out the exact date. They might turn up at the registry office and cause the ceremony to become a nightmare event or even stop it happening altogether. It didn't bear thinking about. Sean worried about it as well.

'Is it just a Glasgow thing, I wonder? he said one day, thinking aloud.

'Is what a Glasgow thing?' Chrissie asked.

'All this religious stuff. Especially at football matches.'

'I don't know. But now you mention it, I haven't ever read about anything like that happening in London, for instance.'

'All the chanting and bawling out sectarian songs.' He shrugged. 'It might be the same in Wembley Stadium but I doubt it.'

'Well, maybe we should be looking for a flat in London.' Chrissie laughed. 'Near Wembley Stadium, of course.'

Sean took her seriously.

'Maybe we should,' he said.

38

Sammy and Alec had been sitting in the Boundary Bar talking over a pint about how so much of old Glasgow was divided into predominantly Catholic or Protestant areas. The new housing schemes built by the Glasgow Corporation were an attempt to eradicate this problem. Up Alec's close, for instance, and in Balornock in general, there was now more of a mixture of different religions.

'But take a Protestant place like Larkhall,' Alec said. 'One of the fastest things on earth is a Catholic going through Larkhall on a bike.'

Sammy laughed. Being with Alec always cheered him up.

'There doesn't seem much, if any, of a problem in Bishopbriggs. Not as far as I've seen anyway. And one of the priests – Father Kelly – is well liked and respected by other flocks as well as his own.'

'Well, good for the people of Bishopbriggs! Can you imagine the likes of Jimmy Stoddart respecting a priest or feeling anything towards him except hatred?'

It was then that Sammy remembered his own hatred.

'What's up?' Alec immediately sensed his change of mood.

'I was just thinking I'm not much better than Jimmy.'

'What?' Alec's voice careered up to squeaking point with incredulity. 'You've never had a bigoted, sectarian or discriminating thought in your life, Sammy.'

'I've felt hatred. I feel hatred. The worst kind – against my own flesh and blood.'

Alec rolled his eyes. 'You mean your old man? For God's sake, Sammy, no one knowing what your father's put you through could blame you for that.'

'I wonder what the Friends with a capital F would say – try to separate the doer from the deed, I expect.'

'How are you supposed to do that?'

Sammy shrugged and couldn't think of any answer. Then, after a few thoughtful moments, Alec said,

'I wonder what on earth made your father into such an awful old devil. After all, he was once a wee baby and a wee toddler, like the rest of us. I mean, even my lot seemed angelic when they were that age. I wonder where things go wrong? What kind of background did your father have? What were his parents like?'

Sammy stared at Alec.

'Do you know, Alec, I've never thought of it like that. Not once.'

'Do you remember your granny and grandpa?'

There was another pause.

'Funnily enough, when my grandfather visited us, that's when I have some of my most vivid memories of my father. He was always worse when his father was there. I dreaded the visits because of that. And because of that my whole attention was on my father. I can hardly remember what my grandfather even looked like.'

'What about your grandmother?'

'She must have died earlier. I've no recollection of ever seeing her at all.'

'That's odd, isn't it?'

'What? Not ever seeing my grandmother?'

'No, how your father was always at his worst when his father was there. I would have thought it more likely to be the other way around. You know, that he'd be on his best behaviour to make a good impression.'

'Well, I certainly don't remember it like that. It was almost as if he was showing off how he could terrorise the whole family, including my mother.'

'Maybe he was.'

Another pause.

'That's a thought,' Sammy said. 'Maybe that's the sort of behaviour that impressed his father.'

'Sounds as if his own father could have been even worse.'

Sammy couldn't quite get his head around that but the thought drifted about at the back of his mind like a dark shadow or an unwelcome ghost.

'Enough about my family tree,' he told Alec. 'Julie wants to know what she should cook for your Sadie and Agnes. Are they still vegetarians?'

'Och, if it's not one fad, it's another with them. Catriona doesn't help either. Telling them all about herbs and stuff. She'll be having them eating grass next.'

'I suppose there's worse things that they could get into.'

'How's Catriona bearing up, by the way? Julie

284

sees more of her than anybody now.'

'About Melvin being whipped off to the hospital, you mean? I think at first she thought it was just another ploy to get her back. So did I, to be honest. But, no, according to the hospital he's suffering from pretty bad emphysema. Catriona says all those years of chain-smoking have finally got to him. I don't think there's much they can do for him now.'

'Has she been in to see him?'

'Yes. Julie says she forces herself for Andrew's sake. He's been so good and attentive to his father, that boy. Far better than Fergus. Yet Fergus was always Melvin's favourite. Fergus is always coming up with some excuse or other about being too busy and not being able to manage to get down to Glasgow. You'd think he was on the other side of the world, instead of just up in Aberdeen.'

'Funny that.'

'Yes, it's a funny old life,' Sammy said, not thinking it was funny at all. He knew what Catriona must be feeling. She hated Melvin and, as far as Sammy knew, with good reason. He felt disturbed again as the shadows at the back of his mind threatened to slink forward.

'Ask Sadie and Agnes if they've got a favourite veggie dish, will you?'

'Oh, right. Fancy another pint?'

Sammy shook his head. 'I'd better be getting home. I've promised to put the decorations up.'

'There's hardly enough room in our house for decorations. By the way, you know you and Julie would be more than welcome at our Boxing Day do but I doubt if you could squeeze in. Sadie and

Agnes's boyfriends are coming and Hector and Willie's girlfriends. The place is going to be bursting at the seams and absolute bedlam. I don't recommend it. Thank goodness they'll all be away at New Year. There's some big do in Edinburgh they're all going to and they'll be there for two or three days. Sadie and Hector have begun to talk about having a double wedding in the spring so they should both be moving out then. I'm going to race down to the housing office and put their names on the waiting list myself, before they get a chance to change their minds.'

'Right enough, it's time they were all married and in places of their own. They must feel too happy and content at home, Alec. You're too good to them.'

'Time I took a leaf out of your father's book then.'

'You couldn't. It's not in you. You're far too good natured. Always have been.'

They had arrived out on the busy Springburn Road.

'See you,' Sammy added with a wave.

'Aye, OK, pal.'

For a moment, Sammy watched Alec's tall figure swagger away, hat on the back of his head, whistling jauntily. Then he went off to catch his bus back to Bishopbriggs. When he got in, Julie was ready to dish his meal up and afterwards, they enjoyed decorating the house with a riot of coloured paper chains and balloons. Already the mantelpiece and dresser were covered with early Christmas cards. It was a bit early for the decorations as well but Julie was so looking forward to the festive season.

Sammy's enjoyment was slightly forced. He didn't feel happy deep down. He hoped that going to church on Sunday would soothe his troubled spirit. It usually made him feel better and so did the cup of tea and chat to everyone afterwards. Julie had long since got into the habit of going with him and it seemed to help her too.

The following Sunday, although nobody openly gave him the reassurance he sought, they all sat in silence. A calmness washed over him and reached deep inside him and he knew, for the first time, without any hatred or bitterness, what he must do.

Julie was astonished when next day he announced to her that he was going to visit his father.

'I don't want to worry Mother. So don't mention it to her. There's no need for her to know. At least not right now.'

'She's so happy at the moment.'

'I know.'

'Why should you go, Sammy, after all this time?'

He shrugged. 'He's a very old man. He can't do me any harm any more. And he is my father.'

'Do you want me to come with you?'

'No, no. This is something I have to do on my own.'

And so he made the journey that he'd thought he'd never make again. It was snowing and the air was a haze of white. His feet sunk deeper and deeper into the snow as he came nearer and nearer to the lonely back road and the isolated cottage. He could hardly see it until he was almost at the garden gate. After quite a long struggle to open the gate – the snow was piled so deeply on either side it just wouldn't budge – he vaulted over it, sinking knee-deep into the snow on the other side. The gate obviously hadn't moved for some time. He had a bad feeling about that.

Eventually he got to the cottage door. He knocked loudly at it and stood waiting. No sound. He turned the handle and the door opened. The first thing that met him was the smell. It was sickening, disgusting.

Rubbish, bits of paper, dirty clothes, even rotting food, lay about the hall floor. He picked his way into the sitting room and found his father sitting on his big chair but not filling it like he used to. Here was a bent, gaunt skeleton of a man, a mere shadow of what he had been. Sammy was shocked.

There was no fire in the grate and the old man looked blue with cold. God alone knew when he'd last eaten. He must have needed help but of course he'd been too proud and 'thrawn' to seek it.

'I'll make you a cup of tea, Father.'

The old man's rheumy eyes swivelled round at him.

'Can ye no' offer me something better than that? A wee half maybe?'

'If I can find some.' Sammy searched in the sideboard, found nothing but eventually dug a bottle out of a cupboard in the kitchen. He handed his father a glass of the amber liquid but had to hold it to the old man's mouth.

'Here, get this down you.'

Hodge smacked his lips. 'By God, that was good.'

'Is there anything in the house to eat?'

'Can ye no' eat in yer own house?'

'I mean for you. I'll cook you something.'

'I don't know. I can't be bothered getting up off this chair any more.'

'Have you had the doctor look at you?'

'Are you deaf or something? I can't get around the house, never mind get out to a doctor. Who are you, anyway?'

Sammy was taken aback.

'I'm Sammy, Father.'

'Sammy? Samuel? From the Old Testament?'

'No, Sammy. Your youngest son.'

'I don't remember you. Where have you been?'

'I'll make you something to eat, Father.'

All he could find in the kitchen was a tin of Heinz tomato soup. He opened it and heated it. He felt so terrible, he hardly knew how he was going to be able to cope, what he should do next.

He had to spoon the soup into the old man's mouth. He was obviously too weak to feed himself.

Eventually he said, 'Now I'm going to carry you through to bed, Father, and fill a hot water bottle to keep you warm until I go and fetch the doctor. We'll see what he says and then decide what to do for the best. All right?'

'What was it you did in the Bible again?'

'Never mind about that just now.'

The old man felt like a bag of bones and Sammy could have wept at the awfulness of it all. He got him settled in bed with the hot water bottle.

'Now, you're going to be all right, Father. I won't be long. I'll be back as soon as I can with the doctor.'

'Aye, Hannah was your mother's name. What was your father's name again?'

Sammy escaped outside and stumbled as fast as he could through the snow.

'God forgive me,' he thought. 'Please, God, forgive me.'

39

To say that she was surprised would be the understatement of the year. Catriona was astonished when Julie told her that Sammy had been to see his father. She'd always understood that Sammy hated Hodge Hunter. And with good reason, as far as she could see. Sometimes she even thought that what she and Sammy had most in common was hatred and their understanding of that emotion. He couldn't have changed, surely. She hadn't changed though, for a time, she thought she had – to some degree, at least. Often the only emotion she felt for Melvin was pity.

He had changed so much, especially physically. The change had been caused by the war and she couldn't blame him for that. The war had wrecked him physically and, she often suspected, emotionally and mentally as well. That was another thing she and Sammy had in common –

their abiding hatred of war. Sammy's beliefs now went even deeper. To him, peace was not simply the absence of war, it was a vision of human wholeness. He seemed so idealistic at times, and Julie was the same these days. They both believed in living adventurously, though, which certainly seemed wise to Catriona and something she wished she had taken to heart much sooner in her own life. Sammy and Julie's religious beliefs also led them to hope for reconciliation between all sorts of unlikely people. It was all pie in the sky to Catriona. She knew from bitter personal experience that there were some people with whom it was simply impossible to be reconciled, no matter how hard you tried. The Quakers obviously meant well but where had their God of love been when she had needed him?

She even doubted if she could be sure of any love from Andrew any more. But, oh, how she was trying to deserve it. He wanted her to be reconciled with Melvin and visit him more regularly at the hospital and she'd forced herself to go. It was during these visits that her hatred had taken root again and outweighed any pity she felt for Melvin.

If she was alone with him for any length of time before Andrew arrived, or on those rare occasions when Andrew couldn't manage to visit, Melvin would nag at her in the same way he always had. She would sit watching the bitter downward twist of his mouth and keep silent. He was also beginning to sound more like her mother every day. He too had begun to say things like how wicked she was for deserting him, and how God would punish her. Meantime, he was doing his nasty, malicious best to punish her himself.

He'd told her that he'd already made the house over to Fergus. 'I know you,' he'd said, 'if anything happened to me, even though Fergus was supposed to inherit my house, you'd contest the will. You'd try to claim at least half. Well, this way, you'll never get anything because the house legally belongs to Fergus now. I've explained to him it's just for his legal protection so that, after I die, if he wants to sell it, the proceeds'll go to him. Every penny. Andrew will get the business.'

'What business?' she thought. The place was barely making a profit any more, despite Baldy Fowler's best efforts.

She listened to Melvin in silence, only able to do so by repeating over and over again in her mind, 'For Andrew. For Andrew. Smile for Andrew's sake. Suffer it, suffer him, suffer anything, suffer everything for Andrew's sake.'

And certainly Andrew's attitude had at least softened towards her. He was pleased and grateful that she was acting in what appeared such a kind and compassionate way to his precious dad.

Melvin was a different man when Andrew was there. His sour face would break into a sweet smile of welcome and he'd put out a hand to Andrew, who'd lovingly clasp it in his.

Maybe Sammy had forced himself to go and see his father for much the same reason as she went to see Melvin. Maybe it was to please his mother although she found that hard to understand. Why on earth would his mother want him to have anything to do with that old horror?

Next time she saw Sammy, maybe she'd get the chance to talk to him about it. Then it occurred to her – perhaps it was something to do with Christmas, the time of peace and love, forgiveness and goodwill to all men and all that. Yet, as far as she'd understood it, Quakers didn't give oh! extra emphasis or value to any particular day. They had no calendar of specially significant events. So it couldn't just be about Christmas.

Catriona herself dreaded Christmas. It was all very well for the likes of Julie and Sammy. They had their love for each other – and Julie had her love for her daughter. She still clung to the hope that one day they would be reunited. Their love made their wee room and kitchen in Bishopbriggs a place of peace and sanctuary, as well as hope. She really liked to visit them there and, no matter what state she had been in before she arrived, she always came away feeling better. She couldn't quite put her finger on the reason. Maybe the loving atmosphere of their home was somehow infectious. She tried to tell herself not to be so daft and think things like that. At the same time, there was no denying that she cheered when she visited Sammy and Julie. They did have some interesting evenings at their house, lively discussions about all sorts of things, with fascinating and unexpected people.

Julie said that's what they did at the end of their Quaker meeting every Sunday – everyone shook hands at the end of it. Once, Julie had said, 'We'll get you there yet, Catriona.'

She'd replied, 'No way!'

Sammy had looked quite annoyed. Not at her but at Julie.

'You shouldn't do that, Julie.'

'What?' Julie looked surprised.

'Try to put pressure on Catriona or anyone to go to Meeting.'

'I wasn't putting pressure on her.'

'It's all right,' Catriona assured Sammy. 'Even the word *worship* puts me off.'

Sammy said, 'I know what you mean. It can sound as if it means bowing and scraping before some tyrannical master. But in fact the word derives from the word *worth* – we see it as the time we give to finding worth in our lives.'

It was all very interesting but did it help her situation, her problems? Could anything help her problem with Melvin? Those moments of relaxation and peace at Julie and Sammy's, those moments of appreciating the love that she experienced there did help to keep her going in a way. And they were such good friends.

Maybe if she paid them a wee visit before Christmas this time ... but before she could make that visit, something happened that neither Julie nor Sammy could help her with.

40

Hodge Hunter was removed to Stobhill Hospital and promptly transferred from there to a nursing home. Beds in the hospital were more urgently needed. Hodge had been diagnosed as suffering from dementia and it was obvious that he had to be in a nursing home from now on in order to get proper care and attention.

'He'll be comfortable and safe here, don't worry,' Sammy was told. It had all happened so quickly, Sammy found it difficult to grasp the situation and get on with ordinary life. He had taken time off work to organise everything and was glad to be able to do so and to see his father safely settled. The old man seemed perfectly happy now. Away in a world of his own but happy. His mother seemed happy too. He thought she'd be very upset but not a bit of it. It was as if she was in a world of her own too. She actually visited the home and sat by the old man's bedside chatting to him.

After the Christmas party was over, Sammy went to clear out the cottage. He had been going to leave it until after Hogmanay but then decided it would be better to start the New Year afresh with all the mess behind him and everything more or less organised. Julie went with him and between them, they swept out the sea of rubbish and mopped the floors and all the surfaces with numerous buckets of strong disinfectant.

Sammy told Julie to go home eventually because she looked so tired. 'I'll just stay for another half hour to clear out some of the papers in his desk.'

'All right, I'll have the tea ready.' She kissed him. 'Don't be too long.'

After she left, Sammy sat down at his father's old roll-top desk and began pulling papers from pigeon holes, glancing through them, tidying some and tearing up others. He opened a drawer and found several notebooks. Another drawer held several more. He discovered, on opening one of the books, that in fact it was a diary. He hesitated to read the small, neat writing but curiosity overcame him. He read on, unable to stop, well into the night. Then eventually, emotionally and physically drained, he shut the desk, leaned across it and wept. His father's diaries had revealed the life of a man he had never known – and the child he had never even guessed at. The tormented, abused child with the strong ambition, as he reached a twisted manhood, of finally getting his revenge on the world.

'We're all just victims of victims,' he thought. 'Why did that never occur to me before?'

Eventually he wiped his face dry and left the house. He was glad of the snow now and the biting cold wind. He needed it to clear his head and help him find some sort of normality before having to face Julie.

'Sammy!' She ran along the lobby to greet him. 'I've been so worried. What happened?'

'I got carried away reading the old man's

diaries. A lot of them went back to his childhood. Sorry I've taken so long. I should have phoned you from the nearest phone box in Balornock. I never thought.'

'As long as you're all right.'

'Yes, fine. I'm glad we got the house cleared and organised. We can forget it now.'

He never wanted to set foot in the place again. Let his brothers do what they liked with it now. That is, if they ever returned to Glasgow. He suspected that they'd only come for their father's funeral. If they even came for that. Not that he blamed them. The way he felt now, he'd never blame anyone for anything ever again.

He was glad now to be going to the big match. It would take his mind off everything else. Alec was looking forward to it – as was every man in Glasgow. Well, maybe not every man. Jehovah's Witnesses John McKechnie and his son Peter would never go near Ibrox Park. They thought football was a sin. Alec maintained they thought everything was a sin. Also up Alec's close was the Pater family. Alec said they believed in keeping themselves to themselves. Alec said he thought the Paters did karate just to warn everybody off.

Jimmy Stoddart would be there with all his Orange Order pals. And Michael, Dermot and Sean O'Donnel wouldn't miss the Old Firm match for the world. They would be at the Catholic end of the park, of course, but not together as a family this time.

Sammy put on his uniform, remembering how the Red Cross had to change the berets they used to wear to caps. The berets had been the cause of

297

some attacks on Red Cross men. Some idiots had decided they must be IRA supporters because IRA men wore berets.

He kissed Julie goodbye.

'Now don't you be getting drunk with Alec afterwards,' she said and he laughed. They both knew he'd never been drunk in his life and only enjoyed the occasional pint of beer. Two or three at the most.

It was a dull, misty day with cold, blustery showers. The pitch was muddy-looking and puddled. Sammy didn't think it was a good idea to play the match in such conditions but knew that there would have to be an earthquake way up the Richter scale before anyone would agree to cancel it.

It soon became obvious that the O'Donnels would be in their element. Sammy could just imagine Dermot singing his heart out, giving 'Land of my Fathers' everything he'd got. Celtic were having a good game, especially when wee Jimmy Johnson scored with a header. The crowd at the Rangers end had begun to leave, were already on stairway thirteen.

Then, hallelujah, Colin Stein stuck one in for Rangers in a goal-mouth scramble. In the very last minute of the game. There was a huge roar and all hell broke loose.

Sammy saw the crush on the stairway. It looked worse than usual. Instinctively, he made his way towards it. As he got nearer, he began to run. So did several policemen. People were being lifted off their feet by the pressure of the crowd. People were slowly falling. Then the crowd stopped moving but the pressure obviously continued because the air was filled with agonised shouts and cries. But, as time went on, these decreased until there was almost silence.

Desperately, Sammy and other ambulance men and police fought to pull people from the crowd and lay them gently down on the field. Nurses arrived and everyone tried to help the injured and the dying. Men and young boys with shocked faces and crushed ribs were given oxygen or mouth-to-mouth resuscitation. Others were carried to the main stand for medical attention.

Amidst all this chaos and horror, Sammy caught sight of Alec's tall figure. He saw him being crushed forward, saw his ashen, blood-smeared face. Like a maniac, Sammy fought his way towards Alec and, praying for a miracle, managed to pull him out.

Lying on the grass, Alec opened his eyes and looked up at Sammy. Sammy cradled him in his arms and leaned his head down close to Alec's face. He was barely breathing.

'Alec,' Sammy said. Alec's eyes closed. 'Alec,' Sammy repeated. 'Friend with a capital F.'

And he believed Alec heard him because he saw a ghost of a smile.

Teresa O'Donnel wondered what all the noise was in the close. But there was usually a lot of noise and singing and carry-on late into the night after an Old Firm match. She opened her front door and listened more intently. It wasn't the usual sort of noise. It sounded like weeping and wailing. Incredibly, it sounded like Madge Jackson. What on earth could be wrong with her? Cautiously, hugging her woolly cardigan tighter over her chest, Teresa ventured down the stairs. The Jackson door was lying open.

'Madge?' Teresa was breathless with the stairs but she managed to call louder, 'Madge, are you all right, hen?'

A distressed-looking Catriona McNair appeared in the lobby. 'Oh, it's you, Teresa. Come in.' Her voice lowered. 'It's terrible. Alec's been killed at Ibrox. Madge is demented.'

'Holy Mother of God!' Teresa whispered. 'The poor soul.' Her eyes suddenly widened. 'Here, my man and one of my boys were at the match.'

'They'll be all right, don't worry. The accident was at the Rangers end.'

Feeling shaken nevertheless, Teresa followed Catriona into the living room, where Madge was thrashing about, sobbing uncontrollably with Julie hanging onto her and trying to clam her down.

Catriona said, 'I'll go and put the kettle on.'

Teresa gazed in distress at Madge. 'Ah'm that sorry, hen. Alec was such a nice big fella, everybody liked him.'

Madge's tragic face fixed on Teresa. 'He was always that good to me and the weans.'

'Aye, Ah know. He thought the world of you and the weans.'

'Did he? Do you really think he did, Teresa?' Madge asked, suddenly, pathetically subdued.

'Of course he did, hen. Ah swear in the name of the Virgin Mary.' She crossed herself. 'Your man thought the world of you, so he did. A lovely big man he was as well. Just try to be glad of aw the time you had him, hen. He wouldnae want you to be so upset now, would he?'

Still weeping, Madge sank into a chair, wiping her face with the back of her sleeve. 'Thanks, Teresa.'

'Nothing to thank me for, hen.'

Catriona came through with the tea, the cups rattling noisily on a tray.

'While I was waiting for the kettle to boil, Sammy looked in. He said to tell you, Julie, that he'd be downstairs at the Stoddarts. Jimmy Stoddart has been killed as well and Aggie's on her own. There's sixty-five dead and another man looks as if he won't last the night. And over a hundred injured.' *Just at a football match. Ugh.*

'Holy Mother of God,' Teresa said. 'Is that no' terrible? Poor Aggie as well. Maybe I should go down and show a bit of support.'

Teresa looked anxiously around as if hoping that someone would contradict her. Big Aggie was not someone Teresa ever had any desire to visit. Nor had she the slightest desire now.

But Catriona said, 'That would be really kind of you, Teresa. She'll appreciate a woman being with her.'

With sinking heart, Teresa shuffled reluctantly towards the door. Before leaving, she turned to Madge. 'Try to keep your pecker up, hen. An' Ah'll see ye again soon.'

Lips trembling, Madge nodded.

Downstairs, Teresa timidly knocked at the Stoddarts' door. It was opened by Sammy who

301

led her into the living room. 'Aggie,' Teresa said, 'Ah've just come doon from seeing Madge. She's lost Alec an' she's in an awful state, poor soul. It's terrible, so it is. Now Ah've just heard about Jimmy. It's terrible, so it is. Such a nice wee man, Jimmy.' It was a lie – she'd never thought Jimmy Stoddart a nice man. 'Ah'm that sorry, Aggie. How are ye, hen?'

Big Aggie had been sitting, straight-backed, like a giant iceberg. Suddenly, with Teresa's words, the ice melted, her body shrank, the flesh seeming to hang loose and water cascaded silently and unchecked down her flaccid cheeks. It was a terrible sight – not like Big Aggie at all.

'Oh, Ah'm that sorry, hen,' Teresa repeated and hurried over to put a comforting arm around Big Aggie's shoulders. Big Aggie unexpectedly clutched at Teresa and gripped her to her now-heaving bosom.

'What'll Ah dae?'

'Ye'll be aw right, hen.' Teresa struggled for breath.

'Ah've naebody,' Big Aggie wailed.

'Chrissie an' Maimie...'

'You know fine Chrissie's no use. An' Maimie's joined the army. Could you beat it? The bloody army and her a lassie. She's gone off her heid. Ah shouted at him before he went.'

'Jimmy, you mean?'

'Aye. Ah told him Ah'd batter him if he got drunk and got into any trouble.'

'Och, Ah dae the same to Michael.'

This was so obviously untrue that Big Aggie actually managed a quivery smile. 'What a

302

bloody liar!'

'Well, OK, Ah huvnae the strength tae actually batter him. But many a time Ah'd like to. Oh aye, Ah'd like to and that's no' a lie. Him an' his drinkin' an' fightin' an' carryin' on. Every week he's the same, no' just at Auld Firm games.'

Sammy said, 'Sit down, Teresa. I've made a cup of tea.'

'Catriona made a pot upstairs but Ah didnae wait. When Ah heard about poor Jimmy, Ah came right down.'

With some difficulty, she disentangled herself from Big Aggie's embrace and accepted the tea Sammy offered. Equally thankful for the chair pushed towards her, she tottered into it and took a few sips from the cup.

'Och, there'll be a lot of sore hearts the night, so there will.'

'Ah cannae believe it. No' really,' Big Aggie said. 'It's no' fair.'

'Ah know, hen.'

'See your God and your Holy Mary? What did they go an' dae that for?'

Teresa trembled at the dangerously accusing tone. Sammy came to her rescue.

'It wasn't anything to do with God, Aggie. It was men. It was men that built the barriers. And they probably got that wrong. And it was men that started the crush on stairway thirteen.'

'Thirteen?' Aggie echoed, subdued again. 'That's an unlucky number.'

'Aye, so it is,' Teresa agreed. 'We once got the chance of a house up close number thirteen. Ah turned it down.'

'Bloody right.'

'Aye.'

A knock on the door startled them both. Sammy went to answer it and returned with a young doctor.

Big Aggie looked indignant. 'Ah never sent for nae doctor.'

'I know. I did,' Sammy told her. 'I was worried about you.'

'Now then.' The doctor had a bouncy, cheerful manner. 'What can I do for you?'

Big Aggie glowered at him. 'Nothin' much by the looks of you.'

She sounded much more like herself. It made Teresa begin to tremble again. She finished her tea in double-quick time. 'I'd better get back upstairs.'

She rose and began shuffling towards the door, managing to escape without Aggie noticing. Aggie had angrily locked horns with the doctor. He must be a Catholic, Teresa thought.

41

'No!' Catriona shook her head in disbelief.

A white-faced Andrew repeated what he'd just told her.

'Fergus has sold the house. Apparently, the university has been looking for a house on the Terrace for ages. They jumped at it. They've been taking over so much of the West End.'

'Does Melvin know?'

'Well, Fergus hasn't told him and I'm certainly not going to. It would kill him. That house has always been Dad's pride and joy.'

'Where will he go when he gets out of hospital? He's bound to find out sooner or later.'

Now she really did feel sorry for Melvin.

'How could Fergus do this to his dad?' she said. 'He's not caring about making you homeless either.'

'He wrote to me. Hadn't even the guts to tell me to my face,' Andrew said bitterly. 'I would have gone up to Aberdeen if it wasn't that Dad expects me to see him every day. I didn't want him to get worried about me either.'

'I can't understand it, Andrew. I mean, he knew he'd be able to sell it eventually but your dad made it clear that it was to be once he was gone – not while he was still alive…'

'I know that and Fergus knows it too. But apparently he was desperate to start a recording studio and fit it up with all the latest gear and God knows what else. He believes he's on his way to fame and fortune now as a recording star. You know how music-daft he is.'

'Yes, but I never thought…'

'No, nor did I. Well, as far as I'm concerned, Mum, he's got his recording studio but he's lost a brother. Not that that'll bother him much, I suppose. I'll never forgive him for doing this to Dad.'

'You're right about trying to keep it from your dad, Andrew. We must at least try our best to protect him from this. Apart from anything else, it would break his heart to think Fergus would betray his trust like this.'

'I'll never forgive him, Mum,' Andrew repeated. 'How could he?'

'You can always come to my place to stay. And your dad too, of course,' she hastily added.

'Thanks, Mum, but it's maybe a blessing that the chances are Dad won't make it much longer. The doctors aren't very hopeful, but I've kept hoping. Now, though, as I say, maybe it's for the best...' He turned away to hide his distress.

'Oh, son.' Catriona didn't know what to say or do to comfort him. At last she managed, 'We'll just have to keep on hoping that he'll pull through and we'll get him home. I'll try and make my house as nice and as comfortable as possible for him. If necessary, I'll get a bigger place. Between us, we'll make everything all right for him again.'

'Thanks, Mum,' he repeated.

She went in to make them both a cup of tea, her mind and emotions in turmoil.

The wedding went without a hitch. Ailish and Sean's workmate Bill enjoyed the tea at Miss Cranston's afterwards. Sean and Chrissie were too excited, too happy and relieved, to bother about food. Later they returned hand in hand to Aunty Mary's flat, hopeful that they might even be able to steal a few hours on their own. Then came the shocking, unexpected news of the tragedy at Ibrox and that Chrissie's father had been killed there. Sean's mother had come to tell them and to ask them to go and be with 'poor Aggie', who was on her own and in a bad way.

'Ah know she flung a lot of angry words at the pair of you,' Teresa said, 'but then so did we all. Sure we did.'

'But does Aggie want us back – even me?' Sean asked.

'Och, once you're there she'll be glad to see you both, I'm sure,' Teresa replied, her anxious face revealing that she wasn't sure at all.

Sean didn't look convinced but he turned his attention to concentrating on comforting Chrissie, who had begun to weep and sob out, 'He was really happy for me getting into the Mitchell. Proud even. Once he came to see me there. He looked around and said, "It's a grand place, this." I can just see his face.'

Sean took her into his arms. 'He wouldn't want you to get so upset.'

Teresa said, 'Alec Jackson was killed as well. Poor Madge is fair distracted.'

'God!' Sean said. 'Two up the same close!'

'Aye, it's a sad place the day. You'll come then, son?'

'Yes, of course. It was good of you to trail all the way over to tell us, Ma.'

Teresa managed a smile. 'Aye, it's high time we aw had wan o' them phones in our houses. Magic, sure they are.'

Sean braced himself for the meeting with Big Aggie. The last time they'd met, she'd done her best to knock him down and trample all over him. She hadn't managed it but he somehow couldn't imagine her feelings changing towards him – even as a result of such tragic circumstances.

As it turned out, at least she made no attempt

at violence against him although she still eyed him belligerently.

'Oh, it's you, is it?'

'I'm so sorry about Jimmy,' Sean said.

'Aye, well, he wisnae the only wan.'

'We just thought it might help if we…'

Big Aggie turned on Chrissie, who was quietly weeping into her hanky. 'Snivellin' never helped anybody. Now, are you gonnae come tae yer senses and come back? No' him, just you, d'ye hear? He disnae belong in this family, and never will.'

Sean said nothing but Chrissie managed, 'Well, I'm sorry you feel that way, Mammy, but I'm Sean's wife now and I belong with him – I always will.'

'Good riddance,' Aggie shouted after them as they left. 'Ye're no' welcome here.'

Sean put his arm around Chrissie's shoulders. 'We've got each other. That's all that matters now.'

'It's so sad.'

'I know but there's nothing we can do about it. We've tried but it's no use. It would be just as bad upstairs. Can you imagine the kind of welcome Dermot would give us?'

'I never want to come here again.'

'Nor do I. How about us going away? Right away from Balornock, from Glasgow, and starting afresh somewhere else? Think about it.'

The visits had been daily for some time now – the visits to her mother and the visits to Melvin. Andrew feared that his father was dying and

308

Catriona didn't know what she would have done without Julie, who practically ran the therapy centre while she was out so much. There were three therapists there now – a physio, an osteopath and a young man who specialised in the Alexander technique. When Catriona managed to spend any time in her consulting room, she concentrated on homeopathic treatment.

Mainly thanks to Julie, everything was running smoothly. The front area of the shop was shelved and stocked with jars, tubs and boxes of vitamins. There were displays of herbal teas, shelves of natural beauty products and books on every aspect of natural health and beauty. A very pretty assistant in a green apron served at the front counter.

The ever-increasing profits of the therapy centre meant that redecorating her flat and furnishing it to her own taste would cause no financial worry. She was successful. Her dream was coming true – had actually come true already. But she worried constantly about Melvin finding out how Fergus had betrayed him, made him homeless. Knowing how much the house had meant to Melvin, she could feel nothing but pity and indignation on his behalf. Nobody deserved such treatment. She could only hope that he would never find out. For the first time in years, she prayed. Then, not long after Fergus's betrayal, she turned up at the hospital for her daily visit and Andrew met her in the corridor. She guessed immediately by the tragic look in his eyes what had happened.

'Mum,' he said, 'I've sad news for you. Dad has died.' His voice broke. 'I was with him. He was holding on to my hand.'

'Oh, son, you were a comfort to him. Be glad about that.'

Andrew managed to nod, then cleared his throat. 'It's for the best in the circumstances. He was suffering and he would have suffered a lot more if he'd lived to find out about Fergus. It's a mercy, in a way.'

'I suppose we'll have to tell Fergus,' Catriona said worriedly. 'But, I wouldn't be surprised if he doesn't come to the funeral. He was too busy most of the time to come and see his dad when he was ill.'

'I'm having nothing to do with him.'

Catriona burst into tears. 'It's so sad,' she said, thinking not of Melvin now but of the two brothers coming to this.

Andrew put his arm around her shoulders. 'You've always got me, Mum.'

She knew then that he would always be a comfort to her.

He saw to all the arrangements for the funeral, a quiet affair with only Andrew, herself and a few friends. Fergus sent a black-bordered card and a large wreath but made the excuse that he was ill in bed with a bad dose of flu, and unable to travel down from Aberdeen. Neither she nor Andrew believed him. It made Catriona feel even sadder.

Andrew moved in with her afterwards, to her gratitude. She knew that one day he would find a place of his own, get married probably, but meantime she treasured every moment he spent with her. On her next visit to Julie, while Andrew was working late in the physio department of the local health centre, she enthused about how wonderful it was to have her son staying with her. The words were hardly out of her mouth when she regretted saying them. She had suddenly noticed that both Julie and Sammy were looking unhappy. When she asked what was wrong, Julie said, 'Sammy can't get over losing his best friend in such tragic circumstances. He's upset about his father as well.'

'It was terrible about Alec,' Catriona agreed. 'I was fond of him. We all were.' Then she added, 'Your father ... is he?'

It was Julie who answered. 'It's sad to see anyone in the state his father's in now. He doesn't recognise anyone, even Sammy. Apart from that, Sammy's read some of his diaries, and he understands why his father was so awful a bit better now. The bits about his childhood were enough to upset anybody. I feel sorry for him myself.'

Catriona understood. She'd eventually felt sorry for Melvin.

The silence that followed was broken by a knock at the door. Julie went to answer it.

'Oh, Mrs Robertson!' They heard the mixture of surprise, confusion and apprehension in her voice. 'Come in.'

'There's something I wanted to talk to you about.' A small, elderly lady entered the room and immediately looked taken aback. 'Oh, I didn't realise you had a visitor...'

'It's all right. Catriona's my best friend. You can talk in front of her. And I think you've met my husband, Sammy.'

311

Catriona and Sammy both smiled a welcome. Sammy rose and pulled a chair over.

'Have a seat, Mrs Robertson.'

Mrs Robertson returned his smile and settled herself on the chair. She hesitated, then looked over at Julie. 'You already know about Alice, don't you? That's why you came to live here. I guessed a while ago.'

Julie's eyes widened with anxiety. 'Yes, but I never meant... I would never try to come between you and your daughter. I'm so sorry if finding out about me living so close has been a shock or a worry to you. I just longed for the occasional glimpse of Alice. I didn't mean any harm.'

'Of course you didn't, dear.'

'Why have you come to see me about this now?' Julie sank on to the couch beside Sammy.

'Alice has started trying to find her biological mother. She asked me first if it was all right with me and I reminded her that I had told her years ago that I wouldn't mind a bit if she tried to find you. But, as I say, it's only recently...'

Julie was trembling so much that she had to clutch at Sammy's hand to steady herself. 'And now she's changed her mind? She doesn't want to see me?'

'Why do you say that?'

'Well, you've come instead.'

'Oh, she doesn't know I'm here.'

'I don't understand.'

'She's like you, Julie. She didn't want to risk causing you or your family any trouble or embarrassment. But I knew you longed to meet her. When I thought back on all the times you asked

312

me about her, I knew. I couldn't convince her, though.'

Julie looked as if she didn't know whether to laugh or cry.

'Can I go across the road with you now?' She jumped eagerly to her feet.

Mrs Robertson laughed. 'Calm down, dear. You've waited all these years, you can surely wait another day. She's on duty tonight but tomorrow's her day off. Come over tomorrow afternoon. I'll have spoken to her by then.'

'Do you think it'll be all right? Will she be all right about me coming?'

'She'll be absolutely delighted.' Mrs Robertson rose. 'I can assure you of that.'

'Oh, thank you so much!' Julie saw her to the door and then came skipping and dancing back into the room, her face alight with joy. Sammy was suddenly transformed as well. He rushed towards her and swung her up into his arms.

'I'm so happy for you, Julie. So happy, darling.'

'It must be infectious,' Catriona laughed. 'I feel as excited and as overjoyed as the pair of you!'

'Impossible!' Julie cried out. 'Nobody in the world could be as happy as I feel right now!'

42

Sean and Chrissie had put their names onto the Corporation Housing List, hoping they'd get something as far away from Balornock as possible. They discovered that the waiting list for a house anywhere was enormous. They even tried Edinburgh, without any luck. They were becoming thoroughly disillusioned, not to mention exhausted, tramping about here, there and everywhere trying to find a decent place to live. They had begun to have nightmare visions of never getting away from Aunty Mary and her icons, her tiny kitchen, with its high hole-in-the-wall bed and her beloved books.

'I'll go mad,' Chrissie said, 'if I've to stay there much longer.'

'Me too,' Sean fervently agreed.

'If we could just get another roof over our heads, a new job in another town would be no problem. The library service is crying out for library assistants all over the place. There are even vacancies in London just now and they can even arrange accommodation for anyone coming from a distance! I could get a transfer no bother.'

'London?' Sean repeated. 'Would you be willing to move that far?'

'I never thought about the London vacancies in connection with us...'

'But would you?'

'Move to London? Well ... yes ... why not?' Chrissie flushed with excitement. 'Sean, that might be the answer!' Her excitement fizzled out again. 'But what about you? You'd need a job as well and I'm not going anywhere without you.'

'Of course not. But I could get help from Mc-Hendry's. They correspond with shipping offices all over the place. I could get the address of a shipping office in London and make enquiries. Oh, Chrissie, I think this might be our new beginning. Just think of it!'

She did and could hardly wait until next day to find out all the details of the London vacancies for library assistants. Sean contacted a London shipping office, found there were vacancies and immediately applied for one of them.

'What with my experiences and the excellent references from McHendry's, Chrissie, I should have a good chance.'

They were walking on air for the next few days. Eventually Chrissie was able to go to Copeland's and tell Ailish.

'Well,' Ailish said, as they made for the tea-room, 'I'm happy for you, of course, but I'll miss the pair of you.'

'I'll miss you too but you'll come and visit us in London, I hope. We won't lose touch.'

'I hope not. But London's an awful long way away. I know people even travel abroad, now-adays, but I've never been out of Scotland.'

'Neither have I. What an adventure it's going to be, Ailish. I can hardly wait.'

'I'll miss you,' Ailish repeated.

'Och, you've got a new boyfriend, don't you?

315

He'll keep you occupied.'

Suddenly Ailish laughed and flung back her blonde head. 'You think you've had trouble with your family! Wait until they hear about my man.'

'He's not a Protestant, is he?'

'No, worse. He's English!'

Chrissie laughed. 'Oh dear, oh dear.'

'Exactly.'

'Whereabouts in England is he from?'

'York. A lovely place, he keeps telling me. He's really interesting, the way he talks.'

'You obviously like him.'

'Yes.' Ailish looked thoughtful. 'I do. We get on so well together. He's a sales rep, travels around a bit, but his heart's in York, he says. He's hoping to buy a house there and settle down one day.'

'Oh, Ailish, maybe that's not all he's hoping!'

Ailish smiled. 'That's what I've been thinking too.'

'I'll keep my fingers crossed for you.'

They parted in high spirits and with high hopes. As soon as Chrissie arrived back at Aunty Mary's, however, her mood dampened a little. The tiny flat had become so claustrophobic and depressing. As soon as Sean returned, though, her happiness leapt into life again. He had good news. There had been interviews held in the Central Hotel in Glasgow for the job he'd applied for in the London shipping office. He had been successful. She had, of course, already asked the Mitchell for a transfer and it had been confirmed a few days before.

Their dreams were going to come true at last. It was so wonderful. Despite Aunty Mary looking on, they threw caution to the wind and hugged and passionately kissed each other. 'Now, now,' Aunty Mary remonstrated.

Aunty Mary didn't know what she was missing.

The publishers hope that this book has given you enjoyable reading. Large Print Books are especially designed to be as easy to see and hold as possible. If you wish a complete list of our books please ask at your local library or write directly to:

Magna Large Print Books
Magna House, Long Preston,
Skipton, North Yorkshire.
BD23 4ND

This Large Print Book for the partially sighted, who cannot read normal print, is published under the auspices of

THE ULVERSCROFT FOUNDATION

THE ULVERSCROFT FOUNDATION

... we hope that you have enjoyed this Large Print Book. Please think for a moment about those people who have worse eyesight problems than you ... and are unable to even read or enjoy Large Print, without great difficulty.

You can help them by sending a donation, large or small to:

**The Ulverscroft Foundation,
1, The Green, Bradgate Road,
Anstey, Leicestershire, LE7 7FU,
England.**
or request a copy of our brochure for more details.

The Foundation will use all your help to assist those people who are handicapped by various sight problems and need special attention.

Thank you very much for your help.
